*"Fire in the straw stack, blazing bright,
You'll be ashes by tonight."*

—OLD NURSERY RHYME

straw

a novel by

WILLIAM MORROW & COMPANY

f i r e

KATHLEEN CRAWFORD

New York, 1947

to MARTHA FOLEY

part one

o n e

Every Sunday morning since she could remember, Frances had awakened to the smell of corn-meal muffins in her house, and the sound of church bells competing with each other across the Virginia valley. She pulled the sheet up over her head to lengthen the moment before the world crowded in. This was the time of day she liked best, the space of time between her mother's passing through her room to prepare breakfast and her father's nudging her before he went down to eat it. And it was like her whole life, bounded on both sides by father and mother, and permeated with the smell of corn-meal muffins. There was every reason to stay on and on in bed, this summer Sunday morning—every reason except that she had risen on Sun-

3

day mornings for Sunday school and church for twenty-three years, and that was reason enough.

There was no more holding back the minutes. From her parents' room came the murmurs of conversation, the noise of drawers and closets being opened, heavy footsteps back and forth to the connecting bathroom. That was her father, of course, dressing with more than his usual care; being a leading deacon in Kingston's largest Presbyterian church was as important a position as being vice-president of Kingston's largest bank, and he passed the plate with the same gravity and concern he bestowed upon negotiating loans or foreclosing mortgages. And this was no ordinary Sunday morning. The First Presbyterian Church was dismissing its pastor because of the injudicious and rabble-rousing doctrines he insisted upon preaching in spite of repeated warnings from the Session to desist.

Or rather, thought Frances, Dr. McDonough had been "permitted to resign." "Preach the Gospel, Dr. McDonough, just the straight Gospel," the board of elders and deacons had cautioned him, mildly enough in the beginning, when he had first been called to Kingston two years before; and later more hotly, "This is Virginia, Pastor, you seem to forget that. These niggers are uppity enough as it is, without your spouting a lot of race talk and Christian brotherhood at them from the pulpit. The war has changed things a hell of a lot around here . . . excuse our language . . . and you'll be having us a race riot on our hands if you keep this kind of thing up."

Mr. Acheson would return from fiery Session meetings late in the evening, to stomp around the living room and shout, "He's going too far, too far, that damfool preacher. Defied us tonight right to our faces. Says he'll preach the ideas of Christ as long as he's got a pulpit under his feet. Christian brotherhood hell! That nigger-lover!"

And finally Dr. McDonough had gone too far even for the tolerant and brotherly Christians of the First Presbyterian Church. He had made them eat with their darker brothers.

Things can move in this town if they want to, Frances thought, but they always seem to move in the wrong direction. She remembered the night of the awful meal in the basement dining room of the church. It had been only two weeks ago. The ministers and leading laymen of all Kingston's Protestant churches were holding their annual supper and unity conference there and, as host, Dr. McDonough had also been in charge of all arrangements. Frances had assisted the supper committee with the serving, and then had left early for home to prepare her mother for the approaching explosion. "We'll be picking Daddy off the ceiling for a week," she told Mrs. Acheson cheerfully, and the two of them sat expectantly in the living room as though they had box seats for a play. Frances always enjoyed her father's performances when they weren't directed at her, and in this one neither of the audience was to be disappointed.

"He *has* gone too far this time, too far, I tell you! Do you know what that man has done now? Niggers he had to dinner! All the damn black jigaboos in town. The preachers and half the congregation of damn near every black church in the county. Sitting right down at the table beside us, beside us, do you hear! Not even at a table to themselves. White, black, white, black, all around every single table. There must have been fifty of them!"

He flailed his arms wildly in the air. "There they sat,

5

with place cards too, place cards. He fixed that. He fixed it so we'd *have* to sit beside them." Mr. Acheson strode the living room as though he were treading vipers underfoot. There was no stopping him, even if his wife and daughter had wanted to.

"And smile, God, how they smiled! With all their goddam gold teeth showing from ear to ear. I'd like to slit their black throats. Didn't they love it! Didn't they just eat it up! Oh, come and eat at my table, for Christ's sake," he minced, imitating Dr. McDonough's voice. He changed his inflection and said it again. "For Christ's sake! He's gone too far this time. This time we'll have him out of the church and out of the whole damn town if I have anything to do with it. God! You should have seen the faces—Sidney from over at Brethren Methodist, and Bill Abbott and Joe Hill. We'll be the laughingstock of Kingston after this."

Another turn about the room. "And then he had the guts, the unadulterated guts, to stand up and say that we should all live together like brothers, the world was looking to us, the church should set the pace, and a lot more crap like that. Brothers, hell! The black bastard on one side of me smelled like a garbage pail. I couldn't eat a mouthful. I almost threw up. But this'll ruin him. You wait. You just wait."

Kingston had to wait only a few days. A short announcement in the religious section of the *Daily Bugle* on the following Saturday had noted gently that Dr. McDonough would preach his farewell sermon at the First Presbyterian Church on Sunday, June ninth; that his tendered resignation had been accepted. The near-by Washington papers had learned the details and featured the incident, which was immediately seized and trumpeted by the Ne-

6

gro press in the deep South, none of which ruffled Kingston at all. The town never read foreign newspapers anyway.

Frances kicked the sheets back with a last reluctant sigh and swung her legs off the bed, feeling sleepily for her slippers. She tied a dressing gown around her and pushed open the door to the bathroom, where her father was shaving. She nuzzled the back of his neck where the mole was.

"Good morning, Pop. I should think you could shave better with your teeth in."

"Hello, honey." The shaving cream mellowed the hard lines of his chin and gave him a wonderfully sabbatical look. "You'd better get dressed. We wouldn't want to be late today."

"Lord no! And miss that final performance? Who's going to be master of ceremonies at the lynching?"

Interested in a tiny nick on his cheek, he did not answer her, but she knew he would follow the point up later. The most certain thing in an unsure world was the knowledge that her father would harry a point into its grave.

She went on into her parents' bedroom where her mother was carefully inserting rubber pads into her brassiere.

"Frances honey, didn't you want any breakfast? I had eggs the way you like them, and corn-meal muffins—"

"For a change?" Frances climbed into the tall four-poster bed, but the smile she gave her mother took the sarcasm out of her words. Mrs. Acheson was a beautiful woman, far more beautiful than she had been as a girl. Maturity had brought her a rich full body, but had not thickened the modeling of her cheekbones and chin. She only hoped that age would do something for her daughter; youth had not yet seemed to.

"Your father likes his corn-meal muffins on Sunday morning, Fran, you know that. His mother used to make them for him when he was a boy. And I think you ought to eat more, darling. Certainly more than you do. You're much too thin for your height."

"At least," Frances pointed at her mother's breasts, "I don't have to wear those things."

"My mother wasn't as smart as your mother," said Mrs. Acheson. "I've told you about the corsets my mother made me wear, laced up to here, and I was a lot younger than you are now. It's a wonder I have any ribs left."

Frances burrowed down into the big bed, which smelled of her father's tobacco and her mother's cologne; which smelled warm and secure and intimate, as though it had secrets it couldn't share even with her. She could see her father in the bathroom in his long checked-muslin drawers which his wife had to make for him now that the stores had stopped selling such things. His paunch kept him from getting too close to the mirror, and every morning he cut himself to the accompaniment of quiet cursing. She tried idly to imagine her father as a lover, but since she didn't know too much about it, the effort failed.

He called in to his wife, "Did you tell Fran that Hannah had her kittens in my closet this morning?"

Frances was on her knees among the shoes and boxes in a hurry. "Mother, they're wonderful. Let's keep just one this time, please?" In the dim light she could count three. "How many does this make in all that Hannah's had?"

"Eighty-eight," Mrs. Acheson said. "And you know we can't keep any of them. At the rate she turns them out, we'd be run out of house and home in no time."

8

"Do you think she'll break a hundred before she dies?"

Hannah, a shapeless black mass against the darkness of the closet, was purring noisily. Frances rubbed her nose in a couple of the little kittens before she backed away and stood up. "Maybe we could find a home for just one, Mother; it's so pathetic for her to go on and on having kittens month after month, just to have them vanish the very next day. How would you like to have babies and have somebody come along and drown them all immediately?"

"If I'd had eighty-eight, I should be very happy to have them drowned," Mrs. Acheson said imperturbably. This was an ancient argument with routine questions and answers. They both knew she would send for the ASPCA in the morning.

Mr. Acheson came out of the bathroom and began to climb into his pants. His teeth were in, his white hair shone, and his face was rosy and cherubic. He practiced his Sunday smile on his daughter. "You can have the bathroom now, Fran, and hurry up. We don't want to have to wait for you."

"She could have used her own bathroom, James," his wife reminded him. "She wasn't waiting for you. She's just dawdling."

"Oh, Mother, you know that shower of mine is so small you have to leave the room to pick up the soap. Besides, I was afraid I'd miss Pop's final words on the Great Schism if I didn't come in here."

"Great Schism?"

"Sure. The Shooting of Dan McDonough. The Decline and Fall of Religious Tolerance in Kingston. How to kick a preacher out of a church in one easy lesson."

9

Very patiently he turned to her. "The board of elders and deacons did not *kick* Dr. McDonough out, as you so crudely put it. We merely accepted his resignation."

"Daddy, what a farce. You all railroaded that man right out of his job like you said you would. Just because he happens to interpret the Bible in a way you don't approve of."

"Look, Frances, I'm dressing. We're late now, and I have no intention of waiting for you. We've discussed this thing before and I don't want to continue it now." He turned away to the mirror over his chest of drawers, but already his neck was flushed above his collar. Frances ignored her mother's warning shake of head.

"There's absolutely no difference between what you all did and the old witch-hunting up in Salem or the religious persecutions in Europe or"—she cast around in her mind—"when Calvin burned Savonarola. Just because a man doesn't agree with you doesn't make him wrong."

Mr. Acheson had been trying to tie his necktie, futilely, and now he wheeled again to her, the loose ends dangling. "You mean Servetus. And listen to me, young lady, get this straight. The pulpit is no place to air a lot of half-baked theories on niggers—"

"Negroes, Daddy."

"They're niggers to me, always have been and always will be. My grandfather owned slaves. My own mother had one when she was a little girl. You think I want to sit down at the table with them, have them in my home, have you marry one? When I go to church, I want religion, Christian religion—"

"Did you ever try reading the New Testament?"

His face mottled. "Don't talk to me like that. I'm as

good a Christian as that man ever was, and a damn sight more sensible about it. If God had meant everybody to be equal, He'd have made us all white. I've been a member of First Presbyterian for over fifty years, and my allegiance is to the church and not to the man."

"You mean to the building and not what's said there!"

Mrs. Acheson stood up from her dressing table and looked meaningly at Frances. "That's quite enough. You'd better get dressed." Her husband belched, long and deep. "There. You see. You've given your father indigestion."

"He'll probably burp in Dr. McDonough's face this morning and love it." Frances trailed off to her own room.

"And another thing . . ." her father shouted after her, but she heard her mother's cool, low voice interrupt, and the noise subsided.

Poor Daddy. Poor darling Pop. Why did she have to tantalize him incessantly? She seemed to have the knack invariably of bringing his Irish boiling to the top no matter what they discussed. And he meant so well . . . But he was so damn right all the time. If he'd ever admit he was wrong, just once . . . She smiled a little to herself at the idea. Mother must have quieted him down all right, because she was going downstairs. Frances could picture her standing in the sunshine at the wide doorway, drawing on her gloves, assured, stately, cool.

Her father rushed to the head of the stairs. "Evelyn, have you seen my new Panama? What the hell did you do with it?"

Mrs. Acheson's voice floated back. "It's in the hatbox on your closet shelf, James, where it belongs."

Footsteps, a moment's Sunday silence, a crash, a cat's agonized wail.

"And get these goddam cats out of my closet before I bash their skulls in!"

Another Sunday had begun.

t w o

Life in Kingston in the summertime, meandering at best, on Sunday afternoons stopped completely. How flat-faced all the houses look with their shutters folded, thought Frances as she walked up the quiet street toward home. One thing certainly. If an atom bomb ever hit Kingston on Sunday afternoon, they'll all die in bed—and their own beds at that.

The Acheson house was shuttered too, of course, she noticed as she turned into the drive. Sleeping off a heavy dinner after an even heavier sermon. In the dim hallway she laid her hat and gloves on the silver card tray and started toward the kitchen. Upstairs a door opened and her father stuck his head over the banisters.

"Frances, is that you? Where have you been?" The whisper curled down out of the darkness.

"I'll tell you all about it in a minute, just as soon as I get something to eat."

"Hush. Your mother's asleep. We waited dinner for you an hour."

"I know. I should have called you. Wait a minute. I'll be right up."

There was a platter of fried chicken in the refrigerator; her mother had saved her a leg. Presently she went upstairs, a bread-and-butter sandwich in one hand and the drumstick in the other, into her parents' bedroom. Mrs. Acheson, who had been taking a nap on Frances' bed, stood in the bathroom door, tying a wrapper on.

"Didn't you have any dinner, darling, wherever you were? What time is it getting to be? It must be nearly four o'clock."

"Don't you all get awfully tired of chicken every Sunday, Mother?" Frances hoisted herself up on the edge of the large bed. She was excited and a little frightened. She did not look at her father.

"Well, honey, you know there's a meat shortage. I had to stand in line at the butcher's the other day for over an hour and then all he had—"

"Never mind that right now," Mr. Acheson said to his wife, politely enough. "You're all excited, Frances. What's all the excitement? Where have you been?"

"Oh yes—uh—" She laughed nervously, and then in a great rush of words, "I've withdrawn my membership from First Church. I signed up to be a charter member of the new church, and that's where I've been."

"You've what? What new church?" Mr. Acheson sat up in bed.

"The new church we're going to organize. Already have organized, I mean. About three hundred people—oh, more than that, I reckon—withdrew their memberships from First this morning right after church, as a protest against the treatment Dr. McDonough received, and we're going to form our own church. And it's going to be non-denominational." She looked from one to the other. This isn't going to be so bad after all, she thought with mild astonishment.

"Have you already signed your name, Frances?" her father asked.

"Oh yes. Miss Cantrick—Dr. McDonough's secretary, you know—went around getting the signature of everybody who was at the Braxtons' house—"

"At the Braxtons'?" said Mrs. Acheson. She sat down on the corner of the dressing table. "Do you mean they have left First Church too?"

"Yes'm. It was their house we held this meeting in, you see. And there were a couple of the elders and deacons there too, Daddy. Mr. Harwood asked me if you were coming along, and I said I didn't think you knew anything about it—"

"When did all this business start, Frances?"

"I guess most of this was fixed up last week after people found out that Dr. McDonough had been asked to resign. I heard about it after church in the choir's dressing room. Gladys Anderson said that she was going over to the Braxtons' house right away to a mass meeting and asked me if I didn't want to go—"

"Do you always do everything people ask you?"

"No, Daddy, and that's not fair either. I thought Dr. McDonough's sermon this morning was wonderful, and I agreed with every word he said, and besides you know how I've felt about this thing all along—"

He was sitting very still against the pillows. "Just because you signed your name to something doesn't necessarily mean that you have to leave First Church. All this nonsense will blow over—"

"Daddy, don't start that kind of thing now. It isn't nonsense and it won't blow over. It's been done now, and when I did it, I knew you wouldn't like it, but you'll just have to get over it somehow. Anyway, Miss Cantrick is sending all our names in a letter to First Church *today* so I can't back out, and you can't make me!"

She jumped off the bed and stood in the middle of the room.

Her mother said, "Frances, don't get crumbs all over the rug. If you aren't going to eat that bread, put it on the bureau."

"I'm not trying to stop you, Frances," said Mr. Acheson, "if you think you're doing the right thing. You're twenty-three and you're certainly old enough to know your own mind."

She was encouraged and reassured by the calmness of his voice. "Daddy, you should have been at that meeting. There were so many people they filled Judge Braxton's library and little den. You know how the house is built with the whole back opening on the garden? And they all spilled out into the garden too. The Thompsons were there and the Bruces, and—oh yes, Mr. Carlyle from the bank—"

He hardly seemed to be listening to her. He was looking at the shadows the leaves made on the window shades. She glanced at her mother, who was sitting quietly on the corner of the dressing table. Frances knew her mother's reactions to these frequent clashes between her husband and her daughter; with what effort no one realized, Mrs. Acheson retained a core of serenity and an aloofness which irritated the both of them even while they envied her. The love between mother and daughter was strong, but Mrs. Acheson never sided with Frances against her father.

How can I make them see how important this is to me, Frances thought. What a wonderful spirit there was at the meeting, and the way everybody looked. Free, I guess

1 5

you'd say, as though they had been honest with themselves for once. What was that quotation Dr. McDonough used for us? "We few, we happy few, we band of brothers." Something like that. People should start new churches more often. At least you know that all the members are there because they want to be, and not because they were born into it. A lot of people want their church service to be like going to a play or a concert or something. They don't like to see signs of struggle, and the performance has to be just so, all timed down to the minute, with the choir getting up on schedule, like puppets on a string. And if something does go wrong, they feel cheated, as if they weren't getting their money's worth. But in a new church you don't feel as though you were just a piece of the audience. Getting in at the beginning makes you really belong.

Frances walked back over to the bed and sat down beside her father, rumpling his hair. "Daddy, Mr. Carew is going to let us use the Old Gaiety Movie Theater until we can get a building built. Wouldn't you like to come to a meeting with me once? You wouldn't have to sign anything, just visit—"

He sat up so quickly that she had to slide to her feet. He threw back the sheet and groped for his slippers. They made a liquid sound on the floor as he shuffled across the room to the chest of drawers and reached for his glasses. She watched him in the mirror and noticed with a little concern how old he looked when he was undressed and uncombed. And with all his hair sticking up like stiff white brushes, he had an oddly wild look.

"I think you've made a damn fool of yourself," he said without turning. He hitched his pajama pants up and re-tied the string. In the silence she could hear the cicadas whirring in the trees outside. Her mouth hung open a little.

"Just a damn fool." He came forward to the bedpost nearest him and shook it slightly. "Flying off half-cocked. Jumping into this thing feet first without a second thought. Without even asking your mother or me. Two hours ago, three hours, you didn't even know there was going to be a split in our church, *our* church by God! The one you were christened in, the one your mother and I were married in, the one *I* was christened in—"

"But Daddy—"

"All your life you've done damfool things. Leaping first, thinking later. And you always regret it. You always come around to my way of thinking after you calm down. But I can't hang over you every minute of the day to keep you from flying off the handle and pulling some damn stunt like this. I have to give you credit for a little sense—"

"Now wait a min—"

"That time when you finished college, you grabbed a job teaching down in Norfolk, right in the middle of the war—Norfolk! Thank God I got you out of that in time. And I fixed it so Mr. Douglas gave you a better job right here in Kingston. You had to admit you were wrong that time too, didn't you? You see, it's always this way—"

She kept trying to interrupt him. She recognized all the symptoms. His face was getting ruddy, and the knuckles of his hand as he gripped the post were white. But she knew now that it was too late to stop him. His rage must run its course, and the pattern of it was familiar.

Yet she didn't have the control to listen to him without retorting. "You don't know everything, you know! In this case—"

He ignored her. "And now you've gone and joined up with a bunch of nigger-lovers. That's all they are, nigger-lovers!"

The ferocity of the attack appalled her. "They're not nigger-lovers. They're fine good people who practice what they preach—" Her voice shrilled, to be heard over his.

"Just nigger-lovers. I suppose you're going to have tea parties and dances with niggers now!"

Her stomach oozed away. "Certainly not! But at least we're not a bunch of whited sepulchres who pray for our brothers inside the church—" she dragged out the words sarcastically, "and then go out in the street and kick them in the teeth because they happen to be black."

"I suppose you'll be bringing some of your nigger-friends here and set them down to dinner with your mother and me—"

"Daddy, I haven't even thought about things like that! My Lord, what's that got to do with it anyway? That hasn't got anything to—"

He plowed on implacably. "Pretty soon, you'll want to marry one, won't you? And have a nice black nigger baby—"

"Stop it! That's no argument. You always drag in marriage, as though they want to marry me any more than I want to marry them—"

He leaned forward, his face contorted. "Where do you get your ideas? Just tell me that! Where do you get your ideas?"

"I told you. Out of the New Testament. Why don't you try reading it sometime?"

"For God's sake, Frances, keep religion out of this—"

"But that's how the whole thing got started! It's religion I'm trying to talk about. I want a church where you get honesty, and not a censored phonograph record."

"You talk like a goddam fool. I'm ashamed that any daughter of mine would consider herself no better than a nigger!"

She realized that her nails were driving into the palms of her hands, and all the muscles along her arms and shoulders were rigid. She unclenched her fists and relaxed so suddenly that her whole body sagged. Her father was watching her. He always misinterpreted her silence for defeat. Even in the most inconsequential quarrels, she saw the futility of her words, realized that her arguments, principles, theories thudded unheard to the floor. Nobody ever won. And now they had spoiled a beautiful Sunday afternoon. She was suddenly exhausted.

"Okay, Daddy. Skip it." She walked around him to the bathroom and then into her own room, where she threw herself face down across the bed. Her mother had lowered the blinds when she came in to nap, and the room was sweet with the faint odor of cologne. She could hear the two of them talking in low tones beyond the closed bathroom door. Frances thought about her mother. Mrs. Acheson had the ability to walk straight away from a situation; without ever having moved, she gave the impression of having gone miles elsewhere. Frances supposed it was a defense technique acquired early in marriage to prevent a nervous breakdown or stomach ulcers. She remembered time and time again the unconcern with which her mother read a newspaper in the living room while her father stomped militantly up and down.

Once Mrs. Acheson had given several pairs of shoes to the Russian War Relief, among them a pair Mr. Acheson called his ice-skating shoes. Naturally he missed them immediately.

"Damn Russians. Why couldn't you leave *my* shoes alone?"

"My dear, those shoes have been in the closet for years. You haven't been on skates since Frances was in high school."

"That doesn't mean I'm never going skating again in my life. What do you think I am, an old man?"

He stormed on, spreading his anger from Russia to Britain to Washington and the whole damn war. And finally, "You're not even listening to me, Evelyn!"

"Oh, yes, I am, James," she said pleasantly above the paper, and had gone on reading.

"Hell, I'm just wasting my breath!"

"I know, James, but you have so much of it."

. . . The bathroom door opened and, without turning, Frances knew it was her father. She heard him tiptoe across the matting. He sat down on the side of the bed in the darkened room and gently turned her over with his strong arms so that she had to look up into his face.

"I didn't mean to say goddam fool back there, honey," he said softly, kissing her on the forehead. "That just slipped out. I only meant to say damn fool, but you know how excited I get."

"That's all right," she muttered, turning her head away. This was the awful aftermath of one of their quarrels. The scene which always followed upset her more than the unreasonable argument.

"Look at me, honey," her father said gently. He put one hand to her cheek and moved her head so that he could look into her eyes. "I don't want to quarrel with you all the time. Looks like when two people love each other as much as we do, we've always got to fly off at each other's throats and say something we don't mean. That's the Irish coming out, I guess. Seems to me you and I are always trying to hurt each other. You know I love you more than my own life."

All the stops are out now, thought Frances peevishly. His eyes were filling with tears, and his glasses misted up. A tear rolled down his cheek and he didn't brush it away. That's for me to see, she said to herself, and knew immediately that it wasn't true. His tears were as genuine and sincere as his rage had been ten minutes earlier. There was never any pretense in his remorse, and his heart was as generous in offering apology as it was adamant in sticking to its own illogical principles. Why doesn't he remember all this aftermath when he starts getting mad, she wondered, and knew that next time would be just as bad.

She smoothed his hair back from his forehead. "When he was good, he was very very good, and when he was bad, he was horrid."

"I've worked all my life just to give you all the things you've wanted. Nothing else matters to me but you. You are my whole life—and your mother, of course. I just don't want to see you ruining all I've built up for you by plunging helter-skelter after *this* crazy idea and *that* crazy idea and so on. And," he added with a sigh, "I wish to God I knew where you got some of your crazy notions."

He blew his nose. "I've lived a lot longer than you have, and I do know a few more things than you think I do —you think I'm a dumb old man—but there are a few things in life that you just can't change. And one of them is human nature. So you listen to your old daddy. I'd cut off my arm before I'd guide you wrong."

In spite of herself she had begun to cry. He's counted on this too, she thought as he tenderly handed her his handkerchief. He knows I always cry. "What a stinker you are," she snuffled into it. "You always know how to get around me."

He grinned at her. "There's some peach ice cream left in the freezer in the basement. Let's go get it."

She slid off the bed and went into the bathroom to wash her face. "Okay. But don't think," she called above the running water, "that you've won. This time I'm not going to back down. My mind's made up."

She heard him laugh. "We'll see," he said.

t h r e e

The Old Gaiety Movie Theater had been built in the days of Lily Langtry, and in spite of the intrusion of moving pictures, it still retained an aura of secret glory, as though it mused inwardly on past delights. It stood in what had once been the center of town, but town had lifted up its skirts and moved half a mile farther from the railroad tracks, and the Old Gaiety, big and badly in need of paint, was left with its memories.

The theater had steadily sunk from legitimate dramas to vaudeville (which Kingston had pronounced "vaw-dee-vill" and had refused to patronize) and finally in desperation, to second-run movies. The crystal chandelier, which had jingled to the orchestras of *Rose Marie* and *The Desert Song*, sagged listless and silent. It had been condemned by the city two years ago, but no one had bothered to remove it. The china wall brackets were empty of candles; they had never been wired for electricity. The grime of sixty years obscured the walls so well that only here and there was the form of a fleshy leg visible, dim reminders of the murals beneath which had once been the talk of the Valley.

When the 372 charter members of the New World Church (non-denominational) held their first service in the Old Gaiety, they huddled wanly together in the center section of the vast dark theater as though in the black corners a nameless something from another century would clutch them by their coattails and pull them into the umbrella closet. A few shifted uneasily in their seats, waiting for the service to begin. "Mamma," said Emmy Leslie, aged seven, in a sibilant whisper, "it's spooky in here," and her mother, who said hush, agreed with her.

From backstage, where they had hastily assembled, the choir filed forward rather sheepishly onto the stage, and stood forlornly among the folding camp chairs set up on either side of the rostrum. Awkwardly, by ones and twos, they sat down. Frances, in the front row of sopranos, counted them from under lowered lids, as she pretended to be meditating. Across the uncarpeted stage from her were two basses and four altos, the women in the simple white dresses they had been asked to wear; on her own side there were six sopranos and four tenors. She could see the men's dark shapes lined up behind her. Not such a bad turn-out, for the first, if they'd only had time to practice something. And of course there was always Mrs. Wellington.

There always had been Mrs. Wellington. She had sung in church choirs since she was a girl, she was fond of telling anyone within earshot—a considerable distance; church just wouldn't seem like church without it, and all that. Although she had no voice at all and sang the anthems in a nasal monotone like a factory whistle at noon, she had a great deal of money, and so it had been only recently that the choir director at First Church had dared suggest that she might enjoy the service more from a front pew than from in the choir loft, a suggestion which had been made with timidity and desperation on the part of the director, and which had been received by Mrs. Wellington with horror and a show of wrath that shook First Church to its Primary Department and caused the church treasurer to acquire a great dislike for the choirmaster. It was this incident more than any conviction that Dr. McDonough was the new Messiah which brought Mrs. Wellington into the New World Church and instantly into the New World choir, but at least, thought Frances, her very size makes us look twice as big as we would have, and maybe her voice will vanish in the folds of the curtain.

The theater was so still that the clang of a streetcar bell cut clearly across the silence. As Frances looked at the rows of upturned faces, she was conscious of a small pang, for there was among the congregation, she felt, a brooding anxiety, even a little doubt, about the success of their new venture—already it was a venture more than an adventure. And there was a faint feeling of foolishness as they reacted to the dank atmosphere of the Old Gaiety. Most of them might be partially reassured because the Braxtons were there, for after all the Braxtons were almost the most important people in town. But who would reassure the Braxtons? Frances wished Dr. McDonough would start the service.

He had come quietly from behind the backdrop to sit in a large oak chair at the rear of the stage; in his heavy black robes his body looked even bigger than usual. He not only seemed perfectly content on the stage of the theater, with his arms resting on the arms of the chair; he looked like a man who at last has come home.

While she was watching Dr. McDonough curiously, Frances heard, as though from a long way away, the music of a violin. It was so faint at first, so thin, she wasn't even sure it came from within the theater. Then, as it grew louder, she saw that in the orchestra pit, half hidden from her by the old upright piano, a young man was playing, unaccompanied and without a score. He was bent away from her to his violin, and she couldn't see his face, but she could watch his fingers along the strings. They were not very long fingers; they were wiry and sure, and the nails were clean and short.

She had no idea what he was playing. Singing in a church choir could scarcely be called a musical education, especially when most rehearsals were devoted to the babbling exchange of gossip. And she had purposely avoided music courses in college because they required too much work. Traveling orchestras occasionally included Kingston in their tours during the winter season, and Frances always attended these concerts, partly from a sense of civic pride and partly because there was little else to do. But the programs bored her, and she usually spent the second half in a whispered conversation with her mother on the fashions and faces in the audience.

But she had never heard music like this before; rather, never before had she listened. It reached down and fished her stomach up through her throat, left her empty and breathless, full and choking, all at the same time. My goodness, he certainly can play, she thought to herself. She thought it so strongly that she was afraid she might accidentally have said the words aloud. She glanced at Mrs. Wellington beside her, but that lady was gazing enraptured at the ceiling. Yes, he certainly can play, Frances thought again, and wondered who he was.

When the music had stopped, the notes of it still hung in the air. "Strangers and pilgrims on the earth," said Dr. McDonough to his congregation, "we seek a country, a better country, which hath foundations, whose builder and maker is God."

After church, while the choir was rummaging through the wings in search of hats and gloves, Miss Cantrick, Dr. McDonough's secretary, moved around the group, shaking hands, welcoming, greeting. She caught Frances going out of the stage door. "Won't you go out front and say something to that nice young man who played for us this morning, Fran? I'm taking him home to dinner, and I'm afraid he's waiting for me all by himself out there." She smiled and was gone without waiting for an answer. Frances looked after her for a moment, wondering for the hundredth time why a woman of her charm and beauty had never married. Then she turned and shouldered open the heavy side door which led to the already deserted auditorium.

From the far ends of the aisles came a chatter of voices and pale light from the street. The chandelier had been turned off, but two unshaded bulbs on the stage spread a brittle film of light on the dirty boards and curtains and first rows of orchestra seats. The young man had put his violin in its case and was now slumped in a seat on the aisle, dandling the case on his knee while he gazed up into the darkness. The light etched his face against the dark; to Frances as she came through the side door toward him, it looked like a mask, lifeless and chalky, and the cords stood out on his neck. His eyes were sunk in shadow behind his high cheekbones, and it was only when he stood up quickly at her footsteps that she saw any life in his face. His eyes were bright, hard and washed with light, like a windowpane with the sun on it.

"Your music was so fine," she said abruptly. "It meant a lot to me—I mean, it helped the service."

He had put his violin case on the seat so that he could shake her outstretched hand. "Thank you very much," he said now. "I hope I may come again."

"You're not a member?" It was not a question at all, but just something to say. Frances knew all the congregation well. "Do you live in Kingston?"

Afterwards, in remembering their meeting, she was always surprised at her immediate awareness of everything about him: the odd inflection in his voice, his taut body, a faint flavor which she identified at once to herself as "foreign." Although she had never been nearer a foreign shore than the ferry at Norfolk, she had read foreign books, like *Jean Christophe* and *Anna Karenina*, with admiration and longing; she could recite whole passages of *Madame Bovary* aloud.

He was talking, however, and behaving in a most ordinary way. "No, I live in New York, but I'm working out

2   7

at Lake Luray for the summer, in the resort there. Playing with their little orchestra, you know." He gestured at his violin, and then turned his fingers up and glanced at them ruefully. "Four years in the Army haven't helped my hands at all—though I managed to practice a little."

She stared at his hands too, and then looking up, found his eyes on hers. She flushed; she knew she flushed. So she said hurriedly, "I'm terribly sorry. I'm being very rude. I forgot to introduce myself. My name is Frances Acheson."

"I saw you in the choir and wondered. My name is Paul Revkin."

Immediately her face changed. She felt it change. She saw his left eyebrow tilt sardonically. "You're surprised to find a Jew bringing music to your church?"

"Why no, of course not," she said hastily. "Really, I had no idea you were a Jew. I mean . . . not, of course, that it makes any difference—" Her voice trailed off as she looked at his eyes. It was as though someone had pulled down the shades on brilliantly lighted windows.

She realized that she was somehow behaving stupidly. It was at times like this that she was conscious of her height, of the size of her feet, of the fact that her arms seemed to have so little connection with her body. But she had known very few Jewish people among her college associates, and there were none in her circle of friends. Anyway, she never wondered about people's religion; beyond the fact that Mr. Revkin looked—well, foreign, she hadn't even given the matter a thought. Then it occurred to her that he was hypersensitive about his race and detected slights where none was intended, so she began again, bravely enough in the face of his glassy silence.

2 8

"Your name sounds Russian, sort of, like Pushkin or Potemkin or something."

"Both my parents were born in Odessa," he said, adding, "that's in Russia."

She hadn't known.

His face changed expression very little as he spoke. Perhaps he's had to learn control of his reactions pretty much, thought Frances as she watched him.

"But I was born over here," Paul was saying. He seemed to feel that his few statements sketched his life adequately enough, for as he picked up his case and stood back to let her precede him up the aisle, he asked if she were waiting for Miss Cantrick too.

"No, she goes a different way from mine," Frances said over her shoulder. "I have to take a bus out to the Hillcrest section. My family has the car, and they go to another church."

It made her feel good to be able to say this, but he didn't comment and she couldn't see his face. It was not until they reached the lobby that he spoke, and then, "Are you going to attend the Women's Club concert this afternoon?"

She gestured rather vaguely. "Well, mother and I are members, of course, but we really hadn't—" and then more quickly, "are you playing?"

"Yes, I am. Miss Cantrick is on the committee of the club, you know, and it was she who arranged for me to play here this morning before the concert."

"I'd love to come," said Frances warmly. "What are you going to play?"

"What would you like me to play?" he countered. She thought he was going to smile at last; but he didn't.

"Oh mercy, I'm not musical at all." She ran her tongue across her lower lip. "But I do like *Intermezzo*. You know that thing?" Humming four notes, "I don't know who wrote it . . ."

"*Intermezzo*," he repeated. "Until this afternoon, then." He bowed and walked out of the lobby toward the parking lot without looking back and without, she realized suddenly, having smiled once. And that wasn't a bow, really, just a gesture, but for one nice minute there, she actually thought he was going to kiss her hand. That would have been—well, foreign, anyway.

With unusual reticence, Frances did not tell her family of her meeting with Paul, at dinner; her reasons were obscure but instinctive. And since the matter of the new church was at best a painful one ("Now Fran, don't give your father indigestion!"), the whole subject was easily ignored. But she managed to overcome her mother's natural Sunday inertia by an appeal to her civic pride, and persuaded her to go to the Women's Club concert during the afternoon.

Mrs. Acheson had allowed herself to be persuaded without too much difficulty, not because of Frances' nonsense about civic responsibility—which she saw through—but because of the very real affection she had for her daughter ("I *like* Frances," she was fond of saying to her church circle, "in addition to loving her,") and because of her desire to be with her whenever Frances would permit it. For all her apparent placidness—phlegm, her husband often said—Mrs. Acheson was a woman of greater perception than her family had ever realized, and now, as Frances drove the family Buick into town, she looked at her daughter's profile and wondered what brought on this sudden

3 0

interest in classical music. In her calm way she doubted that it was the music.

There had already gathered in the concert room of the Club the familiar group of women, poising their weight precariously on the tiny chairs, fanning, panting, twisting their corsets surreptitiously as the perspiration ran down between the stays. If there had been *anywhere* else to go, that hot June afternoon . . .

". . . Mary has taken the children down on the Rappahannock for the summer, but somebody had to stay and look after Will—"

". . . I haven't had a maid since Annie left me to go to Washington and I was so good to that nigger—"

". . . I heard Elsie's son married some English girl while he was overseas—"

"Well, some of those English girls are right nice . . ."

The soft voices drifted sluggishly through the room. Mrs. Acheson had spoken to acquaintances here and there, but she was primarily absorbed by Frances' distraction. You'd have thought she was to be asked to sing or something, she thought, and noticed that Frances was putting her gloves on and taking them off, methodically, abstractedly. It was one of her more objectionable nervous habits. Just as she reached out and laid her hand gently on her daughter's arm, the heavy blue curtains screening the stage parted and revealed a grand piano. Immediately a heavy woman came briskly from the wings and seated herself, staring intently at the music she had placed on the rack, and cracking her knuckles viciously. The talk had died, and the noise of the woman's knuckles cracking was as sharp in the silence as the snapping of logs in a fireplace.

"Isn't that Miss Eng—" Mrs. Acheson began, leaning

toward her daughter, but Frances hissed, "Shh-hh-hh!" without looking around. A young man with a dark face and a sullen look had come to the front of the stage carrying a violin and bow loosely in his hand, and was bowing to the applause the audience offered. Mrs. Acheson watched him while his eyes slowly and carefully surveyed the small group; they rested at last upon Frances. There was no smile on either face, no nod, but a look moved swiftly between them. Mrs. Acheson let her hand fall from Frances' arm.

The violinist said, "I shall play Brahms' *Sonata in G*, the Andante from Mendelssohn's *Concerto in E Minor*, and the second, fourth and fifth movements of Lalo's *Symphonie Espagnole*, without intermission." It was as though he were speaking only to Frances.

After the first few notes, Mrs. Acheson calmly removed her mind from the music, although her face retained its pleasant expression of attention, a trick she had mastered early in her marriage. The nervousness Frances had shown was well accounted for by the look which had passed between her and that young musician, whatever his name was. Where had she met him? Probably at the new church that very morning. Had it been sooner, Frances would certainly have revealed such a secret long since. Every conversation, every encounter, was shared at the dinner table, repeated at length to amuse herself as well as her parents. And she did tell a story well, Mrs. Acheson reflected. The first time she'd ever been kissed, for instance. She'd come upstairs after the boy had left, sixteen or seventeen she was, and had sat in the darkness on her parents' bed. "It was awful," she moaned, "just awful. Like kissing Daddy." Neither James nor she had ever demanded these confidences, Mrs. Acheson reminded herself, but they flattered themselves that they had created an atmosphere of such friendliness that "my daughter talks to me about anything" was one of James' favorite boasts at the bank. But now she wondered. After all Frances was twenty-three. Most girls her age were getting married . . .

She glanced instinctively at the young violinist. His head was turned so that she could take a long look at his profile as he played. Very attractive, in a peculiar sort of way. Almost too lean though, as though he didn't eat the right kind of food. Smoldering fire, she phrased to herself deliberately, smoldering fire. That's very good. I wonder where he comes from. He hasn't the look of *our* young men. Actually, he looks . . .

She turned her eyes to Frances, who was leaning forward, very still, her chin in her cupped palms and her eyes fixed on the man's face. Mrs. Acheson had often wondered what kind of man would capture her daughter's imagination. Ernie had been too dull, and Steve "just a dumb ox" and George . . . "Oh Mother, *not* George!" followed by shrieks of laughter. But those were early college days, when there were still plenty of young men around, before they began to go off by twos and threes to camps and naval bases. In those days they had come quickly, had been dismissed even more quickly. What did Frances want in a man? What could she be expecting of marriage? "You've been reading too many books," Steve had said rudely as he swung onto the train for Camp Lee. And all Frances had to say of him was, "Honestly, Mother, he used to propose between mouthfuls of chocolate candy. He'd say, 'For the last time, Fran, chaomp chomp, aren't you going to marry me?' And when I'd say no, he'd just sigh and eat another piece."

So they had all gone, Mrs. Acheson reflected, and for the last few years the town had been very quiet. Strange boys in uniform turned up on week ends in Main Street, moodily viewing the Civil War relics. Frances had brought some of them home from the USO, but they had all slid in and out of town without a trace, except for a handful of thank-you letters from all over the world . . . To tell the truth, Mrs. Acheson admitted, I couldn't say when was the last time Franny had a date. Or who there is in town to date. Unless . . .

A spatter of applause startled her, and the room swung back into focus. The young man was bowing again, easily, but with that odd remoteness, motioning to his accompanist to share the applause, and finally walking behind her into the wings. Mrs. Acheson watched Frances with some amusement and more concern; her continued and vehement clapping after the original burst had died down was causing several women to glance around at her, but finally produced what she evidently desired. Another little ripple of applause began to flow from their vicinity and swelled until the violinist reappeared on the stage. "For an encore," he said, "I shall play the *Souvenir de Vienna* of Henri Provost, better known as *Intermezzo*."

An encouraging little murmur of appreciation ran through the group; here at last was something they knew.

Frances had been leaning forward all through the concert; now she slid back onto the end of her spine, loosely. Mrs. Acheson whispered, more sharply than she had intended, "Frances, sit up like a lady, for heaven's sake!" and saw her daughter's eyes turn upon her in blank surprise. She'd really forgotten where we were, her mother thought, or even that I was here!

The performance was over at last, and the women began to gather themselves together, patting hankies gently to upper lips, pushing wispy hair under Leghorns. Mrs. Acheson drew her gloves on thoughtfully as her eyes traced her daughter's line of vision.

The young man had been ringed in at the bottom of the steps to the platform by a twittering aviary of women. Like full-breasted robins after a worm, she thought unkindly. But she was forced to admire the cool assurance with which the man dominated the group, cocking his head respectfully to this old lady, moving his hand occasionally in a deprecatory gesture, smiling a few times upon the charmed covey. It was the first time she had seen him smile, Mrs. Acheson realized, and decided to her own satisfaction why he didn't smile more often. He knows how effective it is when he turns it on, she said to herself, and pursed her lips.

Frances, who had been standing irresolutely in the aisle looking sullenly toward the group, now grabbed her mother's arm abruptly. "Let's go. There's no use waiting here all night." Then she stalked toward the door. It's ridiculous for a girl of twenty-three to go leaping through a crowded room like a goat, her mother mused as she followed. I think I know what she needs, but I hope *he* isn't it. With this muddled thought, she walked out of the wide portals of the Club.

f o u r

The idea of the gas chamber had come to Frances early in her first months of teaching English at Kingston High School; in the succeeding two years her mental blueprints for it had been extensively developed. She lay awake at night elaborating upon it; it was her favorite dream.

A fairy godmother came to her and said, "Frances, here is a gas chamber, fully equipped. You may put any pupils into it you want, but not more than ten." The first six or seven came easily; most of them were members of the football team, great hulking brutes who glowered ferociously as they were shoved through the door. For the last three places her choice varied with the day and with the mood. "Move the total up to fifteen," she would plead sometimes; and sometimes, on really bad days, she wished it were fifty.

Frances had been a good student, an obedient student. All through school she had sat in the front row, watching the teachers enviously as they handed out papers, read stories or wrote on the blackboard. One of her great delights was to be allowed to write on the blackboards herself, and since she wrote in a large, clear hand, she was often called on. When she began to teach, she planned her lessons conscientiously, and planned too to write a great deal on the board. In no time at all, however, she discovered that to turn her back on the class, even for two minutes, was not only to lose her feeble hold on its attention, but also to invite bedlam. Paper airplanes whizzed through the room, large boys began to wrestle in the aisles, and chalk splattered on the wall dangerously near her eyes. This was only the beginning of her disillusionment.

During that first year she wasted three months attempting to instill in her classes some of her own enjoyment of English literature. The next three months she compromised on beating a few simple facts into her students' minds. Finally she surrendered to the necessity of just keeping them quiet so that the other teachers in the building might be heard. It was at this point that the roster of her gas chamber read like the roll of the Junior Class.

"The first year is always the hardest, my dear," said the other teachers and the principal and her father, when in June, she demurred at signing a second contract. Unfortunately, she had believed them, and had returned to Kingston High in the fall of 1945, only to find that the Junior Class had become the Senior Class, and she had to teach them all over again.

That was the year she threw herself downstairs one Monday morning when the prospect of five more days was suddenly too much to be endured. It had not been so difficult. The hallway was shadowy, and she could hear her parents' voices at breakfast in the dining room. She put one ankle in front of the other and pitched forward heavily all the way to the bottom. Although she hadn't wanted to kill herself, she hoped that she might at least break a leg or dislocate a vertebra. Actually she had not so much as sprained a finger, and the doctor, summoned frantically by her family, told her she'd be perfectly all right on Tuesday.

The second year had finally crawled by, June had come at last, and now she stood in the rear of the hot, crowded school auditorium and watched wearily as the principal presented diplomas to the scrubbed and shining graduates.

"William Redfield." A tall boy strode forward, swaggering a little, his wild red hair slicked down, grinning at the burst of applause from the students. William Redfield, better known as Buck. He had always occupied the number one spot on her gas chamber list; there had never been any challenger. She wondered if his father were in the audience, and if so, did he have on more than a pair of underpants?

. . . At the end of the first semester, Frances had outlined the English examination on the board and was attempting to explain it in spite of the competition she was receiving from Buck and Thurman Kelly, who were fighting over a comic book in the aisle.

"Leave this room immediately," she finally demanded, and Thurman had left. He was always happy to get out; in fact, he often left without permission. But Buck, grinning apishly, had sat on the desk nearest the door, swinging his long legs. "My father pays taxes and you can't make me leave," he told her insolently.

She walked up to him, so angry she forgot to be frightened. "I said get out, and I mean it. Get out of this room!" The class sat enthralled.

"I ain't gonna leave and you can't make me," he said again.

A year and a half of loathing rose up in her. She slapped his mouth so hard he rocked back on his haunches. "Get out!"

He jumped to his feet and hung over her threateningly. "Ya hit me!" She fully expected to be knocked down on the spot.

Fortunately Thurman had left the door open. She grabbed Buck by the collar and shoved him through it. But she had forgotten that the stairs dropped sharply away right outside the door, and her final furious push sent him hurtling down them. My God! Suppose I've killed him, she thought panic-stricken, hanging over the banisters. But in a moment he had picked himself up, and raising his fist had snarled something unintelligible before he went on down the steps.

As soon as school was over for the day, Frances rushed to Buck's home, an unpainted bungalow near the factory. "Mr. Redfield's in bed," said the sallow woman who answered her ring. "He works nights at the factory. I'll get 'um." Visions of lawsuits and court action, years in jail, rose in her mind as she sat on the edge of a hard rocker twisting her gloves in her hand. And then Mr. Redfield came into the room. He was enormous, hairy, and filthy, with blood-shot eyes and a stubble of beard on his face. He had on nothing but his underpants, and the smell of his feet as he stuck them out into the middle of the room nearly sickened her. "I cain't do nuthin' with Buck, lady," he said moodily, when she had told him the story. "I practically never see him 'cept on Sundays. Anything you want to do is okay with me."

And now there stood Buck on the platform, shaking hands with Mr. Wade, the principal, waving his diploma over his head with both hands while the audience laughed indulgently. Frances could still feel the skin of his loose mouth under her hand as she had in the exquisite moment when she hit him, and her palm itched to hit him again.

"Vernon Wilson," boomed Mr. Wade's voice over the amplifying system, and Vernon shuffled forward sheepishly across the platform. He was a nice kid, one of the few nice ones, Frances reflected, only he should have stopped in the seventh grade. Poor Vernon. He tried so hard. He always sat in the front row, and his eyes followed her around the room with a kind of hangdog devotion which would have been irritating if it hadn't been so pathetic. There was the day when, correlating English and science in the "progressive" manner, she had bravely plunged into Darwin. She wrote *Origin of Species* on the blackboard and under the words she drew a tree.

"Now Darwin doesn't say that men come from monkeys, class, but that men and monkeys are like limbs of the same tree. Is that clear?" She hoped she was right.

Silence, while the flat-faced students accepted, rejected, or ignored the whole idea. Gratefully she drew breath, about to move along to Thackeray or someone equally safe when—

"Miss Acheson." It was Vernon. "I think Darwin's absolutely right, Miss Acheson. I've seen a lot of men who look like monkeys."

Never discourage discussion. "Now Vernon, Darwin did *not* say that men came from monkeys—weren't you listening?—but that men and monkeys are like limbs of the same tree."

"Well"—deeply serious and groping for words—"I still think Darwin's right. Absolutely right. I think monkeys have been getting better looking in the past few years."

Vernon and Buck had been two of the seven seniors she had failed. Or rather, had tried to fail. But *they* had fixed that: Mr. Wade himself had come to see her in the last days of school, after her grades had gone in.

"Please sit down, Miss Acheson," he had said when

she'd risen to greet him. This was not courtesy, she thought, so much as the fact that she towered over him and made him uncomfortable. "I understand that you have failed to pass seven of our senior class?"

She flushed at his manner. "Yes sir. That's true."

"You're quite aware that these students cannot graduate unless they pass their English course?"

"Certainly, Mr. Wade."

"I have the names of these students here." He pulled a list from his pocket and read them pontifically, in a manner, Frances thought, more suited to a reading of a list of war heroes than of seven illiterate adolescents. "Just what was your trouble, Miss Acheson?"

Frances uncrossed her long legs slowly. "It was hardly *my* trouble, Mr. Wade," she said after a moment. "Those boys are illiterate, stupid, uneducated, completely lacking in manners. They should never have got beyond the eighth grade. They would be a disgrace to our school system if we were to give them diplomas."

"Yes. Hmmm. To be sure," said Mr. Wade, twirling the list between his fingers. "What exactly does this course here consist of, Miss Acheson? That is to say, what do you try to teach them?"

"I *try* to teach them," repeated Frances coldly, "English composition, which is based on the premise that they are acquainted with the rudiments of grammar. Fallacy number one. And I *try* to teach them the history of English literature simultaneously, which is based on the equally fallacious premise that they know how to read."

Mr. Wade stared over Frances into the benign face of George Washington floating on its cloud, until the silence in the room became a steady hum and the sounds of the grammar school at recess came through the open windows.

"Isn't it strange, Miss Acheson," he said finally, "that Miss Connelly, who teaches the other section of senior English, had no student failing in her classes?"

"I couldn't say, Mr. Wade," she answered clearly. "I am not acquainted with Miss Connelly's standards." Perspiration began to accumulate at the backs of her knees. Mr. Wade was now engrossed in a picture of the Edgar Allan Poe shrine on the far wall. She waited. She heard him take a short breath.

"Miss Acheson," he said, sucking his back teeth, "the school board is not in a position financially to keep these grown boys—nearly grown, certainly," he tucked in with a wave of his hand, "keep them in school indefinitely. Our schools are crowded to capacity now, and there is still a desperate teacher shortage. Besides, you know as well as I do that if they don't graduate, they won't come back anyway. All of them are over sixteen and beyond the reach of the truancy law—"

She interrupted him, leaning forward and flattening her palms against her thighs. "So they're supposed to get diplomas just because they've reached a certain age? Whether they know anything or not? When they can scarcely write legibly, much less coherently?"

"Miss Acheson, as I said before, if these boys go out of this school now, without a diploma, they won't come back next year, and they'll be handicapped through life—" He broke off and said pointedly, "I suggest that you give them another examination."

"And what about the others, Mr. Wade? The other kids who've worked hard all year to get through while these boys cut classes and read comic books in my face and generally disrupted everything—you just don't realize what kind of boys they are—"

"I hardly think the character of the student has anything to do with the problem."

"Then how about the kids coming along? How can you maintain any standards at all when you just shove them through because they're sixteen and the school's too full . . ."

She stopped. There was no flicker in his eyes. "I appreciate your interest, Miss Acheson," he smiled faintly, "but suppose you let me worry about maintaining standards, and you just worry about getting your classes taught." He began to wipe his glasses with a handkerchief. "And you will have that examination ready by tomorrow, won't you?"

"I don't give a damn whether they all have to write X for their names," she said distinctly and stood up. "I'll give them all D minus and hope to hell I never see them again."

She had frightened herself as much as she had shocked Mr. Wade. Without answering, he had put his glasses on carefully and had walked out of the door, shutting it softly behind him. In the empty room Frances heard the heavy pumping of her heart . . .

The Kingston band crashed into the school song, and the audience rose and sang noisily.

"We're behind you, cheering for you
Glory to your name, rah, rah, rah!"

The 1946 commencement exercises were over.

Near the exit Frances saw her friends Emily and Millicent, who were obviously looking for her. They were in a state of suppressed excitement. They had barely laid their cheeks up against hers when Emily asked, "Have you heard the news about Roberta Lee?" and Millicent threw in immediately, "She's getting married!"

"No!" Frances had reached the sidewalk before she could ask, "Who, for heaven's sake?"

"We don't know him," Emily said. "Some character she met at Columbia this spring."

"How do you all know about it?"

"Oh, Emily and I got a letter from her," Millicent chirruped. "One of those round-robin affairs. It was addressed to you too, but I left it at home."

"She didn't say too much about him," Emily went on, "except that he's getting his Master's in Education too, like she is, and he was in all her classes . . ."

"Oooh Emily, wait. Fran, Emily hasn't told you the best part! He's a widower!"

A little hush fell. They walked along the quiet street for a moment in silence.

"That must make him pretty old?" suggested Frances tentatively.

"She didn't give his age," Emily said. "But she did mention his two children, who're back home in Kansas."

"His name's Claude Flynn," Millicent tucked in. "That sounds Catholic, doesn't it?"

"Roberta would never marry a Catholic," said Emily scornfully. "Her family would die."

"Oh, I don't know," Millicent answered. "Maybe she's just not as choosy as we are."

"Choosy!" cried Frances unexpectedly. "Choosy, my

4 4

heavens! What have we got to choose from? You can't pick daisies in a cement sidewalk!"

"Well, it's my personal opinion," Millicent lowered her voice, "that Roberta went to New York just to get a man."

"Which she did, and more power to her," Frances said shortly.

"I've just about given up." Emily's voice in the darkness was placid. "I guess I'll be teaching the third grade for the rest of my life."

The conversation was settling into its old familiar channel. They always make jokes about being old-maid school teachers, thought Frances, but down deep underneath, they don't believe, for an instant, they ever will be. They honestly think some bolt of lightning is going to crash through the roof of their house and deposit Lochinvar on the bed.

"You probably will be teaching all the rest of your life," she said rudely to Emily. "Look at Miss Connelly and Miss Harris and all the rest of them. They never thought they'd go on and on teaching year after year, but they do. And why? Because they haven't got anything else to do, so they get drier and dustier and pretty soon they're lost."

"But I don't want to get married just to have Mrs. on my tombstone," Millicent protested, and Emily added, "Besides, I don't think men are all *that* important."

"Oh, how would you know? Have you ever had one— I mean to be in love with, and him in love with you? No!" Frances answered her own question bitterly. "Four years in a girls' college, and on week ends they took you out to the corner and pointed out a strange object and said, 'Look out, that's a *man!*' We drove to college and home every night—

might just as well have been still in high school. And on top of that, two years here at home with all the men away at war . . . If we were Catholic, we'd all be ready for the convent."

Emily said to Millicent, "I just love Fran when she gets this way. It doesn't matter whether it's the OPA or the Russians or men or anything. In two seconds she's off like a rocket."

Emily's face was only a blur in the warm June night, but Frances knew that she was smiling indulgently.

"All right, so I rant and rave. But I feel like we're all missing something important! We're getting older and older and never any nearer to it, whatever it is. I feel like I'm in a railroad station," she said more slowly, fumbling for her thoughts, "and there are thousands of people rushing here and there all around. You can hear their noise crashing back at you from the walls. And outside there are trains leaving all the time, trains going somewhere . . . But the trains aren't very clearly marked, so all these people keep on rushing madly about, inside the station—just because they're afraid to get on a train without a positive destination."

She looked at their dim shapes desperately. "Oh, I don't know what I'm trying to say, except that wouldn't you think we'd go out and get on some train, *any* train— just to be going somewhere?"

"We're going somewhere," Emily said mildly. "The country needs teachers. You just get so impatient."

"I am impatient," Frances retorted. "Do you think I want to wake up one morning and find myself as old and dreary as Miss Connelly, same job, same house, same faces, still a virgin." (That shocked them!) "You lie down in the bottom of your nice fur-lined rut and hear the horses' hooves tearing down the road above your head. If you raise your head a little, you could even see the horses going by. But you wouldn't dare go up on the road yourself for fear you'd be trampled to death!"

"Oh Franny, you don't even know what you're talking about," Millicent laughed. "You'd forget all that kind of talk in a minute if some man would come along and marry you. You'd be just as happy as your mother or Emily's or mine. You watch."

They left Frances at her driveway, and she could hear their footsteps up the silent street. The street lights greened the underside of the trees, and the girls' shadows flickered and spread as they walked. Laughter trickled back to her, and off in the mountains an automobile hooted. As Frances listened, she thought she could hear horses' hooves pounding down the road above her fur-lined ditch, and the whistle of a train, going somewhere. She turned and went up the moonlit drive toward the house.

f i v e

Paul's first letter to Frances arrived on the morning after the graduation exercises at the high school. He had written it on Monday, had addressed it to her in care of the New World Church, Old Gaiety Theater, Kingston, Virginia; from there it had been forwarded to Judge Braxton's home which Dr. McDonough was using as a temporary study and office, and where Frances was working for the summer as a volunteer assistant to Miss Cantrick. His letter had been brief and quite formal, inviting her to go to a concert to be given on the following Saturday evening in the Kingston High School by the Washington Chamber Music Society.

"I don't know a darn thing about chamber music," Frances had told Miss Cantrick. "I guess I'll read up on it ahead of time so I can make some kind of intelligent comment." After several attempts she had written Paul a polite little note in reply.

> *Dear Paul,*
>
> *Thank you for your invitation to the concert Saturday evening. I'll be delighted to go with you.*
>
> *Won't you have dinner with us before the concert? Mother was also in your audience at the Club, and would like very much to meet you. Our address is 15 Hillcrest Drive, and the Hillcrest bus goes right by.*
>
> *If I don't hear from you before Saturday night, I'll expect you for dinner at six o'clock.*
>
> *Sincerely,*

"What do you think of that?" Frances handed her note to Miss Cantrick. "Only six tries too!"

"That sounds all right, dear, but shouldn't you ask your mother before you start dragging strangers in to dinner?"

"Oh no, they expect me to have my dates to dinner first, before I ever go out with them—so they can look them over, watch their table manners, you know."

Frances said this jokingly—but it's the gospel truth, she thought to herself. I'm like the girls in the B.O. ads.

One date, and they never come back. Not that I blame them, she admitted.

The pattern had been marked out back in high school, when the first gangling boy had asked her to go to the movies.

"Bring him to dinner before the movie, dear," her mother said, and "Sure, make the boy feel right at home," Mr. Acheson added. "Nothing like good family background to give a girl a start in life."

The new boy would come into the living room—Bill, or Jack, or Joe. "Nice place you got here." He would walk around a little, looking at the pictures on the wall, conscious of his height and his big feet. There would be the first awkward moments of conversation.

"D'jou pass all your classes last term, Fran?"

"Oh yes," and then swiftly, "I only squeezed through a couple of them by the skin of my teeth, though." This was a lie. Frances usually made A on every course, but she would rather have died than admit it. It was her rooted belief that men liked their girls to be dumb; she hid her report card in her pocketbook as soon as she received it. "How about you, Bill?"

"Aw, I flunked English again. Ol' lady Skinner's down on me."

Draw them out on their favorite hobby or sport. "How's basketball practice coming along?"

"Aw, so-so. The team's stale."

The silences would grow longer and longer until she would actually welcome the appearance of her parents and the announcement that dinner was ready.

"Prentice, Prentice," her father would say from the head of the table. "Any kin to the Prentices in Staunton?"

"No sir. Not that I know of."

"Fine family. Fine old family," said Mr. Acheson nostalgically. "When I was a boy, I used to date Martha Prentice myself. I wonder what's become of her. You say you aren't kin to them, though? Ummm."

And later, "Lived in Kingston all your life, Bill? What's your father do?"

"He runs a gas station."

One date and they never came back. Frances couldn't blame them. "Mother," she said once desperately, "Can't you make Daddy stop catechizing everybody who comes into this house? He makes them feel so rootless, like orphans or something. What difference does it make if Joe's father isn't one of the Carters of Cartersville? I liked him!"

"Your father's only trying to watch out for you, honey. You don't want to marry a butcher's son."

"Holy heaven, he hadn't asked me to marry him! I just wanted him to ask me to the senior dance, but he hasn't called since that first night."

"I know, darling, but you have to watch these things," Mrs. Acheson said again . . .

With a sigh, Frances signed the note to Paul, sealed and addressed it, and tossed it in the outgoing mail basket. They'll probably be inquiring into his intentions by the soup course, she thought sullenly, and tried to picture her father probing into what she labeled to herself the dark recesses of Paul's soul. Daddy wouldn't get very far there, she told herself.

Saturday night had come, finally. Frances and her father were both upstairs dressing when Paul arrived for dinner a little before six. Mr. Acheson had never been ready for dinner on time in his life, but Frances had been dressing since four-thirty, so her mother's voice was not too gentle when she called, "Fran, aren't you ready yet, dear? Paul is here."

"I'll be right down," she answered, and hastily rubbed the toes of her shoes with a Kleenex. She went through the bathroom into her father's room where he was leaning into the mirror looking for the part in his hair. "Daddy! Aren't you any farther along than that?" He was still in his underwear.

"No hurry," he said good naturedly. "Your mother hasn't called me three times yet." He sniffed. "Hmmm, you smell good. You smell just like your mother."

She returned his grin a little petulantly and told him again to hurry up.

"You certainly are nervous, honey baby. Who is this fellow?" He had an irritating habit of stopping whatever he was doing when he talked, and now, hairbrush in hand, he turned to her curiously.

"Oh, for goodness' sake, hurry up. Mother will be mad," Frances said and then impulsively kissed him on the cheek. "Please?"

He turned back to the mirror docilely. "Is this that violinist you and your mother went to hear last Sunday or so? What's his name?"

"Yes, that's the one," she said very casually. "Paul. Paul Revkin. How do you like my dress?"

"Why are you wearing black in the middle of the summertime? Hot, isn't it? Looks nice though."

"Oh Daddy, everybody knows that black is very chic for the summer. Everybody wears it in New York in the summer."

"They do, huh?" He grinned at her in the mirror,

looking so like a pixie that she had to grin back. "Perk up!" he said. "Don't look so nervous, honey. I won't eat with my knife, I promise."

"And don't tell any of your When-I-was-a-boy stories either."

"Can't I even tell about when I was courting your mother and she caught me?"

"Nobody ever thinks that's funny but you—least of all mother." Hesitantly, she went toward the stairs. "Do be as polite as you can?"

Laughing he called after her, "Just so you don't scratch your back with your fork!" She wondered if Paul could have heard him.

But Paul was not in the living room, where she had spent an hour that afternoon arranging dragon lilies and larkspur on the mantel and all the tables. Then she heard voices in the kitchen and her mother's nice chuckle. As she pushed open the swinging door, she heard her say, "No, I'd just rather do it myself."

"Do what yourself, Mother?" And then, "Hello, Paul. It's nice to see you again. Obviously you and mother have met."

"Yes, Paul's being a great help. He's going to set the table for me." It seemed to Frances that her mother's voice was even slower than usual, as if to point up her own unpunctuated rush. Paul had smiled and spoken over his shoulder as she came in, but had not stopped taking dishes out of the china closet in the pantry and stacking them on the kitchen table. Now he pointed to a pile of salad plates and said to her, as comfortably as though he'd been living there for years, "Here, you take these, and I'll take the rest of them." They went into the shadowy dining room together. "Can you turn on the light, Fran? I'm afraid I'll drop something."

She found the switch and then followed him around the table with the silver and the napkins. "I'm awfully glad you could come to dinner. You didn't have any trouble finding your way out here?"

"No, no trouble at all. Your directions were fine. I was just telling Mrs. Acheson that I was glad to get here in time to set the table. Makes me feel like home."

"Don't you have any sisters?"

"Yes, I have one about your age. But she isn't much help at home either." He smiled at her across the table.

"Oh, is that what mother's been telling you? That's not fair, you know. It's just that mother does everything so well that she can get it done in half the time it takes me—"

"And you can learn more from watching?" he finished.

"I'll cook you a meal sometime. You'll see. You should taste my mushroom soufflé." She'd never made one in her life, but it sounded difficult.

"Fine," he said. "I'd like to." He looked the table over critically. "You forgot the glasses."

In the kitchen, Mrs. Acheson, who had been bent over the oven, straightened and looked at Frances. "What have you done to that dress, dear? Isn't it supposed to have lace cuffs?"

"Well, yes it is," Frances admitted. "But I took them off to wash them, and couldn't quite manage to sew them on again. I got all wrapped up in my elbows."

"Where are they?" Paul asked. "I'll sew them on for you. Your mother's pretty busy."

"*You* will? Where did you learn to sew?"

"My father's a tailor."

Mrs. Acheson said hurriedly, "I'm a cook, but that didn't seem to teach Frances anything. Do that for her, Paul, please?"

"They're in mother's sewing basket in the living room, through here," Frances told him. She found the cuffs and sat in the wing chair by the fireplace with her arm stiffly stretched toward him.

He knelt on the floor in front of her and began to stitch, neatly and quickly. "What were you trying to do, sew them on while you were in the dress? No wonder you got twisted up."

This was the position Mr. Acheson found them in when he came into the room. "Good evening," he said. "Should I go out and come in again noisily?"

Paul rose. "Good evening, sir." And Frances said, "Daddy, this is Paul Revkin, who's spending the summer at Lake Luray." She watched them shake hands. They were nearly of a height, and the black head against the white head pleased her. She felt remarkably light-hearted and happy. She listened to Paul and her father discuss the summer season at Lake Luray with a big and foolish smile on her face, although what they were saying was not particularly amusing. The room seemed to her full of a great pleasantness and warmth, and her warm pleasure reached to the valley beyond the windows and the cradling misty mountains beyond the valley and back to the bowl of dragon lilies on the table by her side. And when she went into dinner at Mrs. Acheson's announcement and saw that the candles were lit and the blinds drawn against the sunset, she smiled appreciatively at her mother and thought again how lovely she was.

But Mr. Acheson was saying, "Fran, turn on the lights for a while, please. You know I can't read by those candles," and was reaching for the heavy Bible on the china press. For a moment she had forgotten this part of the evening, which never varied regardless of the company. With the bright electric light, her mood vanished. As Paul seated her mother, she sat down gloomily at her place, eying the pattern on the china as though she had not memorized it years before. She could not look across the table to Paul.

"The lesson for today," her father said resonantly, "is from Paul's letter to the Galatians, chapter 6, verses 1 through 10." He followed the First Church's guide for home devotions, and as she listened to his voice intone the words, she thought, He's really missed his calling. He should have been a preacher. He'd have been great. That pewside manner. I can see him now, comforting the widow and the orphan, visiting the sick . . . handsome, distinguished, saying just what they want to hear. He'd have gone far.

"As we therefore have opportunity," Mr. Acheson read the words sonorously, "let us do good unto all men, especially unto them who are of the household of the faith."

God! He couldn't have picked a better passage for his purposes if he'd sat up all night.

Then his evening prayer. As usual when they had company, Frances heard little of what he said; her mind was obsessed with the mind across the table from her. She squinted up through her lashes at Paul, whose face was expressionless in the bright light of the chandelier. His eyes, which were not closed, had a blank look, and he seemed to be staring into some secret place midway between the pale candles and a few inches above the bowl of lilacs. He's gone away, she thought wonderingly; he isn't here at all. He's in the same place he went last Sunday when he played, the same place I've seen mother go so many times. And she wondered bleakly if she alone were lost between the two solitudes of her father's stark world and that other secret garden of bright images that lay above the lilac bowl.

"In the Name of Jesus Christ, our Saviour, Amen," droned Mr. Acheson, savoring the rich round tones as long as possible, and then "You can turn off the chandelier now, Frances."

When the electric light was gone and the room was dim in the candlelight and slow twilight, the earlier mood returned to her—and to the others, she felt. Mr. Acheson discoursed at length on his nephew Jimmy's experiences on a DE in the Pacific: "You certainly should read his descriptions of Hawaii! What a time that boy is having." And Paul told stories about France and Germany. He had gone into Normandy with Patton and had been in an anti-tank company, but he didn't mention the war directly, talking mostly of the people he had met and the places he had seen.

"I'm glad I saw Paris and Vienna ten years ago," he said, and then stopped abruptly, as if that sentence reminded him of something—either too beautiful or too ugly —which he wanted to forget.

But Mr. Acheson persisted. "Were you living abroad then?"

"Yes, I studied over there for a few years," he said shortly.

"Music, James," his wife reminded him. "You know. I told you." She had been more than usually quiet, serving the dinner from a low table beside her, suggesting a second helping of ham or batter bread, asking a question occasionally. When Frances remembered, she practiced imitating her mother's serenity, but she was seldom successful. Tonight, however, she too had been quiet. She knew enough to know, at least, that Paul was storming the more formidable fortress first, and she happily noticed signs of weakness on her father's part. He was now telling some of his better stories, and even though they all began with "When I was a boy," Frances realized that he had somehow accepted Paul into the circle of family-and-friends-at-the-bank. Since Mr. Acheson had not had so good a listener, so new an audience, for a long time, he naturally overlooked asking Paul the personal questions which usually went with the meal.

Which is just as well, Frances admitted to herself. Not that Paul couldn't have got around Daddy, I'm sure, but he probably wouldn't want to. He's likely to get up on his high horse any minute even now, if Daddy so much as mentions Jews. And there he'd be, back in his secret place again, and I'm afraid I'd never get him out.

How different he can be, within the space of two minutes, she went on talking to herself. He can look alive and then dead in no time at all, as though he pulls a switch inside himself to be bright or dark. But even when he's brightest, you have the feeling that his hand's on that switch, trembling, just waiting for one word to plunge him into darkness again.

"What time is the concert, Paul?" asked Mrs. Acheson, about the third cup of coffee. "You all don't have too much time."

"It's at eight-thirty," he said, turning to her. "How

long will it take us to get to the high school from here?"

"Oh, why don't you take the car, Paul?" Mr. Acheson offered expansively. "Then you won't have to rush off so fast."

Frances leaned down the table and put her hand over his. "Thanks, darling."

Her father smiled at her tenderly. "You look mighty pretty tonight, black and all." She glanced at Paul. He had said barely half a dozen words to her during the meal, but the same look passed between them which she had experienced at the Women's Club. In her smooth voice, Mrs. Acheson said, "Suppose we go into the living room for a while. It's cooler." And Frances dropped her eyes from Paul's.

Before they could rise from the table, however, the doorbell rang, and Mr. Acheson offered to answer. Mrs. Acheson, who had begun to explain to Paul that they hadn't had a maid since Pearl Harbor, was interrupted by hearty voices from the hall. "Come in, Tom, come in. Have a cup of coffee with us." Frances recognized the flat voice of Mr. Douglas, superintendent of the city schools. She turned a horror-stricken face to her mother: he was here about the job!

But Mrs. Acheson was rising and going forward to greet the new guest who stood in the doorway, introducing Paul to him, offering him coffee and cake, gesturing him to a chair. Frances was the only person in the room still seated; now she too rose and spoke to Mr. Douglas, and her voice came out so loud that they all looked at her.

"Why don't you all go into the living room, Mother? It's much cooler and less messy. Paul and I will clean off the dishes."

5 8

"No, darling, Mr. Douglas is going to eat a piece of my cake, aren't you, Mr. Douglas? Here, Paul. Pass this coffee down, please?"

They all sat down again. Frances had not told her parents of the argument she had had with Mr. Wade on that awful last day of school. Though at first she had planned to, the new excitement of Paul in her life had driven it completely out of her mind. This is the most horrible thing that ever could have happened, she thought wildly. If only we could get out of here before he starts . . .

"We were on our way to the high school just as you came in, Mr. Douglas," she said brightly. "There's a concert being held there tonight—I guess *you* know all about it. The Washington Symphony Society, no—it's the Chamber Music Society. Eight-thirty, Paul, I think you said?"

"Well, honey, it's just seven-thirty now," her father told her gently, and her mother eyed her with curiosity. Mr. Douglas was eating his cake with deliberation. He was a puffy man with fat fingers about the same color as the cake, and he spoke very very slowly, when he could bring himself to speak at all.

"This certainly is good cake, Mrs. Acheson," he said at last, wiping his lips carefully. "No, no more, thank you." He paused and looked all around the room. "I just came over to see Frances here, for a minute. Brought her a contract for next year. Let's see." He fumbled with a handful of papers and letters he dragged out of an inside coat pocket. They all watched him, mesmerized, as he shuffled through them.

Somewhere in the house a floorboard creaked.

Just as Mrs. Acheson rose and snapped on the electric

light, saying, "Perhaps this will help," Mr. Douglas pulled a sheet out from the pile. "Here we are. Here we are." He unfolded it reverently, smoothing out the creases until it lay flat on the table before him.

"Next year will be your third year, Frances. That's correct, isn't it?" He searched the closely printed page for a long moment. Frances didn't answer.

Mr. Acheson came in a little too heartily. "That's right, Tom. It's Fran's third year. She started teaching in 1944."

Mr. Douglas plowed on. "Third year, yes. Here it is. Right here. That means your salary goes up to $1350 per annum, Frances."

"I don't know what she does with it all," Mr. Acheson laughed. He was always conscious of lapses of conversation at his table, and did his best to keep them from occurring. "It's a good thing she doesn't have to support herself on *that* salary!"

Still Frances said nothing. I don't feel anything either, she thought, that is, unless numbness is a feeling.

"Have to go out and catch my teachers these days," Mr. Douglas remarked to no one in particular. "Not like the good old days when they came to us begging for jobs." He picked up the contract gently and handed it across the table to Frances. Automatically she took it from him and held it in her hand, her elbow on the edge of the table. When she noticed that her hand was shaking visibly, she laid the paper down.

"There's just one thing, Frances." Mr. Douglas' voice seemed to go round and round in hollow circles in her head. "I had a little talk with Mr. Wade the other day. He's the principal of the high school," he informed them all in the manner of one who gives away state secrets, "and he tells me that you and he had a little run-in at the end of the term, Frances."

God! Did he have to keep using her name every two seconds and dragging it out that way? Just get this business over!

"I know how nervous teachers get when June comes rolling 'round. They do get nervous, very nervous. And what they need is a nice long rest. What are you folks going to do this summer?"

"Well, we really hadn't figured, Tom." Mr. Acheson was caught a little offguard at this turn in the conversation.

There was a fine line between Mrs. Acheson's brows, and she kept her eyes on Mr. Douglas' face.

"I think you and Mr. Wade had better have a little understanding, Frances," Mr. Douglas drawled, looking back at her. "He was kind of upset at the language you used to him, thinks you spoke a little out of turn there—"

"What happened, Fran?" demanded her father. "You didn't tell me anything about this."

"—And if you were to drop in on him, say Monday or Tuesday, and kind of straighten things out, then you could bring this contract around to my office, all signed up, and we'd forget the whole thing."

"What the hell are you all talking about?" Mr. Acheson demanded again. He was getting pretty mad, otherwise he'd never have cursed in front of outsiders. But "Be quiet, James," his wife told him, not even looking at him, but looking at Frances.

There was still that no feeling at all. The candle flame doubled and tripled in front of her eyes. Her voice came out, but it was not like her voice. "I have no intention of apologizing to Mr. Wade for my remarks, Mr. Douglas. I meant them then and I mean them now. I am not interested in teaching school ever again." She stuck the contract toward him stiffly. He did not immediately reach for it, so she let it drop on the table. "And now if you will excuse us, Mr. Revkin and I have tickets to a concert. Good night. Coming, Paul?"

Without daring to look at her mother—whose face, she knew, would be composed though grave; nor at her father —whose reactions she would have to hear at length later on; nor at Paul—whom she had actually forgotten for those moments and who was now excusing himself from a damned awkward situation, she walked straight out of the room and through the house to the hall where the car keys were on the card tray. There she stood waiting for Paul, jingling the keys in her hand. He came up to her. She had a desire to touch him, to take his hand, but she merely handed him the keys without a word, and they left the house together.

s i x

Now, in the car, she was suffocatingly aware of him, of his hands on the wheel, of his silence which was not remote but expectant and generous. The next remark, the breaking of that silence, was her responsibility, certainly, and her mind gnawed at phrases, snatches of sentences, none of which made sense: the offhand approach, "I guess you wonder what that was all about?" The apologetic "I'm sorry I got you into such an awful situation." The ridiculous "You must think I'm a dreadful fool" . . . And the longer she waited, the harder it was to begin. She took a deep and trembling breath.

Suddenly he turned the car off the road onto a rocky ledge that looked across the darkening valley, pulled up, stopped. "Do you still want to go to the concert, Frances?"

It was the tone of his voice that did it, the sympathy—no, more, the understanding he was offering. She shook her head, afraid to trust her voice, still staring straight ahead; but even so, it was coming. Her throat tautened, her chin twitched, and she began to cry, the way a child cries, with gulping sobs, tears and then more tears as her tension eased and she started to enjoy her misery. After a moment Paul handed her his handkerchief, and she wiped her eyes and blew her nose noisily.

"I got lipstick on it," she said feebly, giving it back and looking at him for the first time. He had twisted around so that his arm lay along the back of the seat. His hand was so near her face that by moving an inch she could have touched her cheek against it. She wanted to, but she didn't dare.

"Would you like to talk about it?"

She got it out finally, in starts and pauses and rushes and stops. It was such a stupid little tale, really, full of gripes and petty annoyances, frustrations, futility. Telling it to him that way, with his face in the shadow—almost as though she were in a Catholic confessional—it sounded childish and unimportant and foolish. To behave so shamefully to Mr. Douglas, and in her own home, and before

Paul! Lord! Must she always be so thoughtless, so impulsive, just as her father said? She had to agree with him, she *was* a goddam fool.

As though he had read her thought, Paul said out of the darkness, "Are you always so impulsive?"

"I'm afraid so," she sighed. "Daddy says I might get over it when I grow up."

"Are all your impulses good ones?" he persisted.

She was startled. "Do you think this was a good one?"

"Didn't you, when you had it?"

"We-ell, yes, when I had it . . . but I always fly off the handle and live to regret it."

"What will there be to regret about this?"

"Oh, Lord, everything. For one thing, I know Daddy's furious."

"Is this the first time?"

She laughed, really amused. "No, nor the last."

"Then you needn't waste time regretting that. What else?"

"Well, now I'm one of the unemployed. My professional career is smashed to smithereens."

"Was it a career, or just something you fell into?"

"You could hardly call it a career, I admit. I certainly wasn't trained for it, nor really suited for it from the beginning. But—" she stopped, remembering, and he was gracious enough not to prompt her. She was remembering how much she had once wanted to teach school . . . Playing at school teacher with her dolls or, when they'd let her, with the children in the neighborhood, under the peach tree in the garden in the long hot summer mornings. Counseling at camp between college years, Augusts full of lovely loving children. The handcraft classes—grubby fingers earnestly weaving silly baskets. The swimming meets —the day that her Mohican tribe won the swimming meet was one of her favorite memories. Vespers on the hill at sunset—the sweet thin voices piping in the still air, *Day Is Dying in the West*. And the faces of the little girls on the last day, when the station wagons were lined up in the road and the suitcases were piled on the trucks and the train was down in the valley waiting to take them home. "You're coming back next year, Franny? Promise! Can I be in your tribe?" . . . Lord, what a long time ago.

"I honestly did think I could make a good teacher— *once*," she began again lamely, as though there had been no silence. "I had such a missionary spirit!" Bitterly she laughed back on that old self. "I thought if you caught the children while they were young, and taught them to think for themselves—"

"What do the Jesuits say? 'Give me your children until they're seven—' " he offered.

"Well, there I was, all for reforming our evils by starting with the school children—"

"What evils?"

What an irritating habit he had of pinning her down! "Oh, you know—" she groped for big issues which sounded evil. "The Negro situation, for instance, and our general reactionary attitude down here." She didn't like to be confined to details when she was discoursing on lofty principles; she and her father could argue for hours on lofty principles and never once traffic with the specific. "Anyway, by the time the students got to me, they were practically full-grown, and all their ideas were set along the lines their families wanted them to think—"

"So you lost your missionary spirit?"

"Yes," she said quickly, relieved that he'd brought her back to the point, which she had almost lost in her vehemence. "And then along came this miserable business of my being forced to pass those seven seniors. I just couldn't stand it any longer! And I'm not the only one. The schools are losing teachers regularly. If they don't snap out of this rut they're in, they'll have to close entirely." She half-hoped such a calamity would occur; somehow it would vindicate her.

"And now what do you do?" Paul was asking.

"Nothing, if you mean to earn a living. I guess I'll have to start looking for a job sooner or later." Then, not wanting him to suppose that her father couldn't support her, "I could live on and on at home, you know, and not work. Daddy would love to be in the position of doling out an allowance to me every week—" Immediately she regretted the injustice she did her father by the implications of that remark. "No, I mean I just couldn't bear to ask mother for ten dollars every time I wanted something."

"All the money you made, you spent on yourself?"

Oddly enough she didn't resent his questions. It wasn't as though he were prying; he really wanted to understand what made her tick. And she had a driving desire to explain herself, to justify herself to him. "I admit I didn't pay board or anything at home; mother said there wasn't any point in taking it from me when she'd just have to turn around and give it back. But I *do* tithe."

"You what?"

"Tithe. You know, give a tenth to the church."

"Oh. Oh yes. That was another of your famous impulses, wasn't it? Your going to the new church. You mentioned that your family went to the old one."

"It may have been an impulse at the time," she declared, "but we've got that all settled, Daddy and I, and it just doesn't come up any more."

"Your father hardly seems the man to give up so easily."

It amazed her that Paul had discovered that about her father in so short a time. She told him so frankly. "And Daddy was on his best behavior with you tonight. He's got far more control than I have. He'd never have carried on in front of outsiders as I did with Mr. Douglas."

"At least you're honest," Paul said. To Frances his voice sounded a little grim. And she wasn't exactly sure what he'd meant. "But," he went on more lightly, "there must be plenty of jobs around town you could get. Why worry about this one?"

"I don't know what on earth I could do," she told him earnestly. "I can't type or take shorthand. Who'd hire me?"

"What did you major in in college?"

"A lot of poetry and books, a little art and language thrown in. A year of French, a year of German, a year of Anglo-Saxon. Nothing that will ever do me a damn bit of good. People like me are supposed to teach or—" she had started to say "or get married," but she stopped just in time.

"—Or get married?" he finished.

"Well, anyway," she said hastily, "working in an office isn't a profession. It seems so silly to go through four years of college and then take a job right next to a girl out of high school. It just isn't done somehow. Even if anybody would be foolish enough to hire me."

"It would be done if you did it. Would that make you a social pariah?" She suspected that he was laughing at her, but his voice was solemn.

"Oh, I don't know. I guess not," she said roughly. "I haven't had time to think about it." Practically everyone these days had the ability to make her feel like a fool. "Let's go to the concert, shall we? We should be able to get in at intermission."

"If you'd like," Paul said, immediately switching on the headlights. Scared, a jackrabbit leaped away into the underbrush, his ears flattened against his head. That's the way I am, she grumbled to herself, jumping about from bush to bush whenever they turn the lights on me.

They drove toward town in silence. His silence was a new thing to her; immediately it put her on the defensive. She felt always that she had created it somehow, and that she must break it. There was the difficulty—banal chatter just wouldn't come with Paul. "Isn't it a lovely evening? Can you smell the honeysuckle?" Anybody could have smelled the honeysuckle; the air was drenched with it. "Aren't the streets quiet! I guess it's after nine o'clock." You'd have to explain that Kingston had no night-life, such as he was undoubtedly used to in New York and in those gay European capitals where he had lived so glamorously. How dull he must find this town when he remembered the glitter of Broadway and the excitement of knowing famous people; Paris in the spring, the boulevards swarming with chic women and elegant gentlemen in top hats; sunshine on the beautiful blue Danube and the voices of the students in the cafés as they swung their steins of beer aloft and sang Strauss waltzes. Vividly she projected him—poised, charming, assured—into a swift succession of scenes exotically staged by Hollywood; a wide world of romance and derring-do swirled before her eyes. . . . And in Kingston, there wasn't a single nightclub, since liquor was illegal. Of course, you could go to the ABC store in the daytime and buy a bottle if you had a ration book, but since the Achesons were Presbyterian, naturally they never drank. Never in her life had Frances had a drink, not because she disapproved, but because nobody had ever offered her one. Oh, there were a couple of roadhouses out on the Valley Pike, where liquor was sold under the counter, she'd heard, but she would never set foot within one of *those* places. At college they had been on the Dean's blacklist, for it was generally conceded that women who went there were no better than they ought to be . . . She wished she could be silent as he so often was, without feeling dull. I don't know which is worse, she thought, to be silent and seem dull, or to be talkative and prove it.

The car dropped down out of the hills toward the town glowing below in the soft dark. The night was warm and friendly. Suddenly she rebelled at the idea of the stuffy garish high-school auditorium, the fat bright faces of the audience straining to attend to music they neither understood nor liked, the four earnest musicians sawing away on the platform where she herself had so often stood reading announcements and directing the students in the singing of *The Star-Spangled Banner*. Impulsively she turned to Paul and laid her hand on his knee. "Please, I'm sorry I was so cross back there. Would you mind too much not going to the concert? I really don't want to."

"Of course not, Frances. What would you rather do?"

"Just keep on through town, and let's go driving up into the hills. It's a beautiful night."

The glare of approaching headlights carved his face

out of the blackness. That eyebrow was up again, sardonically. But pleasantly he said that was a good idea. "You just pick the road and I'll follow it."

She was very conscious of her hand on his knee; she couldn't decide whether it would be more conspicuous to leave it there or to remove it. Now she wondered if he weren't interpreting her innocent suggestion as a desire to go off into the woods somewhere and "park the car," a situation she carefully had avoided all her twenty-three years. She withdrew her hand.

The narrow road ahead was dappled with moonlight that sifted through the arching trees, and the valleyland rolled away on either side of them, lush and dreamy beneath the moon. The wooden bridges across the creeks, the squat stone walls enclosing the fields, the very houses themselves lay in the lap of the land as though they had grown there. Nothing could ever change.

"It's funny," Frances said suddenly, "the valley must have looked just like this when Jackson came riding through, or Sheridan. They fought all up and down along here, but you'd never know it to look at this beautiful land. The war didn't leave a single scar."

"Not on the land, at least," Paul said obliquely.

"What do you mean?"

He answered her question with another. "How old is your house, Frances?"

"Some of it's very new. The plumbing, for instance, thank heaven! I can remember when I was a little girl, we actually had a pump in the kitchen and a cistern under the house." She could remember some details about the bathroom too, but decided not to mention them. "But the central part, that square middle part, you know, where the living room and the library are, that's the oldest. On a hand-hewn rafter in the cellar there's a date carved, 1769. So it's at least that old. Why?"

"Did one of your ancestors build it? I mean, has it been in *your* family all this time?"

"Oh yes. Daddy can tell you all about it if you ask him. In fact, if you ever get him started, he'll never stop. He knows the family history upside down. I don't recall all the details myself, but somebody came up from Goochland County before the Revolution and staked out a claim or whatever you had to do, and we've been here ever since." Once her father had taken her to the State Library in Richmond and had made her read a book which traced the lineage of the family but, to his disgust, she could never accurately recall either names or places. "So what?" she had said to him, precipitating one of their worst arguments, right there in the hushed vaults of the State Library.

"Are most of these houses that old?" Paul asked. "All full of FFV's?"

"I reckon most of them are pretty old, and some of them are owned by the same families that built them. Of course nowadays we're getting Yan—people from the North down, who buy old places and start breeding horses because it's fashionable or something. They don't know a sulky race from a steeplechase."

He was silent, watching the road. "What were you getting at?" she inquired curiously.

Thoughtfully he answered, "I was trying to imagine how these first settlers must have felt when they came through the pass in the mountains and saw this land lying at their feet, waiting to be taken. God knows what they'd come from, but this is—this *was* the new world they'd come to. Behind them"—he gestured east with a sweeping motion, but his voice was flat—"hell. The Huguenots driven out of France by the Catholics, the Catholics driven out of England by the Anglicans, all your little Protestant sects deserting Europe by the boatload. There they stood, on the crest of those mountains, seeing a land like this, looking down upon a vast earth that asked no questions and drew no lines . . . God!"

Frances was astounded at this tiny break in his armor; never before had she seen him show emotion. She was equally astounded at the idea he'd put into her mind. She had never thought of her family as being "immigrants," the persecuted of the earth fleeing torture and death because they were different. To her the word "immigrant" summoned up a picture of old women with shawls over their heads looking up tearfully at the Statue of Liberty as the cattle boat passed beneath. She had never been different from anybody else in her life, and it was hard to imagine how that must feel.

"What happened to those people, Frances?" Paul demanded. Fortunately it was only a rhetorical question, because she didn't know how to answer him. "How can people forget in two short centuries the very things that once made them strong?"

His voice was still calm and his hands on the wheel relaxed; yet she felt the tension within him, the holding back of the things he really wanted to say. Deliberately he was talking in generalities, she decided, to avoid becoming personal. It was as though he were re-experiencing a memory and a pain on which he consciously closed the door to her, as though his thoughts might be shared, but never his feelings. She wanted to say to him, Paul, don't stay so far away from me. Don't go off into that secret place of yours where I can't follow. I feel as though I've brushed my finger tips on something real and important. I don't want to lose it so soon. Why won't you be fair with me and let me into your life a little? What are you afraid of?

"Let's pull off the road up here at the turn, Paul," she suggested. "The moon's so clear you should be able to see for miles."

He stopped the car and took a package of cigarettes out of his pocket, offering her one wordlessly. She shook her head and watched him as he lit his own; in the spurt of the match she watched him intently as he drew his heavy eyebrows down into the flame. Her eyes traced the way his black hair grew and the cup of his hands around the glare. In the instant before the match went out, he caught her watching him, and his eyes plumbed hers. Her throat was dry, she laughed uneasily without breath, she knew that she was trembling.

The smoke clouded the air between them. "There are worlds and worlds," he said quietly, as though he were continuing an old conversation. "There is my world, and your world. Everything you say reveals your world: your world of dancing school and family prayers at dinner, candles on the table and heirloom silver. You've lived in your house all your life and your family before you—how many generations? You have your church, your friends, your name, your background, your—respectability." His voice wasn't bitter, only toneless.

"So?" she managed to whisper.

"So what else do you want? What else do you need? Aren't you satisfied?"

"But what has that got to do with—" she trailed off

vaguely, not wanting to say "with us," for there was no "us" to him.

"We are too close to be friends and too far apart to be anything more," he said brutally.

Again she was on the defensive, fighting now for something she couldn't see, against something she couldn't understand. "And what is *your* world, as you call it?"

"The Third Avenue El and a three-room flat over a tailor shop, immigrant parents, strictly kosher, 'apartments restricted to Gentiles only', kids in the street to holler sheeny and kike when you go to the synagogue on Saturday. Enough?"

"But all that," she faltered, "is behind you—"

"My dear," he answered her pleasantly, "nothing is ever 'behind' you. Especially being a Jew. And you mustn't ever forget it." He even patted her hand.

But she was not to be put off so easily. She enmeshed her fingers earnestly, as if she were in prayer and leaned toward him. "But Paul, if you've been hurt, and hurt deeply, as I'm sure you must have been, don't you see? You won't give yourself a chance, you aren't giving anybody else a chance. You're letting your fear of being hurt again keep you all bottled up, away from everybody—"

His voice was wonderfully kind, but only kind, just that and nothing more. "Have you ever been hurt, Frances? Have you ever really been afraid?"

She grew up a little in that moment. "No, I honestly never have," she admitted. "And I've never really been unhappy either, I guess." The clashes with her father, the quarrels at school were in retrospect evanescent and childish; her twenty-three years stretched behind her placid as stagnant water, and as untouched.

"How long do you think your protecting mountains are going to shelter this Utopia of yours?" he asked. "Don't you know the Volga runs down the Valley of Virginia?"

"Oh, now you're being melodramatic," she cried and caught him offguard. He gave ground, laughing, but only for a moment. The next, as if conscious that he had again chinked the blind on some secret room, he started the car. "I'd better be getting you home before your father has a posse out for me." It was, incredibly, one o'clock in the morning.

Her house stood brooding in the moonlight as they rounded the drive. It looked peaceful and serene and content, like a Christmas card house without the snow. One war had been fought across its lawn; others had broken open its doors; more, perhaps, loomed over its head. Yet it lay there still, rooted in the quiet land, as though, Frances thought, there were no ugliness or violence in the whole world, only the beauty of moonlight on a June night across the Valley of Virginia.

From the porch she could see that the living room was empty, though a small lamp was burning in the hall. She stood irresolutely by the railings, shredding a leaf from the wisteria vine. "Perhaps you'd like something to eat? Bacon and eggs or something?" She didn't want him to go.

"No. No thanks. Your mother's dinner is still with me."

Finally she sat down on the glider and looked toward him. "Won't you sit down a little while?"

He flipped his half-smoked cigarette onto the lawn with a gesture that was somehow more suited to the pitching of a baseball and sat down beside her. "Is this what you want?" he said and his voice was rough. He kissed her.

She went rigid all over, but her stomach pitched sickeningly. A shiver started at her neck and itched its way down her spine. Slowly she pulled away and stared at him. In the moonlight his eyes were bright and naked—yet he was poised for flight into his other, his secret place; his hand was trembling to switch off the light behind his eyes. All she knew was that she must not drop her eyes.

She willed him to kiss her again. This time his mouth was gentle. Blood poured into her lips as he kissed them open, and she arched her body against his—not willing it so but unconsciously—until her breasts were hard and hurting from the pressure. His lips were tighter now and stronger, almost brutal. She couldn't breathe; at her involuntary gesture of struggle, he drew away immediately.

"I just couldn't breathe," she explained faintly. "I thought the top of my head was coming off." She smiled tentatively, hungry to know that the moment had meant to him what it meant to her. That bright naked look might mean that, but she wanted to hear him say it. Still he sat, looking at her, twining a strand of her heavy hair in his fingers. "I hope you don't think I do this with everybody," she began again.

"I'm sure you don't, Frances," he said gravely. Holding back, holding back, holding back, she cried to herself, but why must he? Why wouldn't he give way a little and let her in? Suddenly she put her hands behind his head and drew him down to her again. Passionately she kissed him, not knowing how too well but wanting to, and the longer she held him there, the more she felt that the something hard and ugly in him was draining away, that at last she was nearing his rich secret darkness.

Paul drew away. "Frances," he said quietly, "do you know what you're doing?"

"Umhum," she murmured. She had no idea what he meant.

"*You're* going to get hurt. Very hurt." She watched the way his lips moved. She hardly heard what he was saying. How could she have thought they were twisted or mocking lips? A little melancholy perhaps, just a trifle sad . . . but not ever bitter. She stopped his questions by lifting her mouth to his again.

She stood in the doorway watching him walk down the drive, and for many minutes after he had turned the corner and vanished. Off in the mountains a train whistled, no longer a mournful sound. She felt that she could stand in the doorway and watch the night forever.

. . . Memories came oozing up through the layers of time, memories with new meaning and richness. A conversation with her father, "Daddy, are you passionate?" she remembered asking him, looking up from some book she'd been reading. She couldn't have been more than thirteen or fourteen. "My God, Evelyn, what are you letting your daughter read?" he had cried, snatching the book and throwing it open here and there with a wild look. When Daddy was displeased, she was always her *mother's* daughter.

"Well, *is* he passionate, Mother?" she asked Mrs. Acheson later that evening when they were alone.

"That's not a nice thing for you to be thinking about, Frances," her mother told her, "and that's not a nice word for you to be using." Frances never knew for sure whether her father was passionate or not; in fact, she had never received a direct answer from her mother to any such queries.

Occasionally, when Mr. Acheson was sitting up late in the library studying the stock-market reports, Frances would crawl into the yellow curly-maple bed beside her mother. "Scratch my back?" Her mother's nails were not too long, and they were rounded at the tip. She would lean over Frances' narrow shoulders in the darkness and draw her fingers slowly from hairline to waist in a long luscious motion that made Frances' skin crawl deliciously and raised goose pimples up and down her legs. "Go farther down, Mother. All the way."

"That's far enough."

"Oh please." Frances' stomach made queer jerky movements. "It feels so good."

But her mother never would scratch her back below the waistline. "Franny, I'm afraid you're passionate too," she said once, rather sadly, Frances thought.

"Why are you afraid?" Frances had asked over and over, but her mother never answered.

"What's it like?" she asked another time. "After you're married, I mean."

She felt her mother grow rigid in bed beside her, a drawing away without movement. "Honey, you embarrass me."

"No, Mother, I don't mean to, but I mean—it seems such a sloppy way of doing things. Why couldn't they have thought of something more decent?"

Her mother made such an odd little noise, a snort really, that Frances was slightly shocked. It sounded so undignified somehow. "*I'd* rather have a cup of hot chocolate myself," Mrs. Acheson had answered after a while . . .

In her doorway Frances stood looking out into the night and at the corner of the driveway where Paul had turned into the street. She thought of her mother and smiled a little before going upstairs to bed.

s e v e n

Never had summer been so beautiful, and so hot. In front of the county courthouse, men in shirt sleeves lounged on the sticky green benches, fanning themselves with limp straw hats, and at noon the office girls from the bright white buildings around the Square brought their lunches in paper bags and ate the wilted sandwiches on the grass under the elms. At the four corners of the Square children from the poor neighborhoods splashed in the horse troughs, and up the side streets and through the back alleys, mournfully chanting, the watermelon men on their carts swayed gently over the ruts. Dust and flies settled on the cut red fruit.

Behind the town, around the town, the mountains were everywhere, blue, misty, folding together in the shimmering white light. They seemed to grow one from another, on and on down the valley; the mountains were the only moving things in a still world.

The road from Kingston to Lake Luray was not long, about eight miles—but it seemed endless. It was a twisted lonesome mountain road, sinuous, torturous, whose turns brought only more turns until, with a start and a spurt, it flung itself forward in a gallant finish at the gates of the Lake Luray Hotel.

The hotel was scarcely worth the effort. It leaned against the mountain behind it with the infinitely weary air, the faintly apologetic look of very old persons who have been expecting to die for a long time and are none too pleased that they haven't. Like its summer visitors, endlessly rocking on the long wooden porches, the hotel belonged to another age, another time, another way of life, a way which had so saturated the walls and passages and austere bedrooms that the air was still sweet with mignonette and lavender, and the night was still shattered with the crashing of chamber-pot lids.

Yet it was just this creaking gentility added to its inaccessibility which had made Lake Luray so fashionably exclusive. The summer guests came to talk about one another, and if you weren't worth talking about, your reservation, of course, was regretfully refused. There was nothing to do, really, except to sit in the branches of your family tree and unravel by the yard the skeins of cousinly connections up and down the Valley. It was a rare day when two strangers couldn't locate at least a third-cousin-once-removed belonging to both of them; it was a rarer day when any two guests were strangers.

Where the hotel got its name remained an ante-bellum mystery, for there was no Lake Luray, nor a lake of any size or name within miles. There was, however, a spring in a little willow-hung hollow behind the kitchens where the water tasted brackish enough to be as medicinal as was claimed, and where the stiff old ladies and bent old gentlemen congregated religiously twice a day, after breakfast and before dinner, to sip and chat and decide to live a day longer.

When Paul Revkin arrived at the resort toward the last

of May, having been sent by a New York agency which had despaired of obtaining, for the location and the salary offered, a violinist who knew *vibrato* from *pizzicato*, he found himself in a sort of purgatory between the extremes of the Negro help on the one hand, and the paying guests on the other. The "domestics," as the manager lumped all the Negroes together with a dismissing wave of his hand, adhered to a caste system of their own, and so returned Paul's courteous overtures with the sullen and suspicious "yassuh" which meant that, though he was white, he wasn't "their white folks," and that was that. To the guests he was only an employee, not to be tipped, of course, but not to be associated with either; they inclined their heads politely when they passed him on the lawns, but they were much more at ease with the waiters in the dining room, or the "niggahs" who made their beds: *these* were on an old and established basis; *these*, at least, would be certain not to presume.

The other two members of the three-piece orchestra which played in the dining room at dinner, six until nine each evening, one evening off a week, were a pianist and a 'cellist, hack musicians of indeterminate age and origin. They too were strangers to the hotel and to each other, but they had discovered a bond in their love of the bottle and the conviction that Hitler was right when it came to the Jews. It was unnecessary for Paul to speak to them except for a word now and then as they played, and this suited all three perfectly.

The situation intensified the isolation which had originally attracted him to the Valley of Virginia. He was grateful for the mountains, not alone for their splendor—he'd had the Bavarian Alps too long for that—but for the sense of otherworldness which their shelter created. He was grateful for the long road up from the valley which like a hand pushing against his chest kept him from the world below. Most of all he savored the long length of yellow lazy days, the time and the solitude he knew he needed to gain back or lose altogether the music that once had been his whole life.

It was not so much the skill of his fingers which he had lost during the war years: he had retaught them their old dexterity in four months of diligence; he could manage a small concert before an undiscriminating audience. Nor was it that the joy of making music had gone out of him entirely; that too was there—but only in his mind. He had lost the emotional urge to create; there was left only the knowledge that he was translating black notes from white paper into sounds correctly. He no longer believed that the world was a place for music. He believed no longer that music was the most important thing in life, and he had learned no substitute. From this sterility had grown the conviction that never would he become the artist he had hoped to be. Worst of all, he no longer cared.

Determined to relearn discipline, if nothing else, he forced the hours of his days into a rigid pattern; all morning, every morning, and sometimes into the afternoons, he made himself work over positions and shifts, bowing, intonation, interpretation. He set impossible tasks for himself, and then stood at his window staring at the mountains beyond, letting the time slide by. One day he played through the entire Brahms twice from memory. But it was misery, both for him and for the chambermaids who cleaned his hall; they were all happier when he flung his violin on the bed and went out for a walk.

Now there was a more immediate complication. There was Frances. It had been almost a week since he had had dinner with the Achesons, and he'd not telephoned Frances since, nor did he intend to—he kept telling himself. He told himself all the obvious things, all the intelligent things, all the things that made sense and had governed his behavior for twenty-eight years, and they all added up to No. No common background, no community of interests, not even a meeting of minds or temperament. But above all and beyond all there was the towering obstacle of race; to these people, he suspected, being a Jew was only a notch above being a "niggah," and relations with either were miscegenation.

Yet as he jogged up a mountain trail on a horse from the stables at the hotel, where two were kept on the off-chance that an occasional guest might be young enough to ride, or walked miles along some back road as lonely as himself, he remembered her. Sometimes, as he grimly practiced in his bedroom, or watched the faces watching him at dinner as he played, he saw her. And he couldn't help it.

It was in contrast to the faces in the dining room that he saw her, for in the dining room he saw faces with the earthy strength of their heritage bred out of them, as blank as the old shuttered houses in town, with eyes that looked neither forward nor inward but backward. And *her* eyes were wide-set and wide-open and receptive, and there was a stubborn strength to her jaw that encouraged him. Her laugh was free and impulsive, reflecting the impulsive emotions underneath, and in this, he thought, remembering that she had left her family's church and had defied the school system, lay his hope.

Sometimes he let himself go, let himself think about

8 3

her without halter or bit . . . And they were driving down the Valley Pike on a hot white afternoon and the wind was catching her heavy black hair and tossing it wildly and they were both laughing at nothing at all; he could see the gurgle of laughter down deep in her throat where the white silk shirtwaist fell back; he could see the dust of freckles on her skin. Or they were stretched out on the slope of a hill with the patterned valley rolling away below, the air moist with the smell of earth turned up to the sun. He could see her lying on her back, looking up into the branches of the trees, her arms under her head and her knees drawn up so that her toes could dig into the ground . . . Desire uncoiled within him and rose like slow blue smoke, making his eyelids heavy. Behind desire, swift anger, smashing his reverie like a mailed fist.

Anger, because of the dry taste in his mouth and the hunger in his heart; like the Red Queen, he ran and ran and ran and got nowhere. Anger, because of the sheets of music scattered across his room and the violin pitched on the bed; he wandered roads that twisted back upon themselves, like his thoughts, endlessly. Anger, yapping at the heels of desire; mind chasing emotion up and down the keyboard of his nerves.

He remembered the first day he had seen her, in the choir at her church, and he noticed her because she looked as though she had just scrubbed her face. Her skin was more than clean, it was shining, and in spite of her hollowed cheeks and shadowy eyes, she looked alive and aware and healthy—God, he made her sound like whole-wheat bread! He had noticed her long-legged, rather awkward grace, which would mature, he realized, into her mother's poise and carriage. Now there was an enigma, Mrs. Acheson: passion quick-frozen and long-dormant, defense perhaps against her husband's more volatile energies. And Mr. Acheson, his passion deflected by his wife's frigidity into fits of temper as fierce and brief as a summer storm. It was an interesting family; he had enjoyed the subtly shifting crosscurrents among the three at dinner. Was that only last Saturday? Where for instance, from what hotblooded Irish forefather, did Frances get the intense sensual response which the faintest whisper of his finger tips could arouse? From what pioneering ancestor did she inherit her instinct of rebellion against the lares and penates of her society? Was it a reasoned hatred of intolerance and hypocrisy and fraud, or was it merely the impulse, the swift unthinking instinct of a child?

Oh face it and be done! he demanded of himself impatiently. Has she got the guts to take a Jew into her life? Or, to be more exact, to give up *her* life for a Jew? He felt like a small boy who tests the ice on the pond gingerly, a toe, then a foot, then his whole weight slowly, step by step. Step by step, he felt his way into the question, fully expecting the ice to crack beneath him and plunge him into the mud below. But he couldn't find the answer; he didn't know. All he knew was that he was in love with her, that he had fallen in love with a little ninny from the blueblooded hills of Virginia, and that made him angry all over again.

Why couldn't it have been someone like his sister Becky, he growled to himself. Always he had looked in other women for what he had found in her—her warm understanding, her deep sensitivity, that tough quick mind which made his run to meet it. But always the search had been futile. Perhaps it was because his parents were worn and old and alien even to him that he had grown so close to his sister. He remembered the way she looked as she accompanied him on the upright piano in the front room of their flat, banging a little louder as the El clattered by. He remembered their standing date to *Parsifal* at the Met on Good Friday, their long climbs up the back stairs to the balcony at Carnegie Hall, her explosive discovery of Kafka whom he abhorred, his transient avowal of Marx whom she detested, the miserable day she had voted for Willkie and they'd barely spoken for a week. And then she had married; he had received the letter overseas one cold December morning when he'd just stumbled back to camp after a shoddy three days in Metz. She had married, but even then he had had no sense of loss. It was not until he'd come home that he realized her new life was full of things in which he had no part. Then, for the first time in his life, he knew loneliness.

"It's high time you were thinking of getting married too, Paul," Becky had said to him very seriously one day. "You remind me of Kipling's cat that walked by himself and all places were alike to him." For three months she had been parading her friends past him, like fillies in a paddock, and in vain. "You know what your trouble is: you possess without being possessed. You'll never be in love until you can't help giving yourself away." He made a moue at her. "Don't go cocking that eyebrow at me like that!" she cried fiercely. "You and your ivory tower! You'll fall out of it one day and break your damn stiff neck."

God, how right she was, as usual. He wondered what she'd think of Frances, and Frances' family, and Frances' background. He could almost hear her crisp voice,

"Well, bring her along! Let's have a look at your Scarlett O'Hara. What are you afraid of?"

It was not a decision. One minute he had no intention of calling the Acheson house; the next minute he was at the telephone in the lobby and dropping a nickel in the slot. He heard it ring a long way off, once, twice, three times. All right, he thought, that's an omen. I'd better hang up while there's time. But he didn't. In the middle of the fourth ring, there was a sharp click.

"Hello." It was Frances. She sounded breathless, as though she had been running.

"Hello, Frances. This is Paul. How are you?"

"Oh, Paul!" He noticed that she didn't even try to disguise the gladness in her voice. "I ran all the way from the backyard. I hoped it was you."

"I've been awfully busy," he covered, "but I'm free tomorrow night. May I see you?"

"Tomorrow? That's Sunday. Oh, Paul—" she hesitated. Was she going to be coy now? "We're having a young people's meeting at our church tomorrow night and I'm chairman. I have to go." She brightened a little. "Wouldn't you like to come? I tell you what it's all about," she went on without giving him a chance to refuse. "We've invited the young people of the Negro Presbyterian church in town to come for supper and a discussion group afterward. It's going to be at Judge Braxton's house. He's our Representative in Congress."

"You don't have to sell me the idea," he said when she stopped for a breath; he felt himself grinning like a Cheshire Cat. "I'll be delighted."

"You would?" She sounded incredulous. "Then meet

me, won't you, at his house? Anybody in town can tell you where it is. It's right near the Square. I have to go early and help the supper committee."

"About six?"

"Yes, or you might come a little sooner if you'd like." The telephone accentuated the soft drawl in her voice; he'd never noticed before what a pleasant voice it was. She made two syllables out of one-syllable words: she said "yeah-us" and "kuh-um" and "li-uk," and it still sounded pleasant. He promised to be at Judge Braxton's by six; he said he was looking forward to seeing her again.

"I'm awfully glad you called," she said at the end.

"So am I," he told her. "Good-by, lieble." It wasn't until later that he realized he had used the endearment saved in his mind for Becky.

e i g h t

At a quarter to six the next evening Paul stood in the library of Judge Braxton's house on the Square; for the first time since he had been in Virginia, he felt at home. The spare old Negro who answered his knock had led him through the spacious entrance hall, with its sweeping white staircase and heavy chandelier, into the library, promising to "go fotch Miss Franny." Paul heard his slow footsteps echoing through the quiet house, and, muted by distance, the sound of women's voices—the supper committee, he supposed, neatly arranging chicken salad and tomato aspic on Havilland plates to serve to the "visitors from the other end of town." Idly he wondered if they would invite the butler to sit down with them too.

French doors opened from the library onto a small walled garden, so informal, so unobtrusive that he knew it must be the work of an expensive gardener. Under the mimosas lilac bushes sprawled carelessly, and with wonderful abandon honeysuckle, clematis, roses, wisteria scrambled riotously up the walls. In every sense it was a room with a view; more, it was a room with a vision, for which even Thoreau might have left Walden. Bookshelves climbed to the high ceiling, packed and jammed with books of all sizes, shapes and colors; shafts of the late afternoon sun indiscriminately picked out heavy volumes of hand-tooled leather and paper-backed editions of old French novels. Over the fireplace hung a massive canvas of a placid Colonial lady, a Gilbert Stuart perhaps; its deep serenity heightened his sense of contentment. Someone had discovered the real beauty of money.

In the corner nearest the double doors was a cabinet phonograph; above it, on tall shelves, more albums of recordings than he had ever seen outside a music store. In the dim light he peered up at the names: Purcell and Viotti and Dohnanyi as well as Bach and Brahms, a catholic taste which missed little from Palestrina to Prokofiev, sonatas to symphonies. The albums were soiled from many handlings —at least the owner had not bought them for show. Vexed, Paul tightened his lips at his own suspicious disposition; he was as great a snob intellectually, he told himself, as these people were socially, and for no better reason.

He wandered back along the bookshelves, pulling down a volume now and then. *Gargantua*, Plato, and Ellery Queen. Rénan's *Life of Jesus* between Faulkner and Rimbaud. Shakespeare in twelve volumes, the creamy paper marked and underlined in a fine spidery hand. Evidently the Judge respected thoughts more than trimmings. He owned his books, they didn't own him.

With Thurber in one hand and Eliot in the other, Paul settled into a shabby Morris chair and put his feet up on the andirons. Even the rising babble of voices in the reception hall didn't bother him; he was well into "Walter Mitty," set for the evening, and lost to his surroundings when a lamp snapped on above his chair and a man's deep voice said, "Wasn't it getting a little dark to read? You'll ruin your eyes." Blinded by the sudden light, Paul looked up, blinking, and rose as the man offered his hand. "My name's McDonough. Frances sent me to find you."

"Of course," said Paul, shaking hands warmly. "I heard your first sermon downtown at the theater. It's a great pleasure to meet you, sir."

"And I never thanked you for your contribution to that opening service of ours. It's a treat to have good music in our churches for a change." Dr. McDonough laughed. "You'll never know how weary a minister gets of a throaty soprano and *Jerusalem the Golden* every other Sunday." Dr. McDonough was neither unctuous nor oratorical; he had the easy manner of a man who never worries about the impression he is making. He looked like a successful insurance man, Paul thought—which in a way he was; but he certainly did not fit Paul's preconceived notion of a Southern Presbyterian preacher.

Dr. McDonough had sat down in an armchair across the fireplace and was looking through the copy of Eliot which Paul had dropped on the floor. He held his finger in his place and glanced up, tapping the cover of the book with his knuckles. "I could preach a sermon from this man every Sunday, and never exhaust him," he said. "You like him?" It was a statement more than a question. "Listen to this: 'I have measured out my life in coffee spoons.' There's a sermon in itself. Or this—" He read as though he were talking to himself.

"*I have seen the moment of my greatness flicker;*
And I have seen the Eternal Footman hold my coat and
snicker;
And in short, I was afraid."

At first Paul suspected that the man had sensed a prospective convert and was deliberately attempting to put him at his ease, to extend the glad hand of Christian fellowship to an outsider, either as a favor to Frances or as part of a canned welcoming procedure. But this was no gesture, no act; this man was as lonely as himself—not lonely perhaps, so much as equally isolated. Talking only with God, Paul imagined, grew a little one-sided at times.

" 'In short, I was afraid,' " Dr. McDonough said again, dropping the words musingly into the stillness. "Fear —and freedom from fear. *There's* something I could preach about every day of my life." Yet Paul had no uncomfortable feeling that Dr. McDonough was preaching to him; it was as though he had forgotten that Paul was in the room, sharing his musings. Like a jeweler who turns a little gem this way and that to catch the lights, he fondled the line of poetry. "Fear that someone will tread on your toes—so you kick them in the shins first. Fear that someone will get his share of the pie—so you grab it all. Fear that someone will discover your inadequacy—so you waste all your strength holding him down."

"That's not a characteristic limited to Southerners, you know." Paul could no longer resist breaking in.

Dr. McDonough looked up sharply and his glance collided with Paul's. He smiled wryly. "True. True." Paul was strangely pleased that the preacher did not labor the point by drawing the obvious comparison aloud; plainly, his conversation would never descend to banalities. "But I am a Southerner, and a minister," Dr. McDonough went on, "and I have to take my work where I find it. Mine is under my nose."

"Frances has been trying to persuade me," Paul offered, "that the solution to the South's race problem is education." He didn't add further that she had given up that method in despair.

"I would say to Frances that the solution is in our churches."

"But the same people who run your schools run your churches."

"The big difference," Dr. McDonough pointed out, "is that the people change the schools, but the churches change the people."

"Do they?" Paul demanded.

"When they can reach them," Dr. McDonough answered confidently. "Do you go to your church?"

"I'm against organized religion, whatever form it takes." At once Paul realized how curt his remark had been; yet he couldn't bring himself to explain: the hatred was too deep, too real and close to him. From the beginning of time, they had all started the same way, those little groups afire with spirit and a new way of life. Isolated, hunted down, murdered, they nourished their ideals and finally grew strong, until their strength convinced them all over again that might makes right, and all over again the weak, the new, the different were hunted down and murdered. He was against anything—organized religion, political philosophy, or a doting parent—that told a man what he could think and damned him to hell for disagreeing.

"It's one thing to be 'against,'" Dr. McDonough noted. "It's a more challenging thing, a more dangerous thing, a better thing, to be 'for.'" He waited.

Paul was glad that words were not coming to him easily, for he wanted no pat answer to give this honest man. "I'm for anything," he said finally, "that helps a man develop all of his potentiality for good, freely, and in his own way."

"You're for God, then."

The suddenness of the statement, its very inevitability, caught Paul off-balance, wordless; it was a good moment, rich with understanding and mutual respect. He savored it. Why, he found himself wondering, why would a man like this stay in a small town, ridiculed, viciously persecuted, where there was neither understanding nor appreciation?

Graciously Dr. McDonough had refused to press his point; instead, he opened the book of poems and was reading again:

"There is only the fight to recover what has been lost
And found and lost again and again; and now under conditions
That seem unpropitious. But perhaps neither gain nor loss.
For us there is only the trying. The rest is not our business."

Paul stared, silent, his question unspoken and answered.

Like King Agrippa, he thought, "almost thou persuadest me."

By now the noise in the hall had grown too loud to be ignored. Through the half-opened doors, they could hear people passing back and forth, chattering, laughing; the front knocker dropped continuously. A young Negro stuck his head around the library door, said "Oh, excuse *me!*" and vanished. Reluctantly, Dr. McDonough laid the book, still open, across the arm of his chair, and rose, gesturing with his head. "They'll all be wondering what's become of us." Behind them, he pulled the doors of the library shut as if he were leaving a part of himself inside.

At the far end of the reception hall was the dining room, where a long table had been laid buffet style. The ladies of the auxiliary, Paul noticed, had attempted to outdo one another in bringing forth their family hoard of china and silver. (Stop it! He told himself savagely. They're really falling over backward to be nice to these youngsters.) Around the table was a long line, Negro and white freely mingled; others, with heaping plates of chicken salad and tomato aspic, stood in little groups, eating and chatting without any obvious restraint. Most of them made a point of speaking to Dr. McDonough, leaning around shoulders and waving over heads; "Dr. Mac" could call nearly everyone by his first name.

Since his invitation from Frances the afternoon before, Paul had suspected that this gathering would be a patronizing cross between a charity bazaar and an old-fashioned revival. Now, for all his contemptuous thoughts, he had the grace to be ashamed. More surely than ever before, he was convinced that the "en masse approach" to human beings was the greatest evil in the world; he stood convicted before himself of a prejudice as blind, as irrational as any. *All* Southerners were not reactionary and fascist any more than *all* Negroes were thus-and-so and *all* Jews were this-and-that. How easy to read the label and stop; how easy to miss the soul of Cyrano for his nose! He was at once piqued and amused to find himself, a Jew, on the offending side.

Methodically he had followed Dr. McDonough down the table, acquiring a dab of chicken salad here and a plop of aspic beside it, a buttery roll and some carrot curls. When he came around the massive coffee urn, he was face to face with Frances. Aspic, coffee urn and all, he wanted to kiss her on the spot. Her face, already rosy from the hot kitchen, colored more, and she gave him the long look he so well remembered, intimate as a love letter. But all she said was, "I wondered what happened to you and Dr. Mac. Did you have a long talk?"

"Umhumm," he said, watching her as though he'd never seen her before. He even forgot to say "No cream and sugar, please," for his coffee.

"Please just make yourself at home. I'm going to be awfully busy until afterwards."

"I won't go away," he promised, and wandered off to strike up a conversation with a solitary Negro in a sailor's uniform.

The preliminaries which led up to the scheduled discussion were complicated and a little tedious to Paul. Folding chairs had been set up in semicircles around the hall facing a raised platform; he sat in the last row, wondering where churches would be without folding chairs. Would the congregation revert to type and sit on the floor? The

Hindus did it; the Buddhists did it. He attempted contemplating his navel from a seated position on a folding chair, and decided that folding chairs were eventually to be the downfall of religion in America.

Beside him sat a red-haired girl of not more than seventeen, audibly gushing about the superiority of Presbyterians over Baptists to the young man beyond her, who was presumably the latter. "At least," she said clearly, "we don't *dunk*. We sprinkle." The young man's reply was lost in a burst of applause which greeted Dr. McDonough's introduction of Judge Braxton. A sturdy old gentleman near the front rose, bowed, and sat down. Dr. McDonough made a few remarks of appreciation for the use of the beautiful Braxton mansion, one of the real landmarks of the valley (applause), and for the generosity of the Judge who was one of the leading citizens of the state (prolonged applause). Dr. McDonough added that this was not meant to be a campaign speech (laughter), although everyone knew that the Judge was up for his third term in the House of Representatives (suppressed cheering). "But most of you youngsters aren't old enough to vote anyway," Dr. McDonough added, "so they can hardly call this politicking."

Then up on the platform stepped an elderly Negro in a frock coat, his arms raised in the traditional gesture of prayer. Just like Jolson doing *Mammy*, Paul thought irreverently; he was having a hard time getting into the spirit of this thing. The Lord was exhorted in a tremulous quaver to bless the Ladies of the Auxiliary for the supper which nourished the meeting, to be with the Men's Club which had provided transportation for the visitors, to spread His light into the hearts of all men everywhere so that the brotherhood of man—and so on and so on. Paul's attention wandered over the bowed heads; in that position it was difficult to distinguish Negro from white.

The prayer stopped, and in response came the deep strong voice of a bass-baritone singing a spiritual: "Lord, I wanna be more lovin'"; "in-a my heart, in-a my heart," the room answered back in refrain. "Lord, I wanna be more lovin', in-a my heart." The singing swelled, deepened, softened, left the soloist singing the last notes alone.

From the row beside him Paul heard the sibilant whisper of the Baptist boy. "I don't see why either dunking or sprinkling makes any difference."

"Then why don't you all sprinkle then?" demanded the red-haired girl with great scorn.

"Oh Lord," said the Baptist, defeated.

As a portable blackboard was wheeled into the room, Frances stepped up on the platform. To Paul's relief he recognized at once all the signs of self-possession and ease. He had wondered whether she were capable of handling such a meeting; he wanted it to go off well for her. But as he listened to her introductory remarks, his stomach subsided: she wasn't trying to make a speech on race relations in Kingston, she was just opening a conversation among some friends.

"We might use the blackboard to point out some of the facts we'll bring up," she said. Paul remembered that she loved to write on the board. "If I draw a line down the center," she illustrated, "and head one column 'Grievances—'" She stopped, chalk poised, and turned to the group. "No, that's not such a good word. Can somebody suggest a better?" A voice called out "Conditions," and a few heads were nodded. "Now for the righthand side,"

Frances went on, "could we say 'Approaches'?" She wrote both words on the board while the audience murmured to itself about conditions and approaches. Paul decided that, under decent circumstances, she would have made an excellent teacher.

Already suggestions for the "Conditions" side were being offered. A girl mentioned the Jim Crow law on busses and streetcars. A man's voice called out, "Discrimination on jobs." Two boys of high-school age stood up simultaneously, and then both sat down, abashed. There was a ripple of laughter, good-natured, friendly. Frances said to the boy nearest her, "You start."

"The school system, the Negro schools don't have half our equipment, and their teachers are paid less," the boy got out in one great rush, blushing furiously. A young woman, older than the rest, murmured, "Poll taxes," in a mousy voice. Frances hadn't heard her and asked her to repeat. "Poll taxes," she repeated in a slightly louder voice. "They were devised to keep the Negroes from voting, and they should be abolished." A ground-swell of comment followed this offering; Paul saw Dr. McDonough duck his head toward Judge Braxton and whisper in his ear.

The lefthand side of the board was filling rapidly; Frances could hardly write fast enough to keep up with the comments that were flung at her. "Now how about this blank other half," she said finally. "The 'Approaches' to our 'Conditions'? We don't have too much time, and we haven't done any *constructive* thinking."

The group was excited and talkative; half a dozen demanded the floor at once.

"Encourage Congress to pass the FEPC."

"Appropriate more money for schools, Negro and white."

"Get the governor to repeal the poll tax. Arnall did it!"

"Refuse to observe the Jim Crow law!" This from a Negro boy. "Sit anywhere in the bus you please." Yes, you hothead, Paul thought, and get yourself thrown out on your neck. That's no way to improve things.

"Write letters to the newspapers," bleated a girl who looked like a young sheep.

Between every suggestion vehement discussion sprang up all over the room. Frances had to rap for order to recognize a young Negro woman who had been waiting patiently. "I'm a college graduate," she began pleasantly, "and I'm teaching school here in Kingston. This is my home. I love the valley, and I hope I can stay." Paul felt a sudden constriction of his throat at the implications of that statement. "Two years ago," she said, "I was elected a representative of our entire Negro young people's organization to a church-wide conference on 'World Brotherhood,' which was to be held at a certain summer resort. I remember the time distinctly," she said without a flicker of expression, "because my brother had just been killed in France. I was elected to this conference," she went on, "but I was not invited, nor were the other three Negro young people who had been elected delegates also. The conference was held at a summer resort which naturally had no rooms for Negro guests; and if they had been so foolish as to allow *us* to come for the special occasion, us four Negro delegates, why, all the regular guests, of course, would have left. It would be unthinkable for them to stay one night under the same roof with a Negro, even a duly elected representative to a church conference on 'World Brotherhood.' "

She took a short breath and continued tonelessly. "So, we were not allowed to attend the conference. I received a letter from a friend of mine, a white girl down in Norfolk, who did attend the conference. She said that all the young people had signed a petition requesting the pastor in charge to wire us invitations; they had offered in writing to share their rooms and beds with us." A small gasp ran around the room. "But the young people were advised to go about their business of discussing World Brotherhood, and leave such trivial matters as the exclusion of the Negro delegates to the committee on arrangements. My friend wrote that somehow the conference was not a success, that occasionally during a very fine talk on 'brotherhood,' someone would snicker."

The room was without sound or motion. "All of the points you've listed on the blackboard," she said, glancing at Frances, "are very important, yes, but they are secondary. All those things are the externals. Nothing can change until the change starts in people's hearts and minds, until the white man on the street stops thinking 'niggah' first and 'human being' second, until he starts thinking *'man,'* man only. Some of us *are* dirty—we're not allowed to live in the more sanitary sections of town. Some of us *are* criminals—we're entitled to our quota, I think. But most of us are decent, ordinary people who feel and love and think, who bleed and die—" (even now her voice did not quiver), "and who want only the same chance that everyone else has."

Not by word or motion did she ask sympathy. Her back was straight, her head high. "The change can come, yes, but slowly, through small groups like this, which are honest and clear-eyed and open-minded, which determine to see beyond color and creed to the *man* beneath." Quietly, in a great stillness, she sat down.

After that, anything would have been anticlimax. Dr. McDonough pronounced the benediction, and the meeting broke up into small groups, earnestly conversing. Through the twisted rows of chairs, around the people, Paul worked his way toward Frances. She saw him coming, and stood still watching him as he came. A quartet at the piano had started "Were You Dere?" and the singing soared above the babble of voices: "Oh, sometimes, it causes me to wonder, wonder, wonder . . ."

"Hello," she said to him. He took her hand. The fingers curled inside his, contentedly, and were still.

n i n e

The logs in the fireplace snapped; little blue flames brightened the soot on the chimney wall. The bricks of the hearth were too hot now for Hannah to curl there any longer; purring noisily, she picked her way with delicacy around the remains of the picnic lunch spread out on the floor, and climbed into Paul's lap as he sat cross-legged, leaning back against the legs of the wing chair. Abstractedly, he fed her a nibble of cold fried chicken.

Outside the living-room windows, the rain poured down. Paul's eyes traveled from the discarded picnic hamper Frances had packed so carefully the night before, through the wet windowpanes to the drenched trees, the gray hills beyond. The rain drummed on the shingled porch roof, and spattered, hissing, down the chimney into the fire; it was the only sound in a still world.

The fire was warm on his eyelids. Nuzzling Hannah under the chin, he remembered contentedly the past three weeks. This was their first bad weather; he hoped Frances hadn't minded too much having her long-planned picnic on the living-room floor instead of down by the river. His eyes found her: she was lying on her stomach, staring into the flames, waving her feet casually in the air.

"Darling, don't you get tired, holding your feet up so long?" he murmured drowsily.

"They're not that big!" she retorted. Then, laughing, "Though Daddy did use to say that the reason I caught so many colds was because there was so much of me on the ground."

He laughed, and his stomach bounced. Jarred, Hannah rose with dignity and gave him an aggrieved look. Paul pulled her back to him remorsefully, and began to scratch the base of her tail.

"How did you learn so much about cats?" Frances asked idly. Hannah was pawing his leg as though she were kneading dough.

"I love all dumb things," he threw at her with mock gravity.

Immediately he caught the sparkle in her eye, the quirk of her mouth. But she didn't make the obvious flip retort, for which he was grateful. For three weeks he had shied away from that word: love, word of one syllable, present tense, first person singular, I love. For three weeks they had walked together each afternoon across the hills, down the back roads, along the twisted old streets of town. And they had talked and they had laughed and they had been serious. But never had he used that word; he had forbidden it to himself. When he looked into her deep eyes, he saw always the same question trembling there, a question she had never asked, which he had never answered. He loved her, yes; but he was still afraid.

Instead of replying to his careless remark, Frances rolled over on her back and put her arms under her head, drawing her knees up so that her feet were flat on the floor. He knew her too well to suspect that she lay so, deliberately to tantalize him; yet in spite of himself his eyes caressed the length of her body, and he felt the skin over his cheekbones tighten as he stiffened his jaw. "Don't you want to hear your new albums, Fran?" he said flatly, no longer looking at her.

"Oh, certainly," she answered at once, gently taking Hannah off his lap as she sat up. "The phonograph plays six records, and then you'll have to turn them over."

He walked over to the cabinet, relieved by the distraction; yet he couldn't help remembering the scene earlier in the afternoon when he had brought the albums to her. Because of the rain, he had picked up an ancient taxicab in town to drive out to the Acheson house. Frances was waiting for him at the door; as always, when he saw her, it was as though he had never seen her before. His heart stopped, hollowly thudded, raced on.

"Hello, Paul, how are you? Let me help you with your wet things," she exclaimed breathlessly, all in a great rush. He shrugged out of his battered Army raincoat and handed it to her, restraining a desire to kiss the back of her neck as she hung it across the banister post. "What's all that you've got?" she asked.

Under one arm was his violin in its case; he set it in a corner and handed her a large squarish package. "Something for you. Here. You want to open it now?" She began to fumble with the wrappings while he shook the water out of his hair with both hands.

"Let me get you a towel?" she said anxiously. "You might catch cold or something."

"I'm more liable to catch the 'or something.' I'm afraid I don't fit into your romantic notion of the weak and sickly artist." He glanced out of the window. "But we aren't going to have a picnic today."

"I don't care, *now*," she purred comfortably, busy with her package.

Paul walked over to the cold fireplace. "Where's your mother?"

"At some meeting of the Presbytery. She'll be gone all day. I was fully expecting a telephone call from you saying that you couldn't make it in all this rain, but now—" She didn't have to finish the sentence; she smiled at him and his heart kicked.

Abruptly he turned to the fireplace. "Does this draw?"

"Oh yes. Just turn the knob to open the flue. Why don't you light the fire? That's a wonderful idea. We could have my lunch basket right here on the floor."

"My God," he said, looking at the hamper, "did you think you were going to feed the Third Army?"

The paper was off her package at last. "Paul! Records! You shouldn't. So many too." She read through the titles. "Brahms' *First*, Brahms' *Fourth*. Excerpts from *Tristan*

1 0 4

and Isolde." She managed a laugh. "Don't you think they're a little advanced for me?" He thought she was very near tears.

"There's a single record inside that top album," he told her. He'd had a hell of a time finding it.

"Intermezzo! I knew it would be." Her hand made little caressing motions across the platter.

Swiftly he went to her and lifted her face in his hand. "Don't, dearest. Don't look at me like that." He bent and kissed her. "Now," his voice sounded queer and strained even to himself, "let's have some of your lunch." Straightening and removing the albums from her lap, "I'll start the fire."

"And I'll lay the cloth." Her tone was bright, but her face had the faintly puzzled look he had seen so often. He turned his back and knelt to light the fire.

After adjusting the records on the machine, Paul dropped back on the floor beside Frances. She had pushed away the remnants of the picnic and was sitting, as he had been, cross-legged against the chair. "May I?" he murmured, and lay with his head in her lap. From this angle he could see the swelling curve of her breasts through the thin silk shirtwaist, the hollow of her throat and the dust of freckles on her skin, the stubborn line of her jaw, her pretty mouth. Resolutely he shut his eyes and the music flooded the room.

So quickly had his days fallen into a pattern. His mornings were his own, his evenings belonged to the management of the Lake Luray Hotel, but his afternoons, the yellow lazy afternoons, were theirs—to swim, to ride, to walk, to talk and be quiet together. Frances had a little game about their time together; at the end of an afternoon, she would announce solemnly, "This afternoon brings our total number of hours together up to seventy-two" or "seventy-six" or whatever it was by then. And, rounding her big eyes, "Don't you think it seems like much longer?" Sometimes it did seem that he had known her all his life; sometimes, as he watched her or talked with her, he doubted that he knew her at all.

Suddenly in the midst of the swelling love music from *Tristan*, "Oh Paul!" she exclaimed. Startled, he cocked one eye up at her. "Hmmm?"

"I was just thinking," she continued, much more slowly, "how sad it is about geniuses who die young, with all their life work still ahead of them and all."

"Whatever brought that up? Wagner lived to a ripe old age."

"It wasn't Wagner I was thinking of," she said, too casually. "I mean, oh—people like Keats and Christopher Marlowe and—and Chatterton." He had the feeling that she was watching him as a fisherman might a bobbing cork.

"Umhmmm," he said slowly. He had no idea what she was driving at, but he took the bait. "It's a hell of a world when a genius like Chatterton poisons himself before he's twenty."

"Damn!" she cried so fiercely that he sat up and wheeled around to her in alarm.

"What is it, darling? What on earth—"

"*How* did you know that? However did you know that about Chatterton?"

"Why, I saw a painting in the Louvre once, showing him slumped over his writing table. The story of his life was on a little card. Why?" He was completely dumbfounded.

"It's so silly," she said, waving her hand vaguely. Obviously she wanted to drop the subject. "I get so tired of your knowing so much more than I do about everything—you've read all the books I've ever read and hundreds more I've never heard of. So I just spent about three hours last night going through some old exams, looking up something I was sure you wouldn't know, that's all." She said it as though she'd caught him taking pennies from her purse.

Oddly enough he didn't want to laugh. He put his hands on her shoulders and pressed her back against the chair. "What beautiful deep eyes you have, beloved. No, don't drop them. Look at me." She did, and what he saw in her face exploded within him. With his lips hard against hers, they slid down to the floor, and when he felt her arms tighten around his neck, he began to fumble with the buttons to her blouse. Again and again he kissed her, eyelids and throat and breast. He felt as though he were in an enormous vacuum out of which had been pumped the last breath of air, in which nothing remained except the exultant music and their one body.

He lifted his head to look at her, a question in his eyes. Aloud she answered his question. "Because I love you," she said simply, "and this is the only way I can make you believe me."

Breath flowed back into him, and consciousness. Gently he fastened her shirtwaist, holding her look with his own. "My dearest, I can wait for you until we're married. I love you too much to take you this way." He kissed her as he might have kissed a child, and sat up, running his hands hard through his hair.

The fact that they were going to be married hadn't come to him as a surprise after all, he realized; he'd known they must be, some day. The most natural thing in the world. No thunder and lightning, no fireworks or shooting stars; just the simple statement of a fact they had both tacitly acknowledged in their hearts. And he was wonderfully content. He studied her as she lay without moving, her arms under her head, wondering how long he could look at her and still find something new in her to love. The way her hair grew, long and straight and heavy; and her eyes, so large that at times her face seemed all eyes; her mouth, by turns provocative, tender, petulant, and always ready to break into a smile. He could look at Mrs. Acheson and see Frances as she would be in twenty years; though the daughter was not beautiful now, she would be, in the fullness of maturity, magnificent. He swore to himself that this awakened passion of hers would never be quick-frozen and stilled through any brutal haste and clumsiness of his.

"Paul, will we have a piano—when we're married, I mean?" Frances was wondering. He reached for her hand and began to kiss the fingers. "That tickles!" But she left her hand in his. "I can just see me now," she went on, playing with the thought, "accompanying you on some great concert stage, Vienna, Paris, London . . . I want to go everywhere you've ever been, see everything you've ever seen, do everything you've ever done—"

"Not that!" he broke in hastily. "You shall have your piano, my dear, and *lessons*," he added, smirking at her insultingly. But a fine line puckered his forehead. This misconception she had of his life, of his work, of his trips to the continent, had been revealed on more than one occasion; no matter how often he had described to her the poverty he had known, the disillusionment, the sheer labor of study and practice, the few small successes which the war had cut short, she flung across it all the tapestry of her imagination, woven out of fairy tales and Hollywood. "But Paul," she'd said, "you did have a recital in Town Hall, you told me so." "Yes, darling, but we paid for it ourselves. *Anybody* can hire a hall." "Well, you'll be world-famous one day," she'd answered, undaunted. And now, what fabulous world was she peopling with herself and with him, with nebulous, applauding crowds from the "romantic capitals of Europe"? Was she only infatuated with the sound of her own dreams? The thought drove him urgently, and he pulled her to him again; her passionate response, as always, astounded him even while it reassured him. He held her without word or sense of time, as if to cork up the moment inside him forever.

The sound of a car on the drive and Mrs. Acheson's clear voice calling thanks smashed the silence. Frances jumped to her feet. "There's mother, and I haven't even cleared away our lunch." Straightening his tie and smoothing his hair, Paul went to the door to greet Mrs. Acheson. He wasn't sure that she would remember him, since she had not seen him since the evening he'd had dinner with the family. But she did.

"Paul, how nice to see you again." She shook hands and let him take her dripping raincoat. Frances turned on the lamps and began to gather the sad remains of the picnic into the hamper.

"Hello, Mother," she called. "We didn't mind the rain at all. We had a wonderful party right here on the floor."

Aghast, Paul stopped short and looked straight into Mrs. Acheson's eyes.

But she seemed unaware of the possible implications of Frances' remark. "So I see." She showed Paul where to put her galoshes, and walked over to the fireplace. "I'm glad you all lighted the fire. It's a nasty day outside." Aimlessly she poked at the logs, not looking at either of them.

Paul, taking the hamper jammed with trash from Frances' hands, saw that her mouth was smeared with lipstick; so was his own, he supposed. It would be better to brazen it out. "You'd better go wash your face, Pocahontas."

"So?" she said, not at all abashed. "You look like Sitting Bull yourself." She wrinkled her nose affectionately at him as he excused himself to go empty the trash.

When he was out of hearing, Mrs. Acheson turned to Frances. Her face was grave. "Were you two here alone all afternoon, Frances?"

"Why, of course, Mother. Except for Hannah, that is."

"Be serious, Fran. Who saw Paul come in?"

"Anybody who was nosing around, I guess. The taxi driver who brought him here, for one."

"Don't you realize that it puts you in a very compromising situation?"

"Mother, you're not serious! Don't you trust me?" But the memory of the afternoon seared her like a flame: Paul was the one who had withdrawn, not she. She dropped her eyes.

"Of course I trust you, Frances. It's not a question of the actual deed at all. It's what people think."

"I don't care what that kind of people think!" she

1 1 0

cried more loudly than she had intended. "I don't think much of them either." Never before had she so addressed her mother. Never before had she had such a strange emotion: almost as though she possessed something her mother —coveted, of which her mother was afraid.

Mrs. Acheson's face had softened. "My dear, please. I'm not accusing you and Paul of anything—well, underhanded. I just want you to remember that people are often convicted on appearances alone."

"They shouldn't be! People around here put too much stock in just the surface of things!" Her mind jumbled memories together like popcorn in a shaker: the colored girl in church, her behavior on the floor with Paul, her mother's embarrassed remoteness. Suddenly, the beautiful afternoon had been pawed with dirty fingers. Guilty, angry, confused, she babbled on, "People like that never give you a chance. They get all their exercise leaping to conclusions!"

Her mother watched her coolly, as though waiting for a toy to run down. "Now Franny," she said quietly, "I merely suggested that it isn't good policy for you and *any* young man to spend an afternoon in an empty house. That's all." She leaned across and kissed her daughter's cheek. "I know you too well to think anything else. Now. Does Paul have to go back to Lake Luray this evening?"

Dully Frances shook her head.

"Well, run and wash your face before your father gets home, and I'll ask Paul to stay for dinner." The set of her back as she walked away told Frances that the incident, though closed, was not forgotten.

t e n

Dinner had been easy and gracious. Flowers and candles and silver worn thin with time and the caress of fingers, the flow of laughter and talk around good food, even the rain outside to remind them of the warmth within. And after dinner, the living room, couch pulled nearer the new-made fire, corners and ceiling and old paneled walls flickeringly lighted by the glow. The copper scuttle on the hearth was made of fire; the hanging trails of ivy danced crazily against the white mantel. In his portrait above the fireplace, an Acheson ancestor in his powdered peruke benignly smiled on the room below.

Mr. Acheson was in a mellow mood. He unbuttoned the two lowest buttons of his vest to let his stomach have its way, settled himself further into his favorite chair, and through the smoke of his cigar gazed into the past. "Used to be kind of an entertainer myself," he confided to Paul, "purely amateur way, of course. Those were the days. This was before the Academy of Music burned, you know," he tucked in, "and that was 19—, 19—" He looked at the glowing end of his cigar as though the date might be blazing there. "When was that, Evelyn, do you recall?"

"Before the first war, James," said his wife, who was attempting to knit in spite of Hannah's waving tail. Frances murmured that the date didn't make any difference anyhow, get on with the story.

"I know it was before the first war, Evelyn," Mr. Acheson said with a trace of petulance, "because Tom Armstrong was killed in France in '17 and he used to be one of our end men. Anyway," he went on, turning to

Paul, who paid him the compliment of listening without interrupting, something Mr. Acheson was not accustomed to, "I was the other end man—this was a minstrel show, you know. And how we used to pack 'em in! Bazaars, charities, benefits, everywhere. I used to do a little soft-shoe number. You've heard of buck-and-wing, haven't you?" He patted his stomach in rueful tribute to the old days. "I sang a little too. There was one song they never stopped asking for, *I'm Afraid to Go Home in the Dark. That* was a song! They don't write music like that any more." His tone was wistful. "They used to tell me I could have gone professional." The fire crackled like the clapping of many hands.

On cue Frances asked, "Why don't you sing it for us, Daddy?" Wickedly she turned to Paul. "I can always tell the times when Daddy is willing to shoulder the role of end man again, and I love to be his Mr. Interlocutor." To her father she said, "I'll go get your guitar." Although Mr. Acheson wasn't making overt gestures of compliance, Paul suspected that he wouldn't refuse either. He remembered Frances' telling him that Mr. Acheson loved to do card tricks and stunts with coins, such as extracting dimes from other people's ears, but these, he suspected, required much light and more moving around, and he asked nothing more than to sit on the couch before the fire, holding Frances' hand and listening to her father's voice as he strummed the guitar.

Listening, he noticed how like a Negro's voice Mr. Acheson's was as he sang—chanted rather—deep-blue and dark-brown all at once, full of cotton fields under the sun and mammies in bandanas, lazy levee days with the fishin' pole and happy darkies way down South in the corn field, the beautiful lost gone-but-not-forgotten days on the old plantation when all the white folks lived like God and the niggahs loved it. "You is mighty lucky, babe of Ol' Kentucky, close yo' eyes and sleep . . ."

"Franny there is the one who can really sing, Paul," Mr. Acheson conceded graciously, after he'd run through his repertory. Paul made the necessary noises and relinquished Frances' hand to let her go and sit on the floor against her father's knee. "Daddy knows I really can't sing," she said, looking up at him cheerily, "but I don't mind making a fool of myself to keep everybody happy."

"Which of our many specialities shall we render first, darling?" Mr. Acheson asked, smoothing Frances' hair. "How 'bout 'Lindy, sweet as the sugar cane'?" They fumbled around for a key which Frances could reach, made several false starts, swung finally into the rhythm. What Frances lacked in quality, she made up in quantity; against her strong melody, Mr. Acheson alternated at will between a tenor obbligato and a tentative baritone, dragged agonizing chords from the guitar, and managed to come in a beat behind his daughter on every measure in a valiant groping toward syncopation. It was home-grown music at its worst, Paul thought, but they were having such a caterwauling good time that he egged them on from one song to another ruthlessly; in the places where he twisted his wince into a smile, they smiled back cheerfully.

"Didn't I see your violin case in the hall, Paul?" Mrs. Acheson inquired. She stopped knitting long enough to rearrange Hannah on her lap.

"Yes, I had to take it by the little repair shop in town this morning," he told her.

"If it's fixed, won't you play for us? It isn't often that

we have a chance to hear really good music in this house."
He had to smile at the gentleness of her voice.

"I like *that!*" cried Frances, scrambling to her feet and
pulling at her dress. "Just because she happens to have
a celebrity in the house, *we* aren't good enough for her."
She mussed her father's hair.

"We just got the hook, darling," he said. "Paul, I
apologize. I'd forgotten we had a real musician around."

"Oh, please," Paul said, throwing his hands out, palms
upward, and lying like a Valley gentleman, "don't stop. I
haven't heard anything like it in years."

"I'll bet you haven't," Mrs. Acheson said dryly. "Hannah here tells me her friends on the back fence would be
ashamed."

Frances came to him and took his hands. "Please?
Daddy's never heard you play."

Only once before had he felt this way: his first public
recital. He had stood on the stage at Town Hall, waiting
for the scattered applause to die. He looked for his parents,
for Becky, in the audience, but his eyes refused to focus.
His bones seemed to melt in his body, and his fingers trembled as he raised the violin. Now, as then, he was certain
that he could never play a note.

For a long moment he stood before the fire, and it was
warm on the backs of his legs. He lifted his violin to his
chin, standing between the two big chairs on either side of
the hearth, and took a deep breath. Slowly, surely, music
rose within him, seeping, exploring, lifting, swelling, surging, pounding to escape. A driving tide of music, it swept
away before it all the flotsam of apathy and sterility which
three years had dammed up. It cascaded from him, torren-

tial, inevitable, Niagara in the sunlight. It drained him, it purged him, it exhausted him, it left him free.

He lowered his violin and his bow, one in each hand, limply standing before them, breathing hard. The light glinted on tears in Frances' eyes; he felt a sting in his own.

Suddenly the doorbell rang, and the little scene broke like a bubble. "Hell," Mr. Acheson exploded, his breath rushing out like air from a blown-up balloon. "In all this rain, who—?" Reluctantly Frances dragged herself into the hall. In the silence, Mrs. Acheson's needles began to click again.

Paul laid his violin in its case, making his movements deliberate and slow to calm the trembling in his hands. From far away, through the exultancy and the tumult inside him, he heard the clatter of greetings at the front door, the sound of people coming into the living room. Lights went up, there was a surging forward, and he was being introduced. He wanted only to go away from all this light and noise and confusion, and to take Frances with him. In a rush of faces and teeth and hands and exclamation of pleasure they came at him, two women and a man; he murmured something vague to all of them which neither he nor they heard. The pushing of the couch back against the bookcase, the bringing of a chair from the library. He felt as though he had scared up a covey of birds; their wings beat against his face.

Not until they had all settled down and he could relax beneath the crosscurrents of burble did he attempt to sort them out, to pair them with the names he had heard. All were relatives, that he knew; "kissing kin," Frances had called them. The bony woman with the large hands and sensible shoes must be Mr. Acheson's sister, Mrs. McIntosh, Aunt Fan, for whom Frances had been named; she sat her chair as though she wished it were a horse. Though pitched low, her voice carried across the room to Paul with the resonance of hounds baying after a fox: So-and-So had taken a bad spill at the Club the other afternoon, he wouldn't be able to ride for the cup, and so on. Frances, beside him on the couch, murmured in his ear, "Somebody told Aunt Fan once that she looked like a horse and she took it as a compliment. She's been buying every nag in the county ever since."

"That's her husband, isn't it, talking to your father?"

"Yes, that's Uncle Cal. He calls himself a farmer, but he really doesn't raise anything except flowers. He's always trying to cross-breed peonies and lilies, all such stuff as that."

"Money?"

"I guess so. Enough anyway. It's a good thing, too, because he couldn't make a living at anything that took brains."

Paul was surprised at Frances' attitude. He had thought that loyalty to family was the predominant trait of the Virginia aristocracy, the "my family right or wrong" kind of thing; she surprised him more and more.

Mr. McIntosh, in the corner nearest the door, was arguing volubly with his brother-in-law; Paul could hear a phrase now and then. "Yankees" and "unions" were the two pegs from which he suspended his monologue. On those words his voice rose above his wife's; between them, it subsided to an angry drone. He was a tall man, so gangling that his clothes, though expensive and padded, could not disguise it. He emphasized the peaks of his discourse by jabbing Mr. Acheson in the shoulder with one long fin-

1 1 7

ger protruding from his clenched fist. "And don't you ever forget it!" Paul heard him declare, one jab per word. Wherever Mr. Acheson shifted in his chair, the finger followed.

At a pressure on his knee Paul glanced down and saw that Frances had laid an opened book in his lap; her finger tapped the page. He read the words, "Say over again and yet once over again That thou dost love me." The words built a wall that shut them off in their corner away from the rest of the room.

> "Say thou dost love me, love me, love me—toll
> The silver iterance!—only minding, dear,
> To love me also in silence, with thy soul."

Without answering, he flipped the pages of the book, looking for words to match his mood, hoping to find Donne and those lines he loved. The passage found, he returned the book to Frances, pointing out the place to read. Then he noticed that the old lady in the wing chair by the fireplace was watching them curiously, her little eyes bright behind their steel-rimmed glasses. That must be Mr. McIntosh's mother, he decided; old and tiny, she was as rigid as a china doll in her high-boned collar of white ruching. One baby-sized hand lay along the chair's arm, so still that a garnet ring caught the light and burned steadily. For a second he wavered before that unflinching stare, which seemed to pin him to the wall like a searchlight on a burglar; he was irritated to catch his hand fumbling with his tie. Then he recovered and gave her back stare for stare, tempering his with a smile that forced her, finally, to incline her head an inch and speak. "Evelyn tells me you are a musician." Her voice held neither curiosity nor interest, only cold courtesy.

"I'm a violinist," Paul corrected her gently. He wondered when Mrs. Acheson had had time to pass the word along. Perhaps she had been discussing him on some other occasion?

"You are from the North?" That classic turn of phrase, which seemed to lump God knows how many people together and regally discard them.

"Yes. I'm from New York."

There was no comment on that, but she sat expectantly. Paul felt constrained to offer something more; just what more she expected, he hardly knew. Gamely, however, he plunged ahead. "It's a fascinating city. Have you ever been there, Mrs. McIntosh?"

"No. I seldom travel, and I certainly have no desire to travel to New York." Why damn it, Paul thought suddenly, I wonder how much money it takes to make people feel like God?

"New York has soaked up a lot of your local talent, you know," he informed her deliberately. "Quite a few of our leading men in the arts and sciences were originally from the South."

"If they want to be traitors to their own kind, let them go," Mrs. McIntosh said without a trace of feeling. If he'd not heard her say it in so many words, he'd never have believed that such a remark could be made in America in 1946. "My daughter went to New York after the last war to paint"—the scorn in that one word!—"and she has never returned." She probably couldn't stand it down here, Paul thought viciously, and hoped the old lady wasn't a mind reader. "How can one leave home, friends, *family*, and go to live among strangers?"

It was obviously a rhetorical question, but Paul decided to give her an answer anyway. "Perhaps in New York she found people who shared her ideas, her thoughts, her plans, more than the people in her own town." There was no flicker in those bright little eyes. Instantly he regretted the criticism implicit in his remark: a woman of such great age merited respect regardless of her ridiculous attitudes. "That happens to families everywhere," he added more gently.

Fortunately, at that moment her attention was caught by Mr. McIntosh. "Mother, I want you to verify something for me."

Paul turned back to Frances, who was tugging at his hand. "That was a beautiful little passage you found for me, darling," she whispered. "I'd never come across it before. 'I wonder by my troth what thou and I did till we loved.' Isn't that the way it goes?" She found the poem again and traced the lines with her finger. "This part too— 'If ever any beauty I did see, which I desired and got, 'twas but a dream of thee.' "

"Why should I try to make love to you when Donne does it so well for me?" he said in her ear. "What did you find for me?"

"I had to go back to Mrs. Browning. Here." He felt her eyes upon him as he read.

"*The face of all the world is changed, I think,*
Since first I heard the footsteps of thy soul
Move still, oh still beside me—"

"—you and Frances there, Paul?" he heard Mrs. Acheson say.

"I beg your pardon, what did you ask me, Mrs. Acheson?" Conscious of the silence and the eyes, he slipped the book onto the couch beside him.

"We've been discussing Judge Braxton's inviting niggers to his house, Paul," Mr. Acheson broke in, "and my wife says that you and Frances were there."

"Certainly we were there, Daddy," Frances answered for him, bridling. "I was in charge of the meeting."

"You never mentioned it to me, Frances."

"I hardly thought you'd be interested." She was almost rude.

"It was a church social and discussion group, Mr. Acheson," Paul explained carefully, "and it was *they* who invited the Negro young people."

"That hasn't got anything to do with it, young fellow!" Mr. McIntosh crackled, forefinger jabbing an imaginary opponent. Paul was glad he was across the room. "In *this* town, decent people don't invite niggers to their houses under *any* circumstances! And to *eat*, too!" he gagged.

Mr. Acheson laid a restraining hand on his brother-in-law's knee. "Just a minute now, Calvin. Paul is from New York," he said courteously, "and just doesn't understand the way things are down here." Directly to Paul, he said, "Most of these niggers down here know their place. Oh, some don't, but they either get in line or they leave. Our niggers are happy, and we know how to handle them—"

Calmly, Mr. Acheson's voice went on and on, explaining the "situation" to an "outsider"; it rang with sincerity and conviction. Remembering Frances' vivid description

1 2 1

of her father's wild outbursts on this very subject, Paul was struck by Mr. Acheson's control and self-possession. Then he recalled that such outbursts were confined to the inner circle of the family; that hospitality—as interpreted in Kingston—demanded quiet voices at all times, courtesy regardless of the provocation. Mr. McIntosh's head was bobbing up and down in agreement with the speech like an apple on a string; occasionally he beat his knee lightly with his fist. Under his hand, Paul felt Frances' hand quivering. Too bad this had to come up to spoil everything, he thought, with a fleeting recollection of firelight and music and the cat purring in Mrs. Acheson's lap. But he could no longer sit quietly, holding Frances' hand, luxuriating in the memory of the early evening and its false peace, while this kind of talk flew at him with the sting of arrows.

"—and the difficulty is, you see," Mr. Acheson expounded with the ease of a lecturer whose audience is convinced already, "Judge Braxton is a representative to Congress, coming up in the primaries next month for his third term. He's been very good. Nobody had any complaints. He would have won hands down—up until *now*. If he'd won the primary, of course, that would have meant the election, because there isn't any Republican candidate, you know. But now, I'm not so sure. This business of having niggers at his house is causing a lot of ugly talk downtown, and his opponent in the primary isn't letting it die."

"I wouldn't vote for a nigger-lover!" Mr. McIntosh cried at the first opportunity. Evidently he felt that Mr. Acheson was putting the case too mildly. "God knows what he'd do in Washington. Have niggers all over the place, running the government most likely."

"Oh come now, Mr. McIntosh." Paul laughed a little,

hoping that he might keep the conversation light, hoping that he might yet avoid locking horns with these blind and dangerous men. "Judge Braxton seems to be a very intelligent person. I'm sure he wouldn't want to turn the government over to any one dominant group."

The women sat, silent. For a little moment, Paul wondered at that. Was this purely "men's talk," in which they had no interest? No, he was sure that Mrs. Acheson, at least, had her opinions; perhaps they differed from her husband's and she shrank from crossing him in public. Could it be, as he had somewhere heard, that among old families in the South it was still considered unladylike and unattractive to have an interest in such masculine matters as politics, to converse on them in company?

Mr. McIntosh had by-passed Paul's last remark, probably because he hadn't quite followed it, but Mr. Acheson took it up, with a steely edge to his voice. "If the well-meaning but short-sighted people from the North would mend their own ways, Paul," he said pointedly, "and leave the South alone, we'd work out our own salvation. Sending to Congress a man who consorts with niggers is not our way of doing it."

Desperately Paul tried to keep his voice smooth. "It's hard to believe, Mr. Acheson, that a district would refuse to return to Washington a good representative because in the privacy of his home he entertains a church group which has broader ideas of tolerance and decency than his neighbors." That did it! He was committed to his course. He tightened his clutch on Frances' clammy hand.

"Now see here—" cried Mr. McIntosh, half rising from his chair. Mr. Acheson ignored his brother-in-law. His voice was shining steel, as he spoke to Paul. "Your choice of words is unfortunate, Paul. We have our standards of decency and tolerance. They are part of our whole framework of living. We intend to protect what is ours."

How futile, how idiotic, to employ reason on men who thought with their feelings, their instincts, their viscera; men to whom a rational argument was as mist before the sun of their emotions; men in whom prejudice was a disease sucked up with their mother's milk along with their burlesqued Christianity. To both of these—the disease and the religion—they clung with the passion of the fanatic, until the religion became a disease, and the prejudice a religion.

But Paul too knew a compulsion as strong as theirs. He was standing now, with a great effort lighting a cigarette, leaning against the old smooth wood of the bookcase, pressing one hand hard against it. He addressed himself directly to Mr. Acheson, for the other man was a complete fool. It was the half-educated, who knew enough to have an opinion but not enough to concede the possibility of that opinion's being wrong, who were the real menace. Donne again: the line ran through his mind, "Who are a little wise, the best fools be."

"Try to *feel* how it must be, Mr. Acheson," he said, appealing to the heart of the man, "to be born a citizen of this country, yet denied the right to vote for your own government. A human being with all the sensitivities you yourself claim, yet forced by other human beings into the dirtiest parts of town. To be educated and capable, yet lose a job, in many cases to less qualified men, because your skin is black. Worst of all, to meet scorn and contempt, often real hate, on the faces of people who don't even know your name, people who hate you *personally* because you're one of a group that's different from them. Never to be given a chance on your individual merit, but pre-judged and condemned already, a 'niggah' and therefore worthless. *You* can't know what that's like! You were born white and Protestant, automatically one of the favored few of the earth. But why take so much credit for it? You had nothing to do with the selection of your parents, your color, your creed. Neither did I, but I know the other side of the picture: the restricted apartments and resorts, the discrimination in education and jobs, the hate on the faces of complete strangers. We Jews don't dare have any prejudices—"

It was not a sound that stopped him, it was the cessation of breathing in the room. The air itself, an animate force, swelled, expanded, pressed upon him like the great weight of the sea on a diver fathoms down. Abruptly faces were cutouts pasted grotesquely against the walls, Halloween masks of shock and horror. Frances' face, stark-white and frozen, tilted up to him. Hadn't she told them he was Jewish? Hadn't she dared?

The tableau crumbled, disintegrated. Someone coughed. Mr. Acheson lit his dead cigar. Old Mrs. McIntosh stirred in her big chair. Mrs. Acheson mentioned coffee and cakes, rose to go into the kitchen. Her sister-in-law dismounted her chair, making helpful noises. The logs in the fireplace spit fretfully. Paul stood by the bookcase, aimlessly tapping his cigarette into a tray, staring down at Frances' smooth head bent over her book. She was turning pages slowly—to keep from looking up at him? His eyes caressed the curve of her shoulder, her long body, her legs stuck out into the room. Suddenly she murmured aloud, opened the book wide, and with a gesture like a priest's at mass, elevating the host, raised the book to him. His heart turned over within him as he read.

> "How do I love thee? Let me count the ways.
> I love thee to the depth and breadth and height
> My soul can reach, when feeling out of sight
> For the end of being, and ideal grace . . .
> . . . And if God choose,
> I shall but love thee better after death."

e l e v e n

Even then, the day was not done. Even after Paul had excused himself on the pretext that he had to catch the last bus to Lake Luray. Even after all the relatives had departed in a great flurry of hugs and kisses and promises to drop in more often, chirruping thanks for the evening and the refreshments, carefully refraining from mentioning the "incident" which had occurred. "So unfortunate, but what else could you expect?" Frances imagined them saying to one another. "Wherever do you suppose she picked *him* up?" Even then she was not to escape to her room and darkness and the sanctuary of the pulled-up sheet.

Upstairs in the back hall, rooting in the linen closet for a clean bath towel, she heard a door open below. Voices came to her clearly. "Where is she?" her father said.

"She's gone to bed." Her mother sounded listless and exhausted.

The steep back stairs dropped into the kitchen. Frances crept halfway down and crouched in the darkness, shamelessly eavesdropping. She knew not only what they were going to discuss, she could have charted all the twists and turns which the discussion would take. Yet she forced herself to stay and listen, holding her hands across her mouth to stifle her heavy breathing.

"How long has this been going on, Evelyn?"

"What do you mean, 'going on'? What makes you think there's anything between them?" Oddly defensive, her mother's voice. Frances knew she was recalling the scene of the afternoon: empty house, smeared lipstick, their conversation later—"Of course, I trust you, Frances; it's just what people will think."

"My God, are you blind?" Mr. Acheson demanded.

—No, Daddy, mother's not blind; she sees a great deal more than you do, I'm afraid.

"Couldn't you see how they were looking at each other, Evelyn? That fellow couldn't keep his eyes off her, and I thought Frances would wiggle herself right out of that dress."

Silence. Sound of nervous pacing.

"I think you're exaggerating the importance of this, James." Mother, not so weary-sounding now, controlled again, the cool hand across her husband's forehead. "Paul will be here for such a short while. At the most it's just a summer flirtation." At least, mother used his name, called him "Paul," didn't say "that fellow," as though he were just another body with a number branded on it.

"Listen, Evelyn, use your head! Use your head! These things happen overnight. Bang! They'll be wanting to get married."

—Bang! There was her picture in the paper. There was the announcement underneath it:

> *Mr. and Mrs. James Curtis Acheson announce the engagement of their daughter, Frances Curtis, to Mr. Paul Revkin of New York City.*
>
> *Miss Acheson is a graduate of Kingston College. On her father's side she is descended from Colonel High Muckety-Muck who was something big on General Lee's staff, and from Fol-de-rol Somebody, spectacular Revolutionary figure. Her maternal grandparents were Senator and Mrs. Blah-blah of Williamsburg, who made all their money selling patent medicines to niggahs. Miss Acheson is a member of the DAR, the UDC, the PDQ and the Society for Prevention of Cruelty to Animals.*
>
> *Mr. Revkin is a Jew. On his father's side he is descended from Jews. His maternal grandparents lived in the most select ghetto in Europe. He is not a member of anything except the human race.*
>
> *No date has been set for the wedding.*

"You seemed to like the boy, James. I thought you and he were getting to be great friends."

—What's this, Mother? Are you on my side?

"Sure I liked him fine. Nice fellow. But I didn't know he was Jewish!" The pacing stopped. "Did you?"

"No. No, James, I didn't."

—Too quick, Mother, too quick. You suspected that he was Jewish, didn't you? Then why didn't you come right out and ask me? Or perhaps you hoped that I'd break down and tell. And why didn't I tell, why didn't I? I knew this business would come to a head sooner or later. It's all my fault that it came out so horribly. But I was so damn scared of what would happen. And now, it has.

"Do you think Frances knew all along he was Jewish?" Daddy, worrying the bone, gnawing down to the marrow.

"Oh, I'm sure she did, James. Paul would have told her immediately. He's not the kind of person to travel under false colors."

—Thanks, Mother. You're right about Paul. I'm the coward in this mess, not Paul. He never dreamed that the family's kindness came out of ignorance.

"I don't see how I could have missed it. I don't see." Sound of fist beating palm. Daddy, trying to justify his blindness to himself. "But, my God! She met him in church, didn't she? I thought—I thought—God knows what I thought. I just wasn't thinking. He doesn't look Jewish, and that name could be anything. It just never crossed my mind. It just never crossed my mind."

—What do you think you could have done about it, Daddy, if you'd known? Locked me in my room on bread and water? Taken a horsewhip to Paul?

Mother, asking the same question. "What are you going to do about it now that you know, James?"

Getting angry now, voice rising. "Don't put it all off on me, dammit! She's your daughter as much as she is mine. Do you want to see her married to this kike?"

"James! That's enough of that! You'll get nowhere with Frances using such language."

—Mother, Mother, stick by me now. Don't evade the issue. Answer him Yes, you want to see me married to this

—this Jew if it'll make me happy. Stop playing politics. Stop appeasing, for once in your life. Don't be a buffer state between us.

"All right, Evelyn, so he's not a kike. So he's a nice Jew. But he's still a Jew, and I won't have Frances throwing away her life after I've worked my fingers to the bone to put her where she is."

—Where is that, Daddy? Where am I? Where are we all? Where does our kind fit into this world of the first year after the war? The war that came and took all the boys away to fight, remember? There wasn't any way you could hold them back. The world's a lot closer to you than you think, Daddy, and it's closing in on you fast. You can either welcome it and go forward with it; or you can turn your back and get trampled to death in the rush. But you *can't* hide out here in your mountains much longer.

"You must take Frances' feelings into consideration, James." Her mother, unemotional regardless of the crisis. If the house were to burn down, she'd manage to appear on the lawn fully clothed, carefully holding the silver chest in both arms. "I think this is an infatuation which will pass with the summer. Paul is new and different. She's never known anybody who so nearly fits her fairy-tale ideas." A snort from Daddy at that. "He's been abroad and has that certain romantic quality she thinks she's been waiting for. She pictures herself traveling all over Europe with a famous musician, meeting all kinds of exciting people, getting herself photographed for the papers."

—That's all true, Mother, but there's much more to it than that. Honestly. Honestly.

Daddy, breaking in thoughtfully. "What she has got to do is get her head out of those woolly clouds, forget all this knight-in-shining-armor stuff, really face up to the situation." Serious now, slow-talking, probably polishing his nose-glasses with a handkerchief.

"She's no child, James. You can't order her around like you used to."

"You're damn right. Look at this business over the split in the church. She's got a stubborn streak up her back a yard wide."

"Now don't raise your voice again, dear. That's no way to handle Frances, ever. You just cannot browbeat her into anything. She responds very nicely to reason."

—Why don't you just hang a carrot in front of my nose and I'll *walk* back into the stable!

"Reason, hell! She thinks on instinct, when she thinks at all. She hasn't got the sense God gave little apples. She hasn't got the faintest idea of what she'd be letting herself in for, if she were to marry this—this fellow. Do you realize *we'd* have Jewish grandchildren?"

"Aren't you being a bit premature, James? They're not even engaged yet."

"That's right. That's just like you. Lock the barn door after the horse has been stolen. It's always up to me. This family would go to hell if I didn't think ahead, think ahead, all the time. Well, I intend to stop it right here and now."

"James, I warn you. If you attempt that tyrannical approach with Frances, you'll lose her. Don't you ever learn? Don't you remember how she wouldn't back down either about the church or that business with the school superintendent? She's an adult and you've got to treat her as one."

"All right. You suggest something."

"I already have. Be rational. Point out all the difficulties she'd have—"

—Yes, Daddy, mass your arguments on the firing line. There's your target, that single solitary girl running down there. She hardly seems large enough to deserve the all-out attack. Was it necessary to call up the reserves? Ready? Aim—

"She hasn't considered that she'd lose all her friends—"

—Let them go! I will use Paul as a yardstick to measure people by, and if they don't measure up, let them go.

"—and she wouldn't be accepted into his world either."

—We'll make a world of our own, he and I. We won't need anybody else.

"I'm sure it's never crossed her mind that the children will be social outcasts too. It will break her heart to see them grow up shunned and despised."

—Oh, Mother, Mother, I'll make it up to them.

"She's never met his family."

—Well, Paul's met mine and that's bad enough. His couldn't be worse!

"Remind her that she's picking her children's grandparents when she picks their father."

Daddy, angry again. "Picks their father, hell! *He* did the picking. Saw a good thing and grabbed it. She's so dumb she didn't know what was happening."

—Oh Daddy, if you only knew how hard I worked to get him! What barriers I had to break down. I was the aggressor, not Paul. And I still don't know why he fell in love with *me*.

"James, be sensible. Paul would be a very good match

for Frances if he weren't Jewish. It's too bad, it really is . . ."

"Hell, they're all alike, they're all a bunch of crooks and shysters, worming their way into your business or your house, pushing, crowding. This fellow's just like the rest of them, only he's been a damn sight smoother about it. He's got what he wanted, hasn't he—"

"Not yet, James. But he most certainly will if you lose control of yourself and begin haranguing Frances. She'll run to him so fast it'll make your head swim."

"Oh, Evelyn, it makes me so goddam mad—" A pause, a sigh. "You're right. You're right. I'll try to reason with her. But my God! She's got to see . . . a Jew!"

—Have you given him a battle map of the terrain, Mother? Does he understand the signals? No frontal assault, as usual, but a flank movement around the end of reason. This ought to be interesting: Operation Frances.

As Mr. and Mrs. Acheson walked out of the kitchen, murmuring now so low that Frances could no longer hear them, she slipped quietly back up the stairs and into her bedroom. Without lighting the lamp, she tore her clothes off impatiently and threw them on a chair. The rain was over. The moonlight lay in slivers on the floor, sliced off by the blinds. She could hear her parents coming up the front staircase as she crawled into bed, carefully, to keep the springs from creaking. Her mother's footsteps turned at the head of the stairs toward the front of the house. Her father's came on to her door.

A long silence. A light tap. She didn't stir. Eyes wide, she stared above her into the darkness, thinking of all the people in the world who had ever lain, trembling and wide-eyed, behind a closed door, waiting for a footstep, a knock. But what was there for her to fear, that she should be trembling, wide-eyed here in the dark, afraid to open the door to her own father?

"Frances, are you awake?"

She felt like a prize fighter entering the ring, flexing muscles, throwing his robe in the corner. She sat up in bed and pressed her back hard against the wall. "Yes, I'm awake, Daddy. Come in."

part two

t w e l v e

Irritably Frances thought that half her life these days seemed to be spent at the dining-room table in unavoidable proximity to her mother and father. During the bright, forced conversation and during the long, strained silences she was equally miserable, and when they had company, as they had this hot Sunday afternoon, she was more miserable because she could not break away from dinner early, go to her room, and write Paul a letter.

Sundays were bad, however she looked at them. Paul was usually tied up on Sundays, and on Sundays, she angered her father more than on weekdays. Day of rest and gladness, my foot, she snorted to herself; I'd just as soon they cut it off the calendar altogether.

She was always late coming home after church, not only because she had to change from her choir robes to her dress, not only because she had to catch the slow Hillcrest bus, but also because she so often indulged in a long backstage conversation with Dr. Mac. He was the only person in her life with whom she could talk freely and glowingly of Paul. Her being late always made Sunday dinner even later—"Why didn't you go ahead and eat?" she would inquire pettishly. "You certainly didn't have to wait for me!" —and her father seldom had time for a long afternoon nap. Mr. Acheson would glower at his pocket watch, har-rumph the longest grace he knew, and have indigestion before he'd swallowed a bite.

Until recently the dinner table, especially on Sundays, had been a place of leisurely dining, hilarious talk, and the three essential F's, her father said, of fun, food, and fellowship. But in the last few weeks—since the "incident" with Paul—all that had vanished. Now they galloped through the meal glumly, if they ate anything at all. There was no more laughter, and, skittish, they reared back from at least five good-sized topics of conversation: churches, schools, Negroes, Jews, and love.

That doesn't leave much to talk about, Frances admitted to herself on more than one silent occasion. Even the most innocuous sentence led, like the roads from Rome, straight into dangerous territory. Politics led to Judge Braxton and the primary, and Frances knew where that would end. International relations led to politics, and just about everything led to love.

Today dinner was later than usual—her fault again; and Mr. Acheson was more than usually provoked because he was entertaining a very important guest, the Reverend

Hugh Andrews, new pastor of the First Presbyterian Church. Across the bowl of clematis and roses in the center of the table, Frances watched him through squinted lids as he talked shop with her father. He was a very young man to be pastor of such a big church, thirty-four or thirty-five at the most. He had the kind of blond good looks which deserved the dark beauty of a pulpit, and an impersonal geniality which probably came from shaking hands with a stream of strangers every Sunday morning at the church door and making each of them want to come to church again.

Remotely she noticed his good teeth, his ruddy skin, his easy smile; he certainly was a good-looking man. He was much better looking than Paul, quite candidly she confessed to herself, and she couldn't help comparing Paul's dark intensity and brooding remoteness with Mr. Andrews' graciousness and easy charm. He's the kind of person everyone takes to immediately, Frances decided, but you have to be a special person to appreciate Paul. Thinking of Paul, she felt her lips curl up contentedly; in her life he loomed so large that all other men seemed tiny and insignificant by comparison. She knew that this was so, and it was the way she wanted it. Yet this attitude made her intolerant of everybody who wasn't Paul, and she caught herself, on many an occasion, saying inside, "Paul wouldn't think that way. He'd think thus-and-so," or "Paul would do it differently." Watching Mr. Andrews, she determined to be tolerant: she would *not* compare him with Paul, she would give him the benefit of every doubt.

Mr. Acheson was in fine form. Smithfield ham and yams candied with butter and molasses were his favorite dish, and he'd had two helpings. "Ah, Mr. Andrews," he

1 3 9

sighed appreciatively, settling back into his chair and almost patting his stomach, "we consider ourselves very fortunate to have secured you for our church. Why, for the past two months, ever since"—he stopped, shot a quick glance at Frances, and started again—"for the past two months, we've had the most wretched collection of whipper-snappers substituting in that pulpit I've ever heard."

Sympathetically, Mr. Andrews made murmurs. "Boys from the Seminary, I suppose, filling in?"

"Youngsters no older than Frances there, telling me how to run my life! It's high time we got a regular preacher. That was a fine sermon you gave us this morning. Fine."

"How did *you* like my sermon, Miss Acheson?"

Frances, who had said as little as decency permitted during the meal, glanced up at him. "I didn't hear it. I'm sorry," she said quietly.

"Oh come now, don't tell me I put you to sleep?" Mr. Andrews persisted.

"Well, you see—" said her mother; and "I'll tell you," said her father. Frances kept looking at the young Mr. Andrews. "I don't go to your church."

His hands sketched the faintest gesture of surprise before they caught themselves in mid-air and fell into an attitude of anticipation.

"I go to Dr. McDonough's church," she went on clearly. "The group that broke away, you know."

"Are you a Virginian, Mr. Andrews?" Mrs. Acheson's pleasant voice insinuated itself into the silence. Frances saw his eyes waver from hers and back again before he turned to answer his hostess. She was afraid she'd seen a flicker of interest there. Truly she hoped not; she didn't want to spend the afternoon with him. On days when she couldn't see Paul, she wrote him a letter for hours . . . She smiled, looking down at her plate. Sometimes, when she'd forgotten to mail the letter, she'd hand it to him on the following day. "Do you want me to read it while you're watching me?" he'd say, with his slow, dark smile. "Of course," she'd tell him. "I've written you all the things I can't bring myself to say out loud in broad daylight. Go on, read it." And as she watched him, warming herself at the warmth in his eyes, he would read it, savoring it, would tuck it away in his coat pocket, would kiss her hands until they burned . . .

"So you're kin to old Professor Andrews down at the University?" she heard her father say. "Fine old gentleman. I remember him well." Yes, that did it: the young minister was going to be a great success. Already her father approved of him; he'd soon be taken into the bosom of the family. As a matter of fact, she thought, narrowing her mind's eye, that is probably Daddy's idea. If Mr. Andrews is single. And if he is single, Daddy will damn well soon find out.

She listened to her father go about it with his usual finesse. "Have you had a chance to look over the manse, Mr. Andrews?"

Gesture outlining height, space and beauty. "Why, yes, Mr. Acheson. Lovely old place, isn't it?" It is *not*, Frances said to herself. It's a disgrace to First Church. The house is about to fall down.

"I suppose you'll be bringing your family here very soon to get settled." Mr. Acheson was pushing his point a little hard.

"There's only my mother, and she will join me immediately. I don't have a family of my own—" Mr. Andrews paused nicely, with one hand lightly on his chest. It was a curiously appealing touch, boyish and diffident, though a trifle overdone. Of course, he *may* have been fingering his tie, Frances reminded herself crossly. Stop your picking on him!

"I'm sure that in no time at all, now that you're here, all the members of First Church will be one big happy family," said Frances mercilessly. For a moment she was afraid she had gone too far in her baiting of him, and she didn't dare look at her father. Mr. Andrews, however, took the remark at face value.

"That's mighty kind of you, Miss Acheson," he said heartily. "As Paul says, we must all work together for the glory of the kingdom of God." At the name her heart thudded—and then she realized that there was a Biblical Paul too. She needed her Paul very much right now, to share this devilish twinkle in her eye; it was difficult to keep her gaze fastened on her plate.

Mr. Acheson ran the ball back into less dangerous territory. "Were you in the Service, Mr. Andrews?"

"Well, no sir, I wasn't." He smiled a little. "I certainly wanted to, of course. Especially when I saw everybody else going. But I just couldn't see my way clear to leaving my little church."

"But ministers were exempt from the draft, of course," said Mr. Acheson.

"Yes, but I wanted to volunteer. Still, my church was a struggling group that had just got on its feet. I finally had to decide that my place was with them."

"How big was your church, Mr. Andrews?" asked Mrs. Acheson.

"Approximately eight hundred members when I was called to Kingston," he told her.

Perversely, Frances commented, "That hardly sounds struggling to me. Our church has barely half that number, and no equipment either." Immediately she was astounded at her own rudeness.

As though death had been mentioned, silence settled around the table. Frances watched the three of them attack their dessert with unnecessary energy. Poor Mr. Andrews was in a wretched position; he could not show great interest in her church for fear of insulting Deacon Acheson, nor could he refuse to discuss it with her when she brought it up, without seeming rude. All he could do was eat his apricot ice cream with a great show of delight and a little too much clatter of spoon on saucer.

She took sudden pity on him. "What was your sermon about this morning, Mr. Andrews?"

Relief rippled around the table. Mr. Acheson leaned back, lit a cigar, and his wife poured coffee. The young minister, resting his elbows on the table, raised his face in an expression of earnestness so perfect that Frances suspected he had practiced it long hours before a mirror. At once she accused herself of spreading her bitterness toward her parents over the innocent Mr. Andrews too; for all his self-righteousness he was honest, and he did not deserve the bad time she was giving him. So she smiled across the flowers and tried to appear interested in the rehash of his morning's sermon.

"The most important thing for us as Christians to do in this world," he was telling her with great seriousness, his pleasant voice ringing against the chandelier, "is to build a united front for Christ. It is the only thing which can save us from the anti-Christ which is flooding the earth. We must march forward militantly, morally strong, knowing that we are on the side of the right. We must fight these atheistic forces which strike at the roots of our Christian society." He stopped and looked at her to see how she was taking it. Frances smiled again, for lack of something to say.

"The war is over, thank God, but the fight for Christian principles is still raging. We must not rest until we have destroyed the evil which flourishes all about us, so that the good may prosper."

Why, he isn't saying anything at all, Frances declared to herself in real astonishment. But he sincerely thinks he is, and he believes that all his claptrap means something. He could never antagonize anybody so long as he keeps on saying nothing. No wonder he's so popular.

Maliciously, she decided to force him out into the open. "How right you are, Mr. Andrews," she said sententiously, "saying that the fight for Christian principles is still being waged. There are outrages being perpetrated right here in Kingston which call for protest and action by all the people who are really Christians." She heard her father stir uneasily in his chair: he believed staunchly that no controversial issue should be aired in company. Regardless of how he seethed within, or how he planned to scold her privately, his tenets of hospitality forbade him to raise his voice or grow angry in public. Frances knew that he would not interrupt her.

"The question of intolerance, for instance. Don't you think, Mr. Andrews, that the churches should lead the way toward the solution of the race problem?"

"The Bible gives us our answer to that," he said gracefully. "All men are brothers, and we must love our neighbor as ourselves."

"Ah?" she said at once, encouraged and pleased. "Then how—"

He flung up one hand, palm toward her, intent on making himself understood. "Just a minute. That is a matter between each individual and his conscience. The church teaches the brotherhood of man; the individual must practice it."

"But of course," she said eagerly. The point was too obvious to labor. "The question is, *does* the church teach the brotherhood of man?"

"Why certainly," he said patiently. "Look in your Bible. That's one of the basic tenets of the Christian faith."

"No. What I am trying to get at is," she fumbled, "the church may teach it, but it certainly doesn't practice it."

"As I said before, the practice is up to the individual."

Constantly he evaded her. They were talking in circles and she'd be damned if she could put her finger on the weak spot in his reasoning. In the middle of the night she would think of a good answer for him, she knew; she was always carrying on imaginary conversations with people hours after the conversation could be effective. She wished Paul were here: he would immediately have sliced through the fatty layers of this conversation to the sickness beneath. She must remember to tell him all about Mr. Andrews and his beautiful platitudes. Perhaps she could introduce them to each other some day soon, just for the pleasure of seeing Mr. Andrews taken down.

There were so many things she had to remember to tell Paul. Whenever she was not with him, she crammed tidbits of talk and events into the drawers of her memory, to be dragged out and nibbled over later with him. And no matter how often they were together, no matter how much they talked, she was discovering always new horizons in his mind, toward which she earnestly plodded, new wells she could never plumb, new worlds she looked upon from afar, covetously. Once or twice she'd tried to explain to him how she felt: "It's as though you'd taken me up on a high hill and had shown me all the kingdoms of the earth that I didn't even know existed—" But Paul would never allow her to sit upon a cloud very long. "Oh, shut up, you beautiful idiot. You must have been reading *The Little Colonel's Knight Comes Riding* again." And if she wouldn't hush, he'd kiss her quiet and she'd laugh up at him, there on the hillside, and say, "But it's true!" between kisses. "But it's true!"

Blankly she looked down at her mother's light touch on her hand. "Frances, dear, don't hum at the table."

"Was I? I'm sorry. I didn't even know it."

"You don't seem to know very much about anything these days."

Utterly astounded, she stared at her mother. Across the table Mr. Andrews was talking with her father, both oblivious to their surroundings—fortunately, because Frances felt her chin tremble. At once she stiffened it and looked directly into her mother's eyes. They were carefully clean of expression, like two gray mirrors which held the inside in and the outside out. And Frances was outside.

Very low, she said, "I'm sorry again."

Mrs. Acheson turned away to her husband. "If you gentlemen want to go into the living room and continue your conversation, Frances and I will take care of the dishes."

"Nonsense!" cried Mr. Andrews, instantly leaning toward her with his wide smile. "You've cooked this fine dinner. Now you should have a rest. Let Frances and me clean up. Besides, I haven't had a chance to talk to this young lady yet, and I certainly want to."

Through her father's too-hearty protests that the minister shouldn't have to wash dishes, through her mother's soft demurring, Frances listened to Mr. Andrews, listened to him remotely, as though she were not within the group nor within the room at all, as though she were perched up in a watchtower somewhere outside, observing through a telescope the movements of four strangers who were rising from the table and pushing chairs back against the wall. The table was small and far away, and the hands of the four people as they collected the dishes were tiny and brown against the white tablecloth. Their talk rose to her faintly. She wondered if she too had found her own secret place.

"Now you must tell me all about yourself, Miss Acheson," said Mr. Andrews when the hot soapy water was in the dishpan and the china was piled on the kitchen table and the family, smugly smiling, had withdrawn to the library. "Or may I call you Frances?" he persisted, leaning down encouragingly from his great height. "My name is Hugh."

"I know," she said, cautiously sliding the plates into the rubber holder on the drainboard. "Your name is Hugh and you may call me Frances and for the Lord's sake, be careful of mother's china. We only use it when we're entertaining the preacher or there's a wedding in the family."

"Oh, I'm used to washing dishes," he informed her cheerfully, holding an enormous platter in his two hands as delicately as if it were a baby about to be christened. "I wash and dry dishes all the time for my mother."

He walked to the table and gently set the platter down. "You mentioned weddings," he commented after a pause. "Is there going to be a wedding around here soon?"

Too quickly she said, "Oh, no, not that I know of," and then wondered why in the world she couldn't learn to keep her mouth shut.

"Well, you never can tell," Hugh mused, appraising her, she thought with a flash of resentment, as though she were up for sale on the block. She could almost hear the counters click in his mind as the grand total soared: money, family, church background—and Presbyterian at that—youth and a kind of coltish beauty, no competition in sight, and a family which had thrown him at her within the first hour. She wanted to inquire if he thought he'd hit the jackpot, but she supposed that he would only stand with his wide mouth smiling and say the Biblical equivalent of 'Huhn.'

Briskly she started to deflate him. "You wanted to know all about me, didn't you say? Well, I was invited to join the Communist Party last week—"

He nearly dropped a Wedgewood cup.

"It's a long story," she warned him wickedly, not offering to shorten it. "I was on a bus going downtown about two weeks ago"—to meet Paul, she wanted to add—"and the bus was very crowded. In the back there were Negroes and white people all standing up together, and in one seat was an old colored woman sitting down between two whites."

She clicked her tongue against her teeth. "Terrible, isn't it, having to sit next to a Negro? Well anyway, the bus driver stopped the bus somewhere on the way downtown and pushed back to the rear, right up to this old colored woman. He hollered at her, he actually hollered at her. He said, 'What do you think you're doing, sitting down while white people stand up? Get up out of that seat! Get up!' Nobody stopped him or said anything to him; they all just stood around and looked embarrassed." Hugh was listening attentively, bent down to her a little as though he didn't want to miss a word.

"So when I got home, I sat down and wrote a letter to the *Bugle*, telling the story and saying that I was ashamed of a town that allowed such things to go on. Oh, I put in a lot of stuff about fighting the war for democracy overseas and losing it here at home—" She waved a soapy hand at him.

"The very next day the letter came out in the paper, with my name in great big black letters underneath. I got home about six o'clock, and there was Daddy waiting for me, right in the middle of the floor, with the paper in his hand opened to the 'Letters' page—and thunder all over his face! Heavens! Was he mad!" Frances laughed aloud at the recollection. "People had been stopping him at the bank all day, saying, 'Well, Mr. Acheson! I see your daughter is in print!' and so forth. Daddy said he'd never hold his head up on Main Street again. He said I'd made him the laughingstock of Kingston."

"But how did the Communist Party get mixed up in this?" Hugh asked seriously. He hadn't laughed at all.

"Oh, them. You don't have to dry the pots and pans, thank you. Just let 'em drain. Well, about a week ago, I got a letter from the State Headquarters of the Party saying that they'd read my letter in the newspaper and they were encouraged to see that young people in Virginia were at last taking an active interest in current problems. They wanted me to send them some money to support them in their work, and they said they'd be very happy if I would join the Party. As a token of their approval, they are now sending me *The Daily Worker* free for a month!" She threw her head back and chortled. "You should see the postman. He brings it to the mailbox as though it had leprosy, and he practically runs back to the street. I guess he thinks we've got a bomb under every rosebush."

"Well, did you?" Hugh asked anxiously.

"Did I what?"

"Did you answer their invitation to join them?" His forehead was furrowed, and his mouth hung open a little.

"What's the matter, wouldn't you speak to me again if I had?" she asked nastily.

This time he did not miss the sarcasm. He drew himself up to his full height. "This is serious business, Frances," he told her earnestly, "and you don't have any idea what you're doing. You'd never forgive yourself if you were to become involved with such forces of anti-Christ as the Communist Party and their ilk."

"Oh, hang up your dishtowel," she said wearily, "and go preach to the family. I didn't even answer the letter."

"Hah, hah!" he exclaimed, his breath spouting geyserlike out of his mouth. "You were only teasing me all the time."

"Hah to you," she said distinctly, splashing the dirty water down the sink and wringing the dishcloth hard between her hands. I was teasing like hell, she wanted to say, started to say, but didn't. After all, what difference did it make? She gave the cloth another wring, as though it were a neck, and then draped it carefully across the sink before she followed his fine shoulders into the library.

thirteen

The coming of Hugh Andrews to the First Presbyterian Church revived the good matrons of Kingston like a frosty mint julep on a sweltering summer afternoon—had they allowed themselves such wicked indulgence. Rocking on their porches behind the vines, they drank in the details of his past with little sucking noises; they savored the large and noble-looking picture of him which the *Daily Bugle* printed twice; they sent all their unmarried daughters up to Washington to buy a new dress ("Something simple, Mary, but expensive-looking"); they almost forgot to discuss the impending primary elections at which, solemnly they quoted their husbands, Judge Braxton was sure to be defeated.

From the Judge's faint frown and Dr. Mac's preoccupied expression, Frances concluded that not even they were too certain of the election. Into the church office came a steady stream of visitors to talk politics; out of the office went wires, phone calls, and letters in which Congress was discussed more than the church and the will of the people was pondered more carefully than the will of God. Once Frances mentioned this, tentatively, to Dr. Mac. "I feel like I'm working for a campaign office rather than a church," she said, laughing a little so that he wouldn't think she meant to be critical. "This doesn't seem like a religious organization at all."

Gravely he came to her desk and stood looking down at her, so seriously that she was startled and wished she hadn't made the impulsive remark. "A real church, Franny," he told her quietly, "is not something which meets on Sunday to sing a little and pray a little and talk about another world. A real church is alive and kicking in *this* world seven days in the week. It jumps feet first wherever there is life, wherever there are people. Wherever there are people, there is choice between good and not-so-good, or in this case, between good and real evil. Political relations, labor relations, race relations, that's all human relations, isn't it? And that's God's business. So it ought to be the church's business too."

As gravely as he: "Isn't there something more I can do?" she asked, wanting to tell him that suddenly Judge Braxton symbolized all her beliefs and secret desires, that the election next Tuesday had become the most important thing in her life, that somehow it was all tied up with her love for Paul and so the Judge just had to win, and she would pass out pamphlets in the streets of Kingston if it would help . . . "I could even work afternoons."

"That's the only time you have to see Paul, isn't it?"

"Yes, but—"

"It's very important that you go on seeing Paul. You're helping us more than you know."

It was the kind of thing she longed to share with her family, the kind of thing once she would gladly have repeated to them, proud that a man like Dr. McDonough talked so richly and inspiringly to her. But now she lived in a house with two strangers, and all things deepest within her were alien to them. From the excitement and high purpose of the church office, from the rich warmth of her afternoons with Paul, she went into a house that was chilly on the hottest nights and silently withdrawn. They knew she saw Paul each afternoon, and they never questioned her, never asked her where the two of them had been or what they had done; in fact, they never mentioned Paul's name at all. They completely ignored his presence in her life. Do they think they can ignore him out of reality, she wondered bitterly, as one would ignore the hallucinations of an idiot? Or worse, the make-believe of a child who sees fairies?

Not since the night of the "incident" had they mentioned his name, not since that miserable night when her father, with a calm and a self-discipline she'd not considered him capable of, foretold the misery ahead for her if she chose Paul's life for her own. She had looked at her father, there on the side of her bed, looked at his familiar face and his sagging heavy body, felt his caress on her hand as he held it between his own, and she did not know him. She heard his words, answered "Yes" and "No" in the right places, but his words meant nothing to her. She heard them without anger and without pain. Carefully he wrote them upon the blackboard of her mind; dispassionately she came behind him and erased them.

The blackboard had been there ever since, slate-hard and cold and impenetrable. Never since had they tried to reach through it to her, behind. Upon it they were content to write meaningless phrases about the weather and business and the shortage of meat, phrases she could read or not as she wished. They were equally content to leave her strictly alone.

Odd, the way she'd started lumping them together as "they," no longer two individuals, but only the separate halves of one enemy. No longer was she free to climb into bed with her mother and giggle funny stories in her ear; to sing at her father's knee while he fumbled for throaty chords on the guitar. Their unity was inviolable. Their eyes sought each other's, not hers. They drew strength from each other and turned it on her. As the three of them had once faced the world, the two now faced her as one, and she was alone.

Did Paul know of the wordless struggle behind the shuttered windows of the Acheson house? she wondered. He'd never even hinted so. There had been no good reason to invite him home in the two or three weeks since the "incident" had occurred; there had been no occasion to tell him the whole long wretched story. No, that wasn't true: any number of times their conversations opened a door onto a full confession, yet she would sit silent, arms wrapped around her knees, watching the cloud shadows spread across the valley, testing and discarding words and phrases in her mind, making up new ones.

"Darling," she rehearsed the thought, "you know what I'm thinking before I begin to think it. You must have realized that I have a terrible problem on my mind—" Or, "Paul, honey, there's something you and I have got to discuss—" Or—but these were all evasions; even in her thoughts she could not bear to smear their love with the festering sore of her parents' prejudice. There's no reason to burden Paul with my problem, she excused herself; nothing must spoil our beautiful afternoons together. So, softly, she would close the door again, and the thought, rehearsed, remained unspoken in her mind, a little puddle of words so near the surface she consciously had to skirt them. But Paul never commented on her abrupt pauses or her odd silences or the long sighs she forgot to swallow.

It hurt her to admit to herself that her own father and mother had become strange to her; even to Paul she could not expose them. After all, she owed them loyalty, whether they deserved it or not.

"And how about the loyalty you owe to yourself?" asked that little voice in her head that kept her awake nights, the same little voice that said, "Aren't you being stupid! You'll get your eyes all red and swollen," whenever she was well started on a tear jag. "If you love Paul as you say you do, are you being fair to shut him out of the most serious situation in your life?"

"But it's not Paul's problem. It's mine and my family's. There's no reason to distress him with it."

"What you really mean is, you don't want him to know how selfish and cruel and unloving your family can be. Isn't that it?"

"Yes. No. I don't know. Oh, shut up."

It always ended this way. The voice got the last word and left her confused and upset and arguing with air. Sometimes she even argued out loud.

"Whom are you talking to, Frances?" asked her mother one night, stopping by the half-opened door of her bedroom. Frances, grimacing in the mirror, caught her arm awkwardly in an outflung gesture and turned to her mother. "Nobody," she said sheepishly. "Myself, I mean."

Mrs. Acheson looked at her for a moment, curiously, before going to the staircase.

"Well, I have to talk to *somebody*," Frances hurled after her. There was no pause in Mrs. Acheson's footsteps as she kept on going downstairs.

Evenings Frances dreaded. Now that Hugh Andrews, in the two short weeks of his pastorate in Kingston, had acquired the habit of just dropping in of an evening to talk to Mrs. Acheson about the great and good activities of the Women's Auxiliary, and to Mr. Acheson about problems of church administration, Frances could no longer go to her bedroom and read until she was weary enough to fall into fitful sleep. As a matter of fact, the first night he "just dropped in," Frances had excused herself within ten minutes, over Hugh's earnest protestations, to go off into her own little sanctuary and read herself to sleep. But the maneuver was outflanked.

Without haste, Mrs. Acheson followed her and closed the door behind them. Attentively, Frances arranged two large pillows against the headboard of the bed, adjusted the reading lamp on the table, settled her shoulders, and ostentatiously found her place in the book. Her mother stood leaning against the chest of drawers, watching her.

Frances did not have the courage to read in her mother's face. "What's the matter?" she said defensively. "Did I do something?"

"I don't think you realize how rude you were to Mr. Andrews, dear. After all, he came to see you, not your father."

"Oh Mother, he did not. Anyway, I don't want to see him."

"Why do you feel that way, Fran? He's a charming young man and quite easy to talk with."

"Oh sure, if you talk his language."

"What language are *you* speaking these days, if I may ask?"

A large bug, drawn to the light, was banging himself desperately against the screen in the window, his wings thudding dully in the thick air. Mrs. Acheson walked over, flicked the screen, and the bug fell away into the night.

"Do you remember something?" Frances inquired unpleasantly. "The year I was a senior in high school and didn't have a date for the Senior Prom. You called up Mrs. Cary and got her to ask Bruce to take me. *That* didn't work out either."

Without hesitation, Mrs. Acheson said, "I don't see any connection whatever." Frances knew her mother too well to believe *that*. "All I'm asking you is, try to be more polite to guests in this house, regardless of whether you like them or not. And if you happen to be downstairs when Mr. Andrews comes again, the least you can do is stay and talk to him."

Wearily Frances asked, "Do you want me to go back now?"

"No, that won't be necessary tonight. I told him you were very tired. I'm talking about in the future. Will you do that for me?"

How different she was from Daddy! He would have taken her in his arms and told her he loved her and asked her how she felt and what was the matter; there stood mother, composed and remote, too proud to show the littlest crack. Yet neither approach had any effect on her at all. She wanted only to be left alone.

Mrs. Acheson walked to the door. "What are you reading?" she inquired in passing, as though she were really interested.

Frances held the book up. "*A Treasury of Russian Love Poetry*." So she had the last word after all.

Within the week, however, Hugh had dropped his pretense of calling at the Acheson house on business. He was jovial, as always, with Frances' parents, but only out of courtesy he demurred when they excused themselves from the living room around nine-thirty. Within two weeks he was calling Mr. Acheson "James" and Mrs. Acheson "Evelyn," something of a feat in itself. "I don't see how you insinuated yourself into mother's good graces so fast," Frances told him in grudging admiration. "I fully expect even her grandchildren to call her 'Mrs. Acheson.' "

He was genuinely surprised and showed it. "Why, my dear," he said in that open and guileless way of his, "your mother is one of the most friendly and hospitable women I've ever had the pleasure to know."

That shows how little you know her, Frances thought, and changed the subject.

By the week of the August primary, Hugh was bringing candy and flowers and holding her hand. She ate the candy and arranged the flowers and removed her hand politely, and all the while she thought of Paul and cherished him in secret.

The night before the Tuesday election she was restless. Disconsolately she wandered about the house, looking blankly at book titles, none of which interested her, fingering phonograph records which she didn't really want to hear, walking to the front door and looking out at the night, close and hot.

"For God's sake, Frances," her father said, rustling his paper with impatience, "can't you find something to do besides moseying all over the house? I've read this damn column three times."

"Are you waiting for Hugh, dear?" asked Mrs. Acheson. "It's rather late."

"No, not tonight. Somebody's sick and he phoned and said he wouldn't be able to make it." She almost wished he had come: at least she'd have someone to talk to.

Two things were on her mind: Judge Braxton's chances in the primary tomorrow, which she couldn't discuss with her family because they were going to vote against him anyway; and her trip to Washington, a subject she had to introduce into the room sooner or later, and it might as well be now.

"Daddy?"

"Hmmm?"

"May I please borrow the car all day tomorrow?"

Suspiciously he peered at her over the edge of the newspaper. "All day? Where do you think you're going?"

"Washington."

"What for?"

She took a deep breath. "Paul's uncle is on his way to Florida. Paul wanted—we wanted to drive up and meet him for lunch."

"In my car! Is there any good reason he can't go on the bus?"

"I told you. I'm going with him, and it would be more convenient for both of us if we could drive."

"Who said you could go to Washington with him?"

"James." Mrs. Acheson's soft word was not quite sufficient warning.

"Oh, goddam it to hell! A man can't get any peace in

1 5 9

his own house any more! Take the car!" Furiously he pitched the newspaper on the floor and stood up. "Go to Washington! Go to New York! Go anywhere you please with that kike, see if I care. It's your life you're smashing!" He stormed to the door. Frances watched him as though she were at a bad movie; he had no power to touch her.

Placidly Mrs. Acheson returned to her knitting. Frances laid her cheek against the cool windowpane and listened to her father's heavy footsteps go up the stairs. Halfway up they stopped, turned, and came back down. I might have known, she sighed, audibly.

He stood in the doorway, making an obvious effort to control his voice. "Is he a good driver, Fran?"

As she looked at him, her heart softened at the concern in his eyes. "Yes, Daddy, he's a very good driver."

Without answering, he turned and slowly went to the stairs again, shuffling a little like an old man.

"Honey," said Mrs. Acheson after a pause, "why don't you ever see your old friends any more? Emily Sydnor and Mary Cary and that other child who taught with you, what's her name . . . ?"

"Millicent?" Frances walked to the couch and threw herself full-length, her arms under her head. "I don't know, Mother. I'm awfully busy, what with church and the election and all—" If her mother wanted to comment on either of these points, there was an opening. But Mrs. Acheson was silent. "—and of course, my afternoons are taken up—" Another pause. Would you like to make something of that? "—and it seems like Hugh's here every single evening. Honestly, I haven't had the time."

Mrs. Acheson managed to make her silence somehow expectant.

"As a matter of fact, I did see Emily Sydnor down-town a couple of days ago while I was waiting for Paul. That was the day, I think, he and I went horseback riding at the Hunt Club." It was so good to say his name aloud. "Paul's a wonderful rider."

"What did Emily have to say?"

"Hmmm? Oh, nothing much, as usual. She can talk more and say less than anybody I know. One thing—remember Roberta Lee who went to Columbia to get her M.A.? I told you she got married to a man from Kansas."

"I think you mentioned it."

"Well, they'll be home about the end of the month, and Emily's having a party for them so that we can all see what she married."

"Does Emily want you to bring a date?"

"She did say something to that effect."

"Hugh would make a very nice escort."

"Well, Paul will be working that night, most likely, so I'll probably have to take Hugh whether I want to or not."

No longer was her mind on the conversation with her mother; she was grateful for the silence between them so that she could recall again, for the dozenth time, the conversation with Emily in the back booth of Sadwell's Drugstore over a tuna-fish sandwich and a chocolate malted milk shake with two scoops of ice cream. It *was* true that Emily could talk more and say less than anyone of Frances' acquaintance, but from the babble there had fallen, from time to time, a word or two, a phrase, the lift of an eyebrow, which deserved collecting and examining at leisure.

"Honestly, Fran, I don't see how you can drink milk shakes and stay so thin." Emily made a face at her own sour limeade. She had been on a reducing diet since high school, without any visible change in her heavy body or full face. "You aren't really fat, Em," people often said to her. "You've just got big bones." This had been known to make her cry.

"But you know, Fran," Emily went on, "I think you *have* gained a little weight, haven't you? At least around—" Her hands made curving motions over her own pendulous breasts.

Well-kissed! The two words flashed like an electric sign in Frances' mind, and she laughed aloud at the idea of saying them to Emily, just to watch her mouth drop. What was that thing Paul kept saying, laughing and cocking his head sideways at her, something about darkness at noon and champagne glasses? And every time she'd draw him to her and kiss him and beg to know what he was talking about, he'd pull his brows down over his black eyes and say, "Haven't you read *any* good books lately?"

"What are you laughing at?" Emily wanted to know.

"Never mind. It's nothing." Frances took Emily's hand. "My! I'm glad I happened to see you. I haven't seen anybody since the day school closed."

"I know. Nobody's seen you either. What in the world do you do with yourself all day?" Emily sighed. "Nothing ever happens in this town. I'll be glad when school opens again. I get so bored just sitting around the house."

"Well, my Lord!" Frances looked at her. The blankness of Emily's life was mirrored in Emily's face. With sudden intensity the awareness of her own full life tingled through her, and she wanted to jump up and stretch tall and feel the health in her body and run out of this dark drugstore into the sunlight, stand on the street corner and shout and conduct a meeting, clutch people by their buttonholes and tell them to wake up, look around, stand on tiptoe, fall in love, cry, get on a train and go somewhere. She longed to take Emily by her plump shoulders and shake her and shake her until her flat blue eyes bugged out. Her palms itched and she pressed her finger tips against the table top until the nails were bloodless-white. Don't you know? in her mind she threw the words at Emily's round face, don't you know that there's a terrific adventure right here in this town, on every street, in every house, if you'll open only one eye halfway. "Bored to death" is the truth! They might as well come and bury you right now. You're just using up air that other people enjoy breathing. Churches break up. New ones catch fire and burn out of the rot of the old. The school system cracks right down the middle out of the sheer weight of age. The most important election since the Revolutionary War comes off here next week. And you say nothing ever happens in this town. Oh, Emily, Emily, there you sit on your fat fanny eying my chocolate milk shake with two scoops of ice cream and wishing you dared order one. Is that all you'll ever think of?

And the big difference between Paul and herself, she knew, was that Paul could have—would have said it all out loud.

"What do I do all day?" she answered at last. "I work at the church office all morning, and that keeps me pretty busy—"

"Oh, you have that wonderful new preacher, Mr. Andrews!" Emily sighed explosively. "When he came along, I almost decided to become a Presbyterian myself."

"I don't go to Mr. Andrews' church."

"You don't? But I thought—" Light dawned. "Oh, now I remember! You go to that new church down in the moving-picture theater. Dr. McDonough's. That's the church father said—"

Suddenly Emily decided not to finish the sentence. She buried her nose in the sour limeade.

"What did your father say about us, Em?" Frances asked gently.

"Nothing much, honey. I mean, it wasn't important. Anyway, if he'd known the Achesons were down there, he wouldn't have said it."

The girl was miserable, and picked at the cuticles of her blunt fingernails. Frances prodded her implacably. What Emily's father had said assumed tremendous significance. For the first time in two months, Frances was in touch with the world beyond her own cocoon of church-Paul-and-family. Only now was she realizing how isolated she had become.

"The Achesons aren't down there. Just me. My family stayed at the old church, so what your father said couldn't hurt them. What did he say, Emily?"

"Well, all right," in a great rush, "he said the church was the greatest travesty on Christianity he'd ever heard of, and all the people were riff-raff and Communists and nigger-lovers, and it was a shame that a fine man like Judge Braxton had got all tangled up down there because it just meant that he was going to lose the election. But honestly, Frances, father was mad. He didn't mean it."

"What brought all this on? What did we ever do to your father?"

"Lord, I don't know. I wish I hadn't mentioned it. It

was something to do with one of the men who work in father's office."

"Do you remember his name?"

"Darcy, Darby, something like that."

"Darrity? Was it Darrity?"

"Yes, that's the name. Do you know him?"

"I used to. He was very active in our new church until he withdrew his membership about three weeks ago."

The changes of expression across Emily's face were painful to watch: perplexity, gradual understanding, incredulity, and finally protective indignation. "You can't mean you think my father influenced—"

Coldly Frances said, "Your father runs an insurance office. Mr. Darrity sold insurance for him. Obviously your father didn't want riff-raff in his office, and a Communist and nigger-lover to boot. So he told Mr. Darrity to stop being riff-raff or get out of his office. Mr. Darrity stopped being riff-raff. It's simple." Her voice was as tight as the knot in her stomach.

"Now look, Frances." Emily's pout was not attractive on her round face. "My father believes in freedom of religion as much as yours does." She did not pause at the ironic lift of Frances' eyebrows. "He wouldn't stoop to such a trick, and I don't think you ought to make such insinuations!"

"I'm sorry, Emily. Let's not talk about it any more." Frances was not sorry, she was merely limp. She was weary of fighting, constantly, wherever she went, whomever she talked with. What had happened to the serenity and bliss of last year and the year before that, the easy love at home, the placid relationships outside, the pleasant flow of days around school and church and friends and family? Now, like a river at flood tide, the days came roaring upon her and she stood teetering on a slippery rock in the middle of them, the way back as dangerous as the way forward. Something Paul had said to her, their first evening together, crashed into her mind. "You have your church, your friends, your name, your background, your respectability. What else do you want? What else do you need? Aren't you satisfied?" He had known she wasn't satisfied. With that incisive perception of his which X-rayed to the bone, even then he had known what she needed: awareness. He had known the price, in peace of living and ease of mind, which she would pay.

Was it worth it?

Indignantly she answered herself "Yes!" and saw from Emily's astonished face that again she'd been talking to herself aloud. "Don't mind me," she laughed a little. "I was thinking about something else. Go on. You were saying you're having a party for Bobby Lee and her new husband?"

Emily's heart held no rancor; forgotten were the ugly remarks about her father. "It's going to be a small buffet supper," she said cheerfully, with the anticipation of someone whose chief pleasure in life is eating. "Our crowd, you know. The only thing that bothers me is, there won't be anywhere near enough men."

"That certainly sounds familiar. Who's coming?"

"Well, Mary Cary said she guessed she could get her brother to come, and Millie has had about two dates with a man from Winchester, so if he asks her again between now and the night of my party, she won't mind inviting him. That makes four and Bobby and her husband make six . . ." Her voice trailed off wistfully; she looked at Frances. "That leaves you and me."

"How's *your* love life?" Frances turned Emily's unspoken question with a straight face.

"Oh, stop it. Listen. I haven't had a date since I took my second cousin to the Senior Prom at college. Maybe something will turn up between now and the end of the month."

"You can't pick daisies in a cement sidewalk," Frances observed cheerfully, but for some odd reason, she had a funny feeling about what was coming next, and she was not so cheerful as she pretended.

Her premonition was well founded. "I heard," Emily began in a I-really-don't-believe-this voice, "that you were dating some musician out at Lake Luray Hotel. A friend of mother's saw you riding at the Hunt Club the other day, and she said he looked like a foreigner." She waited.

"Oh, Paul!" Frances exclaimed, as though the name had just occurred to her. "I *have* been seeing him quite often."

"Paul who?"

"Paul Revkin."

"Revkin?"

"He's Russian," said Frances firmly.

"How fascinating. Why don't you bring him?"

"Well, he works nights." The words were carefully spaced. You wouldn't appreciate him anyway, she thought deliberately. You have to be very special to appreciate Paul.

"Oh dear. We need another man so badly. Couldn't he come after work?"

"How would you like me bring Hugh Andrews?" Frances refused to think through the words themselves to the motive beyond.

Instantly distracted, Emily cried joyfully, "Hugh Andrews! I thought you said you didn't know him."

"Oh, I've had about ten dates with him, I suppose," Frances said as casually as she could. The awe on Emily's face was intoxicating.

"Frances Acheson! You stinker! And we've all been simply dying to meet him. Wait 'til I tell everybody. Honestly! Ten dates in two weeks. He must be serious."

"Oh, I don't know," said Frances, despising herself. Like an avalanche, the conversation gained momentum, and she could no longer stop it. "I don't reckon he brings flowers and candy to my mother."

If the angel Gabriel had appeared to reveal the wonders of Paradise, Emily could not have been more reverent. She sank her chin in her cupped palms and heaved a sigh. "Some people have all the luck! Well, I'm glad it's you and not that Agnes Hitchens. She took two Sundays off from our church and went over to First Presbyterian just to meet him. But she didn't. Her mother told my mother she'd bought a new dress and everything."

Frances made interlocking rings on the table top with the bottom of her wet glass.

"What's he like, Fran? He must be a wonderful preacher to have such a big church so young. But I mean personally. Is he as good-looking as his picture? Everybody says so."

"Better."

"What do you all talk about?"

"Him."

"What about him?"

"What he's going to do and how he's going to do it and what he thinks about."

"What does he think about?"

"Nothing."

That stopped her, but only for a moment. "Franny, does he—has he kissed you?"

Poor Emily. Greedily she drank of other people's lives and vicarious kisses would have to satisfy her always. "Yes, Emily," Frances lied, "he's kissed me lots of times."

Now, sprawled on the couch idly watching her mother's knitting needles flash in the light, Frances remembered again the jealousy on Emily's face and the envy in her voice. More bitterly, she remembered her own sordid aggravation of that envy and desire. To be admired was fine; but to be admired for the wrong reasons was worse than nothing.

f o u r t e e n

It was ten-thirty when Frances swerved the car around the corner of Main Street and plunged to a stop behind the bus station. Paul was not on the loading platform; he must be inside. In her haste, she almost rushed into the "Colored Waiting Room," to the amusement of two men in shirt sleeves lounging on a bench beside the swinging screen door, trying to outdistance each other in spitting tobacco.

After the glare of the sun on the streets, the room inside was cool and dim. When she saw Paul, standing in the corner examining a map of Virginia taped to the wall, she went to him softly and slid her hands around his neck from behind, feeling the pulse in his throat beat against her palms. Without turning he took both her hands in his own and kissed them. For a moment she closed her eyes tight and let herself sway against him before she pulled away.

He wheeled and grinned at her. "A diller, a dollar, a ten o'clock scholar . . . My God, a hat! And shoes with high heels! I didn't think you had any. Why didn't you tell me you had pretty ankles?"

"Paul, behave. Stop looking me over like that! People are watching you. Anyway, we'd better hurry. I'm sorry I'm so late. Have you been waiting long?"

"It doesn't matter, darling. Where'd you leave the car?"

"Out this way. Do you want me to drive?"

With exaggerated courtesy he opened the righthand door of the automobile and helped her in. "Thank you ma'am, no. I want to get there. I drove with you once, remember? And once was enough." He shut the door after her and leaned in the window.

"Well, I must say," she reminded him firmly, "pedestrians in this town are a lot more agile since I started to drive."

He kissed her. "And a lot nearer their Maker, too, my love." He kissed her again, gently this time. "Okay, let's go. I could be doing that all day. I think I found a shortcut on that map which will get us to Washington by noon."

"Believe me, Paul, I left home in plenty of time to get to the bus station by nine-thirty like I promised," she assured him. "But I had to go vote first, naturally, and I nearly had a big fight with the man at the polls."

"What kind of a fight?"

"Well, maybe not a *fight,* actually. What happened was, there was this man behind me in line, I forget his name right now, and I was talking to him about Judge Braxton and what a fine man he was, and how we ought to send him back to Congress for a third term—"

"And he thought the Judge was a louse and a stinker?"

"No, no. Let me finish. He didn't say what he thought. He just let me talk. It was the man at the polls that started it, the registrar I guess you'd call him. The one who looks you up in the books to see if you've paid your poll tax. He hollers at me and says I'm electioneering at a voting booth, and if I don't stop, he'll throw me out."

Paul threw back his head and roared.

"Oh, stop laughing!" Frances demanded indignantly. "It wasn't funny. It was kind of embarrassing. There were about ten people standing around and they were laughing at me too."

"Dearest, I wasn't laughing at you," Paul said when he could find a breath. "Did they search you for a bomb? Or subversive literature like the New Testament?"

Exasperated, she cried, "Be serious. I just informed the registrar very quietly that I was expressing a private opinion, and that I guessed I had a right to say what I thought to an old friend."

" 'Old friend?' That's wonderful. You said you didn't even know the man you were talking to."

"I've seen him around town somewhere. Anyway, the registrar decided I could have my own opinion provided I didn't express it so noisily."

"And he let you vote?"

1 7 1

"Surely. He couldn't stop me. I had my poll-tax receipts for the past three years."

"What does Dr. Mac think of the Judge's chances?" Paul asked soberly.

"Lord, I don't know. Neither of them would say one way or the other. But they never let themselves show the least little bit of uneasiness. Except sometimes last week, I thought they looked awfully worried."

"But," Paul offered hopefully, "there's more to this district than Kingston."

"I know, but the people in the country are even worse than the people in the towns. And you should hear some of the things the other candidate has been saying about Judge Braxton and Dr. Mac and our church. It's sickening. You'd think we had a platform of anarchy, atheism, and mixed marriage."

"Do you mind one-arm drivers?" Paul pulled her to him and held her. "Don't get so excited, Frances. You did everything you could. Now relax and stop worrying."

"You don't seem to realize how much this means to me!" she cried to him fiercely. "The Judge is just one man fighting a whole vicious system. He's a symbol or something. If he can win—if he can win— Don't you see? He's just got to win!" Under his arm she felt herself trembling with the intensity of her desire to be understood. Didn't he realize how important the Judge's triumph would be to— *their* love?

"God, it must be wonderful to reduce abstractions to a simple black or white the way you do," Paul said with a funny shrug. "Listen, Frances lieble, I want the election to go our way as much as you do. Believe me, it means something to me in a sense you'll never be able to comprehend.

But if Judge Braxton should lose, it's not the end of everything. There'll only be the fight to get back what's been lost, and found, and lost over and over again. And if he wins, the fight's just well begun. Either way, there's never any stop to the fighting. And the rest is not our business."

Paul had arranged to meet his uncle Sol for lunch at the Willard Hotel at twelve-thirty; as they neared Washington, he was amused at his own eager impatience to arrive. He felt he'd been far away in a strange country, speaking another language, and for a week he'd looked forward with real excitement to this little link with home.

He was happy that Frances had come with him; not only could she meet one of his family, but Uncle Sol could see for himself that all Paul's glowing accounts of her were true. Better yet, Sol could report to his parents and to Becky that he was not in love foolishly. Chuckling to himself, he remembered passages from his father's letters, full of love, concern, advice and bad spelling. Did this girl understand him? Did she understand what his music meant to him? Had she realized that she must accept his poverty, his moods, and his singleness of purpose along with his love? When his family heard the good things about Frances Uncle Sol would have to say, they'd find the reassurance they craved. Tenderly he looked down upon her, curled in the crook of his arm, her head resting on his shoulder, her eyes contentedly shut, and he warmed to her nearness until he could barely resist stopping the car and kissing her passionate sweet mouth.

Oddly, he was delighted that she had dressed up for the occasion. She was wearing a new dress—or at least, one he'd never seen before, white and plain, of a silky flowing material that molded her high pear-shaped breasts and caressed the lean clean lines of her body as she sat or walked. He couldn't recall having seen her wear a hat before, and it was a concession that he appreciated. "I can't stand anything that holds my hair down!" she had exclaimed, tossing it with an impatient gesture on the back seat of the car as soon as she sat down. In the afternoons on the grassy hillside, he loved to watch her stretch out on her back and in a lovely liquid movement, like Hannah arching her back after sleep, with both hands lift her mass of heavy hair from under her head and spill it on the ground in the shining sunlight.

"The way you look at me, you make me feel so beautiful," she told him time and time again, eyes beseeching.

"You are beautiful, dearest. Why don't you believe me?"

"Ah, you're just prejudiced!" she would exclaim, and then at once, "Do you really, truly think so?"

By this time Paul knew that Frances had no idea how attractive she was, and with all his heart he hoped that she would never learn. Perhaps her most remarkable quality was her complete lack of duplicity or affectation, the level, candid gaze she turned upon the world, the straight line between emotion and reaction which her father labeled "impulsive." In her it was but one leap from feeling to action, a movement neither hampered nor encouraged by thought processes. He envied her freedom from the shackles of rationalization and mental distortion which so often went under the name of "mature judgment" and immobilized the judger. Here was no weighing of the consequences, no balancing of advantage and disadvantage. To feel was to act, and hotly she plunged from instinct into conflict without a thought for herself or the future. Thank God her instincts were sure! Gently he tightened his arm about her shoulders, remembering her break with the church, her tilt with the school superintendent, her impassioned avowal of Judge Braxton and his cause. But there lay a great danger.

Looking ahead no further than the conflicts into which she leaped so precipitously, she was unprepared for the consequences, either good or bad; and being good herself, it was not in her even to contemplate the bad, much less to conceive that the bad might win. In the case of the primary at the polls today, for instance, not once had she faced the fact that the Judge might easily—would probably —be defeated. She had allied herself with his beliefs and with his stand until it was a personal identification. The political defeat of Judge Braxton would be a slap in the face of Frances Acheson; unarmed, unprepared as she was, she would be grievously hurt.

As much as he desired Judge Braxton's triumph, not only for Frances and for Dr. Mac and the congregation of the New World Church, but for Kingston and Virginia and the South, Paul was anticipating his defeat. He had worried considerably over Frances' reaction. It was well, certainly, that she learn to reckon with disappointment, and in this case despair; yet he wondered. Had she had time to acquire the necessary strength to absorb despair? He doubted that ever in her life had she been denied anything she really wanted, except, perhaps, the right to her own opinion. She had not been nursed on disillusionment nor reared with an awareness of reality. Reality hovered over her now, with a beating of wings that filled the air.

Again he pressed her to him in the crook of his arm; if it had been within his power, he would have held her there, safe and sheltered, forever.

In Washington they left the car in a parking lot on Tenth Street and walked toward the Willard. "Are we on time?" Frances asked, poking at her hair under the wide-brimmed straw hat.

"Plenty of time, darling. It's barely twelve-thirty now."

"It didn't seem to me you were driving particularly fast."

"Well, no," he admitted, "compared to the way you drive, I confess I just creep along."

She smiled at him and tenderly laid her hand on his arm. "By the way, is this your father's brother, your mother's brother, or what?"

"I thought I told you—"

"Maybe you did, but I've been in a dream world so long I don't remember half what you say. Tell me again."

"Uncle Sol is my father's brother. His name is Revkin too."

"How remarkable!"

"I'll kiss you right here on the street if you don't behave."

"A threat or a promise? Oh Paul, don't! I'm sorry. I'll be good, honestly. Go on. His name is Revkin, just like yours."

"He married a very wealthy woman and practically doubled her money in real estate. Ruth—that's my aunt— is very sick, and has been for years. That's why he takes these trips alone."

"What a shame. What's the matter?"

"Tuberculosis. They've spent a fortune, but she neither dies nor gets well. Just lies in bed day after day."

"Oh, that must be awful on your uncle. Poor man!"

"The tragedy is that they've wanted children so badly. When Becky and I were growing up, we practically lived at Uncle Sol's house. I remember how big and dark and empty it seemed, and how quietly we had to play because Aunt Ruth was always sleeping."

They reached the hotel and went through the revolving doors into the lobby. It was crowded with people, and Paul asked Frances to wait while he took a quick glance around. After a moment he returned to her. "You're getting the double take from about half the men in here, darling. Shall I offer to go in the alley with that fat guy over there who can't take his eyes off your legs?"

"Don't be silly. He is the perfect traveling salesman type, isn't he?"

"I resist the obvious reply. I didn't see Sol."

"Oh?"

"Let's look in the dining room."

"Surely he would have waited for us? It's only twenty minutes to one now."

"He probably wanted to be sure of getting a seat."

The dining room was equally crowded and there were several groups of people clustered at the doorway waiting for tables. By pushing through, Paul managed to get a good view of the room.

"There he is, darling. Excuse me," he said to the headwaiter, as Frances, elbowing through the close-packed people, joined him.

"You'll have to wait your turn, sir," the headwaiter informed him stonily.

"No, that's all right. Someone is saving us a table. See, over there." Paul pointed toward his uncle, who was standing at his place, waving a napkin above his head.

Frances and the headwaiter looked across the room in the direction Paul was indicating. "Very well, sir." The headwaiter bowed frostily and moved back an inch to allow them to pass. Someone in the crowd said one word clearly, "Jews." Swiftly Paul looked at Frances to see if she'd heard, but her face gave no sign.

Bouncing a little in his eagerness, Uncle Sol came forward to meet Paul and Frances as they approached the table. "So, Paul!" he cried, taking Paul's hand in both his own. "Hello, hello!" He peered up at his nephew with affection, his eyes curiously distorted behind his thick glasses. "You're looking good, boy! Sunshine, huh? And love! Is this your young lady?"

He freed one hand and clasped Frances' outstretched one. "Yes, Sol, this is Frances you've heard so much about," Paul told him, watching his uncle's round face curl up in an even wider smile.

"How do you do, Mr. Revkin?" Frances said in a formal, polite voice.

Mr. Revkin examined her with an unabashed stare. "She's a pretty girl, Paul; you got yourself a pretty girl."

Paul noticed that they were blocking the passage and gathering in tip-tilted glances from the diners. Gently he pulled his hand out of his uncle's warm grasp. "Let's go sit down, Sol. People are waiting to get by." And to Frances, "Go ahead, dear." He stepped back to let her follow his uncle.

"Well, Paul, what gives? What gives?" Sol demanded as soon as they were seated. "How is the music?" Then, without waiting for an answer, he threw his palms out toward him and exclaimed to the world, "See how brown he is! It's good to see him looking so healthy." Immediately he spoke to Frances. "You must have been keeping him out in the sun. I'm telling you, I never seen him look so good."

"Yes, we've been out in the sun practically all summer," Frances began. Paul saw her eyes come to his, full of remembered pleasure.

Sol interrupted eagerly. "Swimming? Dancing? Horseback riding? Tell me everything this boy here has been doing. I want to know."

"Everything?" Paul said and laughed good naturedly. "You know, Frances," he added, turning to her, "you and I haven't danced together at all."

"And Paul is such a good dancer!" Sol exclaimed. "I ought to know. I paid for his dancing lessons since he was a little kid."

"Well, you see," Frances started again, "there aren't very many places in Kingston to dance—"

Again Sol broke in. "Why don't you bring her to New York, Paul?" He darted his eyes to Frances. "In New York you could dance every night at a different place and never get to them all. Why don't you bring her to New York, Paul? Ruth would love her."

"I intend to," Paul assured him and took Frances' hand.

"Well, what is everybody eating?" cried Sol as the waiter handed menus around. Frances leaned toward Paul and murmured that she wasn't terribly hungry. "Of course you're hungry, a big girl like you!" Sol informed her. "Come on now. Dinner's on me. You got to have the most expensive meal on the menu." He leaned across the table to Frances and waggled a finger in her face. "Nothing's too good for Paul's girl."

"What would you like, dearest?" Paul opened her menu and looked into it with her. "How about—"

"Bring us three steaks! Everybody loves steaks!" Sol ordered the waiter who was hovering near by. Paul was suddenly conscious of his uncle's loud voice. "The best in the house! And everything that goes with."

"I hear," Frances said very quietly, "that you're going to Miami for a while, Mr. Revkin."

"Not for pleasure this time," Sol answered, leaning across the table to her again. "This is a strictly business trip. I got a real hot deal over on the Beach," he confided to Paul. Back to Frances shot his eyes. "You ever been to Miami?"

"No, I haven't."

"That's the place all right. But you got to go in the wintertime. August is no time to go to Florida. But this is extra-special business."

"What's up, Sol?" asked Paul.

Sol rubbed his hands together and squeezed his cheeks into a smile until his eyes vanished and his face was a cat's face. "I know a guy who knows a guy who knows a good thing," he said. "Why else do you think I drive all the way down to Miami in this weather? We always go down January, February," he explained to Frances, "Ruth and me."

"How is Ruth?" Into Paul's mind came a picture of his aunt as he had last seen her, frail and listless, a slight ripple under her silk quilts, wanly smiling as she held out a hand to him, in her eyes all the sorrow of a childless woman who loves another's child. "How's she feeling?" he asked again.

The waiter brought the steaks and served them. Sol waited until he had gone. "Oh, Paul," he said, running his fingers up under his glasses and pressing the bridge of his nose with a weary sigh. "No better, no worse. She just lies there, day after day, without a change, never complaining, never complaining. I don't know." He brightened a little. "She sent you her best love, and thanks again for the flowers."

"God, don't mention it," Paul muttered, cutting his steak. "I'm glad she liked them."

"You don't know what those kind of things mean to Ruth, Paul," Sol persisted, laying his hand on Paul's arm and leaning into his face with great concentration. Behind his glasses his little eyes misted, and he blinked rapidly several times.

"Sure, Sol, sure," Paul said tenderly, covering his uncle's hand with his own. "Eat your dinner. Your steak's getting cold."

"No, Paul, I want to tell you. That's all Ruth's got in the world, Paul. Sure, she's got everything money can buy, you know that. But a little bunch of flowers, Paul . . . just a little bunch of flowers from you. Do you think I could buy that for her?" He reached up and took off his glasses with a slow, hesitating movement. Paul noticed with concern the sagging lines of his uncle's face and the droop to his mouth; without his glasses he had a naked, vulnerable expression. Gone, suddenly, was the sharp, aggressive contour. Sol was an old, weary, helpless man whose money could not buy him the one thing he wanted.

"How's Becky?" Paul asked, and was pleased to see his uncle's face grow firm and warm again.

"That girl!" Sol put his glasses back on his nose. "How she does what she does! Runs here, runs there, keeps a house, keeps a baby, keeps a husband, all with one hand tied behind her back. And she's on this committee and that committee, Rent Controls and P.A.C. and concerts and I don't know what all. Tires me out to talk to her."

Paul laughed. "Becky thrives on it. How's the baby?"

"Becky said to tell you he's cutting his first tooth."

"So soon?"

"So soon? He's nearly seven months old, for Chrissakes," Sol spluttered, his mouth full of steak. "He's—he's —" he waved his fork wildly in the air, at a loss for words. "He's the most wonderful baby I ever saw. He knows me! Sits up when I come over to his crib—"

"Could I please have the salt if you're through with it?" Frances requested in a faint, polite voice.

Paul whirled to her. "Darling, I'm so sorry! We didn't mean to shut you out. What did you want, the salt?"

Smiling apologetically, Sol handed it across the table to her. "Paul and I, we could talk like that all night. He's like my own son to me, this boy."

"That's quite all right," Frances murmured. Paul saw that she had barely tasted her lunch.

"Aren't you hungry, dear? You're not eating."

"What's wrong with the food?" Sol asked anxiously. "We'll send it back and get something you want—"

"Oh, no, really," Frances pleaded. "There's nothing wrong with the food. Honestly, I'm not hungry."

Paul looked at her for a long moment, and she looked away.

Sol gave her his undivided attention. "I haven't had a chance to talk to *you* yet," he informed her, lighting a fat cigar and sucking at his hot coffee with noises of pleasure. "Have you lived in Virginia all your life?"

"Yes, I have."

"Go to school there, too?"

"Yes."

"What's your father do?"

"He's with a bank."

Paul laughed and touched his uncle's arm. "Hey, don't you think this quiz program has gone on long enough? She's not on trial, you know."

"But, Paul," Sol said, shrugging his shoulders, "I have to know all about this young lady. How can I tell your Mama and Papa what they want to know, like I promised?"

Paul glanced at Frances, who was examining the tips of her fingernails with absorption. "She's not so easy to know," he said gravely to his uncle, and shook his head warningly.

"Okay, okay," Sol said, waving the subject aside with a gesture. "Let's get out of here. It's hot." He called for the check, recalculated it carefully, paid the waiter and tossed a dollar bill on the table. Paul handed Frances her gloves, which she had dropped on the floor. His hand brushed hers, and she withdrew from his touch.

"What shall we do this afternoon? You don't have to go back yet, do you, Paul?" Sol asked as they threaded their way through the half-deserted dining room.

"No, I needn't be back today," Paul said. "I have the evening off. And Frances has nothing to do."

"I tell you," Frances said brightly and suddenly to

Paul, "I ought to do some shopping, and you two want to be alone to talk. Why don't I come back here and meet you about five-thirty or so?"

"But then I won't see you again," Sol answered. "I'm leaving about five myself. I like to drive at night. I can go much faster."

Paul said nothing.

"Well, then, thank you so much for the delicious dinner, Mr. Revkin," Frances said, shaking hands. "I hope to see you again very soon."

"Maybe I will come and visit you when I'm on my way back from Florida, if Paul's still there."

"Oh, that would be nice," Frances said. "Paul, I'll meet you here at five-thirty."

"All right," he said at last, and watched her as she walked hurriedly down the passageway and out through the lobby into the street. He glanced down at his uncle's hand on his arm.

"She's a nice girl, Paul," his uncle said gently. "A nice quiet girl."

"She's not usually so quiet," Paul told his uncle thoughtfully, still watching the revolving doors through which Frances had gone into the street. Then, impatiently, like a man who throws a blanket off on a hot night, he took a deep breath and threw his arm around his uncle's shoulders. Together they walked down the long passageway of the hotel.

Ahead of them the road home wound up and down over the hills and through the little towns that nodded in the wash of tawny sunset. As far as Frances could see, the valleys rolled up into the hills and the blue hills piled upon each other to the sky. When all the world is lovely and at peace, she thought, why can't we go on and on and on riding this way, he and I, the two of us, and never anybody else, never getting anywhere and never looking back, a little bit of road through a peaceful valley without Washington on the one end and Kingston on the other? But even while she tried to fix her attention on the arch of trees above the road, the curve of a flight of birds swooping across the land, the zigzag pattern of wormwood fences around green fields, her memory wrenched out of hand and raced backward to Washington. —And again she sat across a table from Mr. Revkin with his loud insistent bark and his coarse swarthy face, his grossness, his vulgarity, and worst of all, those cunning little eyes behind his glasses which seemed always to be sneering at her. All at the same time her memory raced forward to Kingston and her father in the dimness of her bedroom, leaning to her kindly. Suddenly she could feel his warm hands over her own and hear his gentle voice in the half-light: "Remember, honey, when you pick your children's father, you pick their grandfather too."

The two memories merged and overlapped until she could hardly tell which had happened first or when or why or what it was all about. Trembling and weary, desperate for reassurance, she turned to Paul and saw him, too, as though he were a stranger, saw him for the first time—his hands on the wheel brown and strong, with the black hairs growing at the wrists, his proud head sharp against the flushed sunset light. "I love you so much I've stopped remembering what you look like," she had said to him a long, long time ago. Now she looked at him again, and not with her heart, saw the high, beaked nose and the firm set of his mouth and the flare of his eyebrow charcoaled against the skin. She hardly recognized him. Paul, she said in her mind to him, hearing the name as if it had been spoken aloud. Paul.

"Paul." Had she said it aloud?

"Yes, dearest?"

She snatched at the uppermost thought in her mind. "Are your father and your uncle much alike?"

Did he think that was a curious question? He didn't answer for a moment, and then, "My uncle is very dear to me," he said. "For three years he financed my music studies in Paris and Vienna. My own father couldn't. He was too poor. That's only one thing Sol's done for me—for all of us. He's as dear to me as my father."

She recognized it as an answer, oblique though it was, and more than an answer: a challenge and a warning. She turned her head away and withdrew her half-lifted hand; then she began to cry. It had to come out somehow, the trembling in her body and the fighting and the strain of the past few weeks. No matter how hard she squeezed her eyes together, the little trickle of tears wouldn't stay behind her tight-pressed eyelids. She hoped Paul wouldn't see them and she turned her head even farther away and clenched her hands and her teeth and her stomach muscles. But the trickle swelled to a little stream that slid out under her lashes and down her cheeks and saltily into her mouth until she could stand it no longer and drew a long, shuddering breath that was nothing less than a sob.

"Dearest, you're crying." Swiftly he pulled the car to the side of the road and turned and took her in his arms, holding her wet face against his own and brushing the hair back from her cheeks, kissing her ears and throat and the salty hollows of her eyes. Over and over he murmured her name and called her lieble and dearest. He held her face in his two strong hands, looked deep into her eyes, his voice crooning meaningless words of love.

But he did not ask her why she was crying. Some small part of her consciousness noted this with pain: that he should know her better than she knew herself, that he should have no need to ask her why she was crying. In the grip of his hands she could move her head only slightly, swallowing hard over the knot in her throat, digging her fingernails into his shoulders. How could *he* know what she was crying for? She didn't know herself, unless it was for her whole world and the people in it, the people trapped on both ends of this little lovely road between Washington and Kingston, the little road that should go on and on between nowhere and nowhere, but couldn't, and had to end somewhere in a reality of faces and cold eyes and words sharp as knives. She was crying for her world as it used to be, of light without shadow and days without rain, in a walled garden where she played with paper dolls under the lilacs and believed in fairies and God. How could she tell him that? He wouldn't understand.

"Dearest, precious, don't. Don't cry like that," she heard him say from far away. "Please, lieble, I love you so dearly. You know how much I love you, don't you?" Gulping, she nodded her head, felt her lashes brush his cheek. "God, I love you so," he said again, and his voice in her ear was rough, urgent, in a way she'd never heard it. "Nothing else matters but that, does it? Does it?"

But even as he spoke, Paul knew that there *was* something else which did matter very much, which mattered so much that it had changed the whole shape of his thinking. Even as he held her close to him, he forced himself dispassionately to re-examine the situation. If an hour-long meeting with one of his relatives could so distress her, could shake her into near-hysterics, how in God's name dared he hope that she could bear the brunt of years in an "alien" society?

Once more he went back to the beginning and tried to think it through, intelligently and without emotion. With all his reason he had fought this relationship; after their first evening together, when he knew he was falling in love with her, he had determined never to call her again. Yet he had called her again against his judgment and against his will; because he loved her he had taken the necessary first step which inevitably led to the next, and the next—and to this moment. Strangely enough, it was his reason which had overthrown his last barrier. At the church social in Judge Braxton's home Frances' purpose and beautiful sincerity, in a situation which was for Kingston a daring innovation in race relations, finally had persuaded him that she had the strength and the courage to take a Jew into her life. Or, more exactly, to give up her life for a Jew.

And then today! The blow was so unexpected! He felt his control drain away as, all over again, anger at her behavior welled up in him. Before this noon, he could never have believed Frances capable of the churlishness and intolerance she had displayed. By her standards, of course, she had been quite polite, outwardly maintaining all the cold good manners with which Virginia gentlefolk always masked their ugliest feelings. Damn such hypocrisy! Courtesy was a poor substitute for honesty . . . And yet, to be fair, perhaps he had expected too much of her. He had expected that her warm, generous heart would see through Sol's exterior into the loving and unhappy man beneath.

Well, he had found her blind spot. How deep was her blindness, how irremediable, he didn't know. But he had to know, and soon.

Still, he told himself desperately, there was always the possibility that he was exaggerating the importance of the incident. So much did he want to believe in her that he would make allowance for that possibility, slight though it was. Frances had been nursed on fairy tales and reared in a dream world; he must never forget that. No matter how fiercely he had fought to kill her romantic illusions, no matter how often he had explained to her that he was not the Little Colonel's Knight come riding, that he was not Lochinvar out of the west, that he was not the most promising concert violinist of the twentieth century, that he was poor in a way she'd never imagined, and not yet even a reputable musician—might never be—still, with her romantic soul, she had looked at him starry-eyed, completely convinced that he was the answer to her dreams. Now, brutally, she had been shocked into reality. Her fairy prince had human connections, and, on the surface, not too prepossessing at that. It was high time she was faced with a few bare facts.

And it was time he faced the same facts, coldly and realistically, all over again.

In his arms Frances lay quiet now, without tears and without words. He held her close to him, gently caressing her hair, and over her shoulder, thoughtfully, he watched the long shadow of the twilight deepen, far across the valley.

f i f t e e n

The Square lay blazing in the noontime. Feebly a bubble of water pulsed up out of the fountain and spilled down into the green and stagnant pool. Overhead the heavy leaves of the trees hung still and dry in the air, rustling only when a lazy squirrel flicked his tail across them. Now and then a truck hooted and the hollow echo bounced wearily from the bright white buildings that surrounded the Square. Each glassy August day dragged out its length as unmoving and unchanged as the high blue hills.

Day after sultry day, following the defeat of Judge Braxton at the polls, Frances walked wonderingly through the Square and down the streets of Kingston. It didn't seem possible but it was so—everything was as it had always been, and there was no change anywhere, nor would there ever be. There were the same blank faces and the same empty eyes and the same hollow lives, on and on in a wretched circle of days upon unchanged days.

If she could only take the town by its shoulders and shake it until its teeth fell out and its eyes flew open: See here! Look! Because your father slept in a feather bed, must you? Where are your tallow candles and your wood cookstoves? Cut down the telephone wires and pull up the railroad tracks! Sit back here behind your wall of mountains. Let the world outside race far ahead of you. How long can you resist? Don't you know something strong and new has brushed your lives? Don't you realize that last Tuesday, right here in this town, you had a chance to shake hands with the future? But you wouldn't hear or heed and the future lies stillborn in your laps.

What good would that do? There was no change, nor could there ever be. Here was the Square through which she had walked all her life—a little girl, holding her mother's hand and skipping alongside with quick steps to match her mother's long ones; to and from school, scuffing the leaves on the paths with her high-laced shoes and watching the autumn die into winter and the winter break into spring, swinging her school books on a strap through the years. On the corner there, Sadwell's old drugstore with its green shutters and frayed awning and outside the door the wooden bench where the big boys waited after school and whistled as the girls ducked by. Down this street and around the corner was Emily's house, with its big hot kitchen where they could make gingerbread on cold afternoons or play paper dolls on the floor in front of the fireplace in the library. What happened to all those paper dolls they cut out so carefully, named so lovingly, traded so shrewdly? Lost and forgotten like the stories the little girls made up by the hour on those warm spicy afternoons after school. "Today my girl is a princess in disguise. She lives in this poor little house because nobody knows she is a princess. And this is my hero. He is a prince. He's going to come riding down out of the mountains to rescue her from these wicked people who are making her live in this dirty old attic. He'll carry her off on his steed into the hills to his castle where they'll live happily ever after." They never got tired of playing that story, and when the paper dolls were yellow and old, she and Emily would cut out new ones and go on and on telling the same story a million different ways, but always with a happy ending.

Emily's house hadn't changed and Emily hadn't changed and the Square and the streets and the town hadn't changed. Nothing had changed except Frances herself and, in a world to which she once had belonged, she was alone.

The election was over and Judge Braxton was defeated. Though to Frances it was a shattering fact, to Kingston it was a passing ripple on the surface of the days. The *Bugle* printed the returns and dropped the issue. The daily routine of the New World Church contracted to normal, and Dr. Mac, not looking back, wholeheartedly plunged into plans for a hospital benefit. Only for Frances did the defeat assume larger and larger proportions; it became a personal humiliation.

This is my town, my own home town, she reminded herself stubbornly, hearing the words fall onto the numbed surface of her mind like pebbles plunking onto an icy pond. Here are the streets I've walked so often, the people I've known so long. Only yesterday they were as familiar to me as the faces of my mother and father. But even they are secret and strange today. I am the one who is changed.

There was a time, it seemed so long ago, when she walked with pleasure and without surprise along this very street which led toward home, loving the bumpy red bricks in the sidewalk and the arch of a purple fanlight over a wide white door, cherishing the majesty of the old oaks and magnolia trees in the yards. Sauntering, she would make up stories about the people who had lived in all these noble mellow houses behind their grilled iron gates. As she gazed through the floor-length windows into a high-ceilinged drawing room, she could see fair women in hoop skirts pivoting gracefully in the arms of tall young men in the crimson and gray of the Confederate Army while the candles guttered in their sockets and the musicians fiddled into the dawn. It had been a street of romance and wonder, wearing its age proudly, serenely conscious of its own dignity and worth.

Now, it was just an old tired row of houses, listless, almost shabby in the harsh sunlight, without romance and without pleasure, smaller somehow than she had remembered, even hostile in its withdrawn and waiting stillness. Like Alice on the wrong side of the looking glass, she felt that everything was backwards and could be set to rights only if she could climb back through the mirror and be on the inside again.

One day, wandering downtown at noon while she had an hour to kill before meeting Paul, she walked through the open-air marketplace behind Stonewall Street. Here, ranged alongside the old Armory, were rickety wooden stalls piled high with vegetables and fruit, carrots and purple eggplant and unshucked corn jumbled wildly together against beds of green lettuce and spinach still streaked with dirt and curly kale by the armfuls. In the gutter were pushcarts, their shafts propped against the cobbles, and horse-drawn wagons in from the country with their loads of fat watermelons, ready for plugging, bushel baskets of tomatoes, potatoes, cantaloupes, squash, snap beans, peaches soft with fuzz. The little passageway between the stalls on the one hand and the carts on the other was jammed with people, sunup to sundown: Negro maids with deep shopping bags come to do the family's marketing; housewives poking fingers into the tomatoes; children tagging along behind, swiping a peach off the rear of a wagon; the peddlers themselves, Negroes and Italians and Jews, calling, cajoling, haranguing, dickering, tempting. The watermelon man, grinning over his wet white teeth, "Lemme plug one for you, missy?" offering a sliver of dripping red from the heart of the melon. His little black four-year-old sat on the edge of the cart, swinging his bare feet and waving flies off the tomatoes.

"Fresh feesh! Fresh feesh!" In the steamy air the plaintive wail rose constantly, a haunting singsong chant that floated above the creak and rattle of iron wheels on cobblestones. Frances moved slowly between the stalls and the carts, smiling, shaking her head, "No, thanks, no thanks," watching, listening. As often as she had been in the market, never before had she been so aware of the rich heavy odors of bodies and earth and fish and cut fruit, the crackle and babble of voices from peddler and shopper, the sweaty, greasy, dark-skinned faces feverishly swarming about her—the faces of the Jews. With a curious, painful intensity she was conscious that all the Jewish men she saw, here among these Negroes, looked much like Mr. Revkin—the same short, heavy bodies and close-set, crafty, peering eyes, the same wet unctuous smiles, and those insistent, aggressive barks which contrasted so harshly with the crooning music of the watermelon man's song and the low liquid voices of the Italians.

She couldn't remember ever having seen so many Jews in Kingston before. As she worked her way along the crowded street, covertly she inspected all the faces as they poured toward her and classified them "Yes" and "No" in her mind. Across the stream of Negroid or Gentile features she slid her glance, unsatisfied, until out of the mass a dark and swarthy face would leap at her and, fascinated, she would study it through half-squinted eyes for a brief and bitter moment, intently observing the color of the skin, the shape of the nose and the body, the slant of the eyes. "He's one!" she would exclaim to herself, or "No, he's probably only Italian."

This consciousness of the faces of Jews grew on her, why she didn't attempt to explain, until she could no longer walk down a street or sit in a bus or even pass a solitary stranger in her own neighborhood without examining closely his features, his walk, his body, and answering "Yes" or "No" to the question that was always with her: "Is this one Jewish?" Finally even the question receded into the murky background of her thinking and only the answer remained whenever she saw a face; methodically she labeled it Yes or No. Once she saw a little boy fall off his bicycle onto the pavement; when she picked him up and brushed him off, straightening his wheel and setting him on it again, she noticed that he was a little Jewish boy. All children didn't look alike to her any more.

Now she read the society columns greedily, even buying a Washington paper from the newsstand behind the drugstore, hoping to find notice of marriage between Finkelstein and Ryan for a change, or Seidenberg and Smith, instead of Finkelstein and Seidenberg all the time, Ryan and Smith. Once there was an announcement that Haufmann was planning to marry Ellison, and with avid interest she read the entire column, only to learn that Haufmann was the son of a German Lutheran minister, his first name was William Frederick, and he couldn't possibly be Jewish.

Superficially her life went on as usual throughout the sticky August weeks. In the afternoons she went to Paul with an urgency and passion even stronger because she was hiding from him the turmoil and twisted confusion of her mind, her new awareness of Jews and all things Jewish, the nearly unbearable pull upon her of her roots and background. In the evenings, with the family and with Hugh, she behaved—she hoped—in a normal and rational manner. But now she had lost the ability to stand off and see herself through the eyes of others. Now, to herself, it was apparent that she no longer walked the clear straight road from belief to action, but scurried about in a tangled underbrush of irresolution and hidden fears.

And one day all her fears rose up and defeated her. One day, alone, face to face with reality, she denied all that she believed in—and she knew it when she did it.

It was on her way to the Hunt Club where she was to meet Paul at one o'clock. She boarded a bus at the Square, carrying a small bag into which she had stuffed her riding boots and jodhpurs. As the bus lurched forward, she held the bag clumsily under one arm and fumbled in her pocketbook for a dime, paid the fare, and stumbled back toward the center where she had seen a single empty seat. The route of the bus ran through the Negro section—"Niggertown," it was called—and through a wealthy suburb before it reached the end of the line, the Kingston Hunt Club. It was not until Frances reached the empty seat that she realized she would have to share it with a middle-aged Negro woman who was sitting by the window, looking up at her.

Frances stood in the aisle, holding onto a strap with one free hand and balancing the suitcase and her handbag in the other. A quick glance at the front of the bus showed her that all those seats were taken by well-dressed women with shopping bags who were evidently going nearly to the end of the line themselves. Nor was there a vacant seat in the rear of the bus among the Negroes, to which the woman could move.

As she swayed back and forth with the bumpy bus, hot and uncomfortable, she wondered why in the world she didn't just sit down. A few weeks ago she would have sat down, without even thinking anything of it one way or the other; *that* she knew. She's not dirty, she told herself furiously. There aren't any bugs crawling on her. You certainly won't catch a horrible disease. Why don't you just go ahead and sit down?

Because she was afraid of the consequences.

She imagined what the Negroes in the back would say, buzzing and whispering among themselves, with perhaps a titter or two. Perhaps the bus driver might make a scene; she had known it to happen. And if some of those ladies in the front—friends of her mother's, probably— turned and saw her, what would they think?

"But you've eaten supper with Negroes," the little voice in her head reminded her. "You conducted that meeting at Judge Braxton's house, remember? Didn't you mean any of that?"

"But that was different," she protested. "There were lots of people around then, and they were all eating and talking with them too. I wasn't all by myself."

"In other words, you're afraid to stand up for what you believe when you've got to face it alone, aren't you?" the voice jeered, but she paid it no attention and stared with great interest at the advertisements of soap flakes and cigarettes on the sides of the bus. On and on the bus went, and nobody got on and nobody got off.

"It's too late to sit down beside her, now, even if I wanted to," Frances soothed herself. "I'd only embarrass her, and it would look so stupid after I'd been standing all this time."

She ventured a glance at the face of the woman and saw with a shock that the woman was looking at her. Their eyes collided. Immediately Frances averted her gaze, but not before she had noticed the peculiar expression on the woman's face. Not wistful, certainly, but proud, dignified, and yet inviting. It was as if she were wanting to say, "I'm not going to get up and give you the whole seat, but you're welcome to your half." And there was something of amusement in it too!

Abruptly Frances leaned forward and rang the bell. The bus stopped at the next corner, and she left by the front door, carrying her suitcase under one arm and unreasonably scowling at the driver as she passed. When the bus pulled away, she looked around and realized she was a good two miles from the Club and that there would be no more busses for half an hour. Angrily she kicked at the dirt as she began to walk down the road, watching the bus grow smaller and smaller in the distance.

s i x t e e n

"Who are the Sydnors?" Hugh asked. He and Frances were driving into Kingston for Emily's party.

"What do you mean, *who* are the Sydnors?" Frances demanded irritably. She was irritated with herself because that was the kind of reply Paul would have made, and her making it reminded her of Paul. This evening she was trying very hard not to think of Paul.

"I don't think that's such an unusual question to ask,

Franny," Hugh answered reasonably. He was always so patient with her, as though he were humoring a petulant child. "Who are the Sydnors? What does Mr. Sydnor do?"

"Well, they have quite a bit of money, if that's what you want to know. Lots more than we do, certainly. Mr. Sydnor runs an insurance office."

"Where do they live?"

"Around the corner from the Square. Back of Judge Braxton's house. I'll show you where to turn."

Hugh had a new car, a shiny black two-door sedan with somber maroon upholstery. "Thank God," Mr. Acheson had remarked to Frances in private, "you won't be borrowing mine every time *Hugh* wants to go to Washington." Frances watched Hugh drive sedately down the streets, creeping to a full stop at intersections, genially waving pedestrians and other automobiles to go ahead, go ahead. Savagely she wanted to get her hands on that wheel, to feel her foot down on the gas, to see a long, straight, empty road ahead of her, to drive faster and faster and faster until the needle flickered madly at eighty, and trees and fields and houses on either side of the road were a blur and a streak, until all her pent-up anger and misery were lost in a burst of speed which would carry her over the farthest hill and out of sight forever.

"Can't you drive a *little* faster?" she demanded. "We'll hold up Emily's supper!"

Unruffled, Hugh inquired, "What time is she expecting us?"

"Six-thirty."

"It's probably just a little past that now." He took one hand off the wheel to extract his pocket watch, and verified the time. "It's exactly six-forty-three."

"Well," Frances sighed resignedly, "we're practically there," looking out of the car window. It was suppertime: the streets were hushed and the rockers on the porches were empty. The rich sunset air was heavy, mellow, and in the linden trees the raucous starlings chattered frivolously. Oh, why does it have to be me? Frances thought, and twisted her hands in her lap.

In front of the Sydnors' house several cars were parked and Hugh pulled carefully into the curb at a distance. "I don't want anybody bumping my new fenders," he observed.

Together they walked back along the silent street, Hugh touching her elbow gently, his body bent slightly to her as he talked. "What a fine old house!" lifting the iron bar on the grilled gate and standing back to let her precede him up the short walk to the wide white door. "I didn't know the insurance business was so profitable."

"Oh, it's not all insurance money," Frances told him in a low voice. "It's Mrs. Sydnor's money they've got."

Twice Hugh dropped the heavy twisted bronze knocker with the two-headed eagle, and the sharp sound echoed in the street. Immediately the door was flung wide.

"Frances, dear! Come in, come in! We've all been waiting for you."

"Good evening, Mrs. Sydnor," Frances said, finding a smile. If, right now, she could only turn tail and go home —no! not home. But go somewhere, anywhere. "May I present Mr. Andrews, the new pastor at First Presbyterian?"

Mrs. Sydnor had enough money to afford to look just as she pleased—dowdy. She was fat and uncorseted and her pendulous breasts sagged nearly to her waist. In her plain, loose, brown dress she waddled when she walked and spilled over the edges of chairs when she sat down; yet on her fleshy face there was a trace of early beauty, and her smile was sweet and warm. "Mis-ter Andrews!" she said in her soft voice, taking his hand and looking up at him with bright eyes, like a round brown bird. "I'm so happy you could come." Still holding his hand, she led him through the entrance hall. "I think everybody is waiting for you all in the drawing room." She extended her other hand to Frances. "Come along, Franny. We don't mean to leave you behind."

Through the double doors to the drawing room, Frances could hear the faint murmur of voices, mostly girls' voices, the occasional rumble of a man's laugh, now and then a tiny shriek of delight. Hugh turned the knobs with his free hand, threw open both doors at once, and the three of them stood in the doorway holding hands, like actors taking a curtain call. A highly melodramatic entrance, Frances thought scornfully, and wanted to curtsy.

In the sudden silence, Mrs. Sydnor exclaimed, "Look who's here!" and pulled the two of them forward into the room, beaming and nodding her head with quick, pleased motions. "Emily! Emily, dear, do come here!"

There was a chorus of Hello's and How are you's. All the men rose and the girls surged forward in little ladylike rushes. Frances said "Millicent" and "Mary Cary," pressed her cheeks to her friends', took both Roberta's hands in her own and pulled her into her arms, declaring "Bobby! Married! How wonderful!" and "You're looking fine, just fine!" all the while watching and listening to Mrs. Sydnor introduce Hugh to Emily.

Emily was broadly smiling and sucking on her lower lip as she always did when she was excited, and Mrs. Sydnor, clasping and unclasping her hands, looked sweetly back and forth between them. "We've heard so much about you, Mr. Andrews," cried Emily, color high in her cheeks.

"Emily's been trying *so* hard to persuade her father and me to become Presbyterians, Mr. Andrews," her mother said, laughing softly and curling her hand in the air.

"We're always happy to have more members in our church," Hugh said, laughing too and glancing around the luxurious room. "Yes, indeed." The three of them laughed merrily together, as though he'd said something wonderful and hilarious, and looked at one another with bright warm eyes.

"This is Claude Flynn, my husband," Frances heard Roberta say to her. "Claude, this is Frances Acheson, one of my dearest and best friends."

"How do you do," Frances murmured vaguely, consciously focusing her attention on the man with whom she was shaking hands. "You're from Kansas, isn't that right?" It was the one fact she could recall having heard about the man Bobby Lee married.

"That's right. The Sunflower State, we call it."

"But," Roberta put in, "his grandmother came from Virginia."

"Oh, you're all right, then," Frances said lightly, hardly listening to her own words. "Just so long as a fourth of you belongs."

"We think Kansas is mighty fine too," Claude Flynn said, not too lightly.

For the first time Frances really looked at him. He was a little man, not so tall as she, about forty years old, with thinning hair and circles under his eyes. His handshake, she remembered it now, had been firm and hearty. In spite of the crow's feet at the corners, his eyes were young, sharp, blue as a crayon sky. They were laughing at her, and suddenly she laughed with them. "I'll bet Kansas is fine," she said. "You'd better drop that grandmother as soon as you can."

Old Jackson, the butler, came in and turned on all the lamps, shuffling among the chattering groups with half-lidded eyes and the impassive dignity of a mummy. Near the windows a little breeze stirred the girls' summer dresses, and on the walls soldiers and statesmen in their mahogany frames disdainfully gazed from the past.

"This is the first time I've ever been so far South," Claude Flynn remarked. "It's amazing. It's like walking into the pages of a history book."

Frances started; she'd forgotten he was standing beside her. "Oh. Oh, yes, it is, isn't it?"

"Where were you then?"

"When?"

"Just now, when I spoke to you. You were looking out of the window with the most woebegone expression on your face. You looked like you were a hundred miles away."

"Only ten," she said, and then quickly, "I'm sorry, excuse me. What do you do in Kansas?"

"Teach at a little college. I teach English."

Wryly Frances pulled in the corners of her mouth. "I wanted to teach English once. I did, as a matter of fact, for two whole years. I was probably the worst teacher the school system of Virginia ever had."

"You don't teach any more?"

"No, I stopped last June."

"What do you do now?" He sounded really interested,

not as though he were merely making conversation until time to eat.

"Nothing. Nothing at all."

Something about that raised eyebrow impelled her to go on. "There isn't much I *can* do, you know. I haven't any money of my own, so I can't go away. And I wasn't educated to be anything except a teacher or a wife—" She broke off and self-consciously smiled at him. "I don't know why I'm telling you all this. It's not very polite to bore strangers with your own personal problems." The entire conversation had a familiar ring, and she remembered saying the same words to Paul their first evening together.

Claude ignored her polite evasion. "Why don't you pull out and go away, money or not? Washington, New York, San Francisco. You could get some kind of job after you got there."

"Don't you see?" she said desperately. "I haven't even got enough money for a railroad ticket. Besides, my family never would let me."

At that moment, Mrs. Sydnor clapped her hands together gaily. "Supper, everybody! Supper!" Relieved that her conversation with Claude could go no further, Frances looked around for Hugh, and saw her hostess lay a plump hand on his arm. "Won't you lead the way to supper, Mr. Andrews?" Mrs. Sydnor requested. "I'd like you to say the blessing."

Hugh, towering over her, smiled down and without a backward glance tucked her hand through his arm. "I'd be delighted, Mrs. Sydnor," he assured her.

Making sweeping arcs in the air with her arm, "Come along, everybody," Emily cried and followed her mother and Hugh into the dining room. In a corner Mary Cary and her brother Bruce were talking with Roberta and Millicent and Millicent's young man from Winchester, whom Frances had not yet met. "Shall we go in?" Claude said at her elbow.

"Why, thank you," Frances said doubtfully, "don't you want to wait for Bobby?"

"No, that's all right. She'll be along. She hasn't seen her friends for a long time."

The dining room was square and high-ceilinged, richly paneled in oak. The table had been laid buffet-style; on either end of it and on the massive mahogany sideboard stood four-pronged candelabra, the candlelight blurring the corners of the room and reflecting itself a hundred times in the mirrors on the wall and the shining china, in the silver and the gleaming coffee service. Behind her Frances heard Claude say "Whew!" under his breath; she wondered if it weren't a little vulgar of him.

After the supper guests were gathered in the room, standing around the table and in the silence looking awkwardly from one another to Hugh, Mrs. Sydnor clasped her hands and murmured, "Now, Mr. Andrews." Everyone bowed his head except Hugh, who, privileged, looked upward. "We thank Thee, Heavenly Father," he said, rounding his vowels, "for this, another expression of Thy goodness to us. Go with us through this night. Keep us in Thy love. Bless this food to the nourishment of our bodies and bless our work in Thy service. Forgive our sins and teach us to walk in Thy straight path. For Jesus' sake. Amen."

"Amen." Mr. Sydnor's voice boomed from the doorway. Frances opened her eyes and saw him standing there, a bluff, hearty man with an unlined face and a Rotary Club expression. Through the movement and talk of guests around the supper table, he caught sight of her and, with a big smile, made his way across the room to greet her. "Hello there, Frances!" Genially he shook hands. "Haven't seen you around for a long time. Where've you been keeping yourself?"

"Good evening, Mr. Sydnor," Frances said flatly. "Have you met Mr. Flynn, Bobby Lee's husband?"

"How d'you do? How do you do?" Mr. Sydnor shook Claude's hand with a great show of cordiality. "Glad to have you." Immediately he turned back to Frances. "Saw your father on the street the other day and told him we never saw you any more. He said he never did either." Mr. Sydnor laughed uproariously. "Guess *he's* been keeping you pretty busy, eh?" He jerked his thumb in the direction of Hugh Andrews.

Frances looked at Mr. Sydnor. This was Emily's father, whom she had known since she was a little girl with a boyish bob and knee-length ribbed stockings. He didn't look a bit different from the way he had looked fifteen years ago. Yet all she could see was poor, plain-faced Mr. Darrity who once had been a member of the New World Church, where all the riff-raff and Communists and nigger-lovers worshiped, who had withdrawn his membership from the church after two months, quietly and by mail, who was still selling insurance in Mr. Sydnor's office six days a week, sitting at home on Sundays. The wildest ideas raced through her head. "How's Mr. Darrity?" she wanted to ask this stranger whom she'd known so long. "Has he been selling lots of insurance now that he's respectable again? Did you give him a raise when he came back into the fold?"

What she did say was, "I guess I have been pretty busy," and she managed a thin, tight smile.

Mr. Sydnor leaned down to her ear and murmured confidentially, "You've got a fine young man in that Mr. Andrews. He's going places, I tell you." He patted her shoulder and winked. "Fine."

"Have you had your supper yet?" Frances asked, moving away from him toward the table.

"Go ahead, go ahead. Enjoy yourself." Hospitably Mr. Sydnor beamed. "I'll get something in a minute. I want to speak to some of these other people."

Although Frances had no appetite, she could look about the table with appreciation. There were platters of cold sliced breast of chicken, each slice as fragile and white as the china; a whole Smithfield ham, crusty with brown sugar and cloves, garnished with broiled pineapple slices and steaming sweet potatoes dripping butter; baskets of beaten biscuit, each no bigger than a twenty-five-cent piece; chunky squares of yellow corn bread; three or four kinds of molded salad. At the far end of the table, old Jackson was serving from a deep bowl. As Frances approached, he looked up and his calm old face split into a grin.

"I declare, Miss Franny," he said warmly. "Haven't seen you in a coon's age. Lord, you haven't got nuthin' on your plate. Lemme give you some of this here lobster salad I fixed up myself this morning." With the serving fork and spoon he tossed the salad in the bowl a couple of times. "Lookit them big pieces of lobster meat in there. All fixed up with my own salad dressing."

"Honestly, Jackson, I'm not hungry," Frances said.

"But that looks so good, I've just got to have a little bit." He heaped a double spoonful on her empty plate. "Oh, that's too much."

"Go on, eat it. It's good for you. You're looking peaked, Miss Franny. Something bothering you?"

"Me, Jackson? Why no, of course not. I feel fine. And I promise you, I'll eat every bit of this."

With plates piled high, most of the guests had flowed back into the drawing room. Claude had been caught up in Roberta's group and alone, Frances wandered over to the sideboard where Mrs. Sydnor was pouring coffee for Hugh and Emily.

"I'm so glad you shook loose from that Flynn man," Mrs. Sydnor said affectionately, moving her shapeless body so that Frances could join the group. Both Hugh and Emily looked uncomfortable and said nothing. "I've been wanting to talk to you all evening," Mrs. Sydnor went on. With her fat graceful hands she poured a cup of coffee and hesitated above the sugar and cream.

"I take it black," Frances told her.

"You really could use a little weight on your bones, dear." Mrs. Sydnor shook her head in motherly disapproval. "I don't like to see you looking so rundown." Without pausing for breath, she turned to her daughter. "Emily, you should be in the drawing room with your guests. I'm sure Mr. Andrews hasn't met *all* those young people."

Remotely Frances watched Mrs. Sydnor's machinations; she deplored only her hostess' lack of subtlety. "You aren't looking well, Franny, not at all," she persisted as soon as Emily and Hugh had excused themselves. "Not like your usual vivacious self." Fondly she patted Frances' arm. "Have you tried taking vitamin pills?"

Frances put both hands at the nape of her neck and pressed as hard as she could. "They don't make pills for what's wrong with me," she said ruefully.

"Oho!" Conspiratorially, Mrs. Sydnor pursed her lips and jiggled her head. "Oho," she said again, obviously feeling no need for coherent speech.

She thinks I'm in love with Hugh, Frances remarked to herself in an offhand manner. Not that she'd let that interfere with the little scheme she's concocting for Emily!

"Is there anything I can do for you, Mrs. Sydnor?" she inquired courteously, picking up her plate and preparing to go into the drawing room. —Except to get out of Emily's way, that is! How she wished she could say these things aloud!—"May I fix a plate for you or something?"

"No, no, you run along, dear," Mrs. Sydnor smiled affectionately. "Go talk to that nice boy from Winchester. And tell everybody I'll have Jackson pass the dishes again in a little while."

Aimlessly Frances wandered into the drawing room. Everyone was sitting in twos and threes, the girls laughing, chattering, the men balancing plates and cups and saucers uncomfortably on their knees, trying to eat without spilling the lobster salad on the rug. On the hearth Mr. Sydnor, feet apart and back to the cold fireplace, was regaling Bruce and Millicent and the young man from Winchester with what sounded suspiciously like the story of his life; from time to time he interrupted himself to laugh heartily, and eventually his listeners would join him. Claude Flynn had placed his supper on a low coffee table and was eating with obvious enjoyment and a singlemindedness which, in the face of Roberta's and Mary Cary's chatter in his ears, was admirable. On the loveseat, which was barely big enough for the two of them, Emily had Hugh cornered—yes, cornered was the only word for it. Leaning forward like a skater into the wind, her supper uneaten, Emily was talking with eyes, eyebrows, hands and shoulders, vivaciously, intently, unceasingly. Hugh won't like that, Frances commented inwardly. He likes to do all the talking himself.

As though she were beyond the long French windows, standing in the street and watching from afar, she surveyed the room. She saw their smiles and did not feel a warmth; she listened to their voices and did not hear a meaning; she stood outside the inner circle of their eyes, alone.

Setting her plate on an end-table near the door, she turned and went upstairs to Emily's room.

Two little lamps with pink shades glowed on the dressing table, and on the double bed was a crimson taffeta spread that swished against her legs as she passed. Propped against the pillows, her flat blue eyes wide-staring in her round pink face, sat Diana, Emily's favorite doll—she looked amazingly like Emily herself—and in passing, Frances rumpled her coarse blonde curls. She wondered if Emily still played with Diana in the night, after the doors were shut, still made up stories of gallant princes and magic mountains and shining dreams with happy endings. She supposed *Emily* still did.

As Frances sat down at the dressing table and idly ran a comb through her hair, Millicent and Mary Cary came into the room, softly and with anxious faces. "Frances? Are you all right?" asked Millicent, sliding an arm around Frances' shoulders.

2 1 0

"We wondered if you felt bad or something," Mary Cary said.

"My goodness, do I look that awful?" Frances demanded, peering into the mirror with exaggerated intentness. "Everybody has been telling me how dreadful I look. Jackson, and Mrs. Sydnor, and now you all." She turned and looked from one pretty face to the other. "Really, I feel fine."

With a sigh, "That's all right, then," Millicent said. "It's just not like you to be so quiet." She sat down on the cedar chest at the foot of the bed and stretched her legs out before her. "New shoes. Like them?"

Frances, still combing her long straight hair, glanced down. "Umhum. Pretty."

There was an odd silence. Mary Cary walked to the window and perched herself on the broad sill. For lack of something better to do, Frances put on some more lipstick.

"I saw you talking to Claude Flynn," Millicent began with an upward inflection. In the mirror Frances saw her dart a quick glance toward Mary Cary.

"Honestly!" Mary Cary exclaimed and tsk-tsked her tongue against her teeth.

"What's wrong with that?" Frances asked, swinging around on the dressing table stool and staring them down. "Shouldn't people talk to him?"

"But whatever did you find to talk about?" Millicent, with a shrug, wanted to know. "He's so dull. He just stands around."

"And he's so funny-looking, too," Mary Cary threw in. "Why, I can remember when Bobby was in college, she used to tell about the kind of man she was going to marry. He had to be *this* and he had to be *that*"—she waved her hands here and there to emphasize her words—"and then she turns up with this character! How could she! Honestly!"

"I tried to talk to him," Millicent said again. "I tried real hard. I asked him about his children. He's a widower, and has already got two children, you know—"

"I know," Frances murmured. "You were the first to tell me."

"And all he did was answer yes and no. He didn't try to help me along in the conversation at all. I asked him if he was Irish, since his name was Flynn, and he said No, he was just from Kansas."

"Maybe he thought you were prying," Frances suggested, lightly, so that Millicent wouldn't be offended.

"Prying? Good grief, you've got to talk about something. You can't just stand and look at each other."

"I'd like to know if he's Catholic," Mary Cary mused from the windowsill. "Flynn. I've never heard of a Flynn that wasn't Catholic."

"I've heard of a lot of Steins that weren't Jewish," Frances offered unexpectedly. She surprised herself, and almost looked around to see who'd made the statement.

Millicent ignored her. "If he is a Catholic, you'll never find it out from him. He won't tell you anything."

"Why don't you ask Bobby?" Mary Cary inquired.

"I intend to."

"She probably won't admit it if he is," Mary Cary decided.

"What's there to admit?" Frances interrupted. "That's nothing to be ashamed of, being a Catholic."

"Well, *I'd* think thirty times before I married a Catholic," Millicent asserted. "How about the children? They make you bring them up in the Catholic faith, too."

Mary Cary was off on another tangent. "Kansas is so far away. She'll practically never get home. Just imagine, going way out there with a whole lot of strangers you've never even met. She hasn't met any of his family, and that's important, you know."

"She just *might* love him," Frances cried desperately. "That's the important thing!"

"Oh, there are lots more things to be considered than that." Airily Millicent shrugged off Frances' cry. "That's movie stuff. What are you going to do when the passion wears off and you have to settle down to everyday living?"

"What do you know about passion?" Frances began contemptuously, but Mary Cary said "Hush!" and Emily came into the room, followed by Roberta.

"What are you all gossiping about?" Emily inquired in the strained silence, not looking at Frances. "It's not nice to leave Bobby and me downstairs alone with all those men."

"You certainly didn't want *us*," Millicent said pointedly. "You were doing all right." Frances heard Mary Cary giggle.

Emily walked over to the chest of drawers and rummaged in her handkerchief box; then, jerkily, she dabbed cologne behind her ears.

Roberta came to Frances and affectionately looked down at her. "Claude thought you were charming. I'm awfully glad you got a chance to talk to him."

"I'm glad too, Bobby." Frances wanted to take Roberta's hands in her own, but she supposed it would look affected. So again she said, "I'm awfully glad. I like Claude so much."

"I knew you would," Roberta said proudly.

"He certainly is nice," Millicent chirruped. "So intelligent and everything." She stood up and looked significantly at Mary Cary.

"I guess we had better go back downstairs," Mary Cary agreed. Gracefully she sauntered to the door, and then, over her shoulder, remarked, "I haven't had a chance to talk to Claude yet. I certainly want to. I've heard so many nice things about him."

"And I," said Millicent with a round-eyed smile, "will now get a chance at that beautiful Mr. Andrews!"

Frances could not resist glancing at Emily's broad back. Emily neither turned from the chest of drawers where she was brushing her hair, nor answered. "We'll be down in a minute, you all," Frances called after Millicent and Mary Cary. Her voice floated down the stairwell after their staccato footsteps.

"How have you been, Franny?" Roberta sat on the cedar chest and leaned forward, arms on knees and chin in cupped palms. She seemed settled for a long conversation.

"All right, I guess, honey. Though if people keep telling me how dreadful I look, I'll get sick just to favor them. I'm tired from so much running around." Again she couldn't resist glancing at Emily's back. "It's been a hectic summer."

"That's wonderful. I want you to tell me all about it," Roberta said.

I wish to God I could, thought Frances. "How much longer will you and Claude be in town? Maybe we could get together?"

"Not more than a couple of days, I'm afraid. Claude's college starts the first week in September and we have to get out there and get ourselves arranged a little bit."

Handkerchief in hand, Emily turned to them stiffly. "Are you all coming along pretty soon?" Her smile was wide and nervous.

"In a little while," Frances said calmly. "Don't wait for me."

"I'll never get a chance to talk to Fran downstairs," Roberta said. "We'll be along directly."

As soon as Emily had closed the door behind her, Roberta leaned even more closely toward Frances. "I should think she would be embarrassed! I've never seen such a shameful exhibition in all my life! And she's supposed to be one of your best friends."

All innocence, Frances asked, "What do you mean?"

"You know perfectly well what I mean. The way she's gone after Hugh Andrews. Why, Mrs. Sydnor deliberately —*deliberately* threw Emily at him." Indignant, Roberta struck her knee with her fist. "Everybody in town knows he's yours!"

"Mine!" cried Frances, shocked. "Mine? Everybody in town knows a lot more than I do."

"Ah listen, honey," Roberta said softly, patting Frances' wrist. "You don't have to put up a front with me. The first thing mother told me when I got home was that Hugh Andrews was at the Acheson house every single night of the week—"

"Except preaching nights," Frances reminded her.

"All right, six nights a week. And my mother heard it straight from your very own mother that he was bringing you flowers and candy all the time until the house practically bulges at the seams."

"It's just some place for him to come in out of the rain."

"Stop it, Frances! What's the matter with you? Couldn't you see him watching you all the time that Emily was sitting practically in his lap? And you should have seen the look on his face when you didn't eat your supper and came upstairs. That man's in love with you."

"He is *not!*" Frances cried out in terror. "He doesn't even know what love means."

"Hasn't he made love to you yet?"

"If you mean—has he so much as kissed me, no, he hasn't."

"Hasn't he tried?"

"We-ell, once or twice, I did think he was going to, so I got up and moved across the room."

"You see, what did I tell you! Why are you fighting him?"

"Oh, Bobby—I—" Frances flung her hands out. If she could only talk to somebody! "I don't know."

"You've changed, Fran. You're not at all the person I knew before I went to New York."

"How have I changed?" It was almost a whimper.

"Well, you're so restless. Your hands are never still. I had the feeling tonight that you're always watching for something or somebody, and you're all tensed up waiting for that something to happen. You're closed away from all of us, and sometimes it's as though you're watching everybody from the wrong end of a telescope."

"Really?"

"Really? Really?" Roberta mimicked. "Is that all you can say? You know it's true. You know you're different. What's happened to you?"

Now could be the time. Here was someone who might possibly understand. Perhaps she could say it now. And she opened her mouth, drawing in a deep breath like a swimmer coming up from way down—when Roberta said gently, "It *is* Hugh, isn't it? Are you in love with Hugh?"

And the moment was gone. Frances let all the air out of her lungs in a long-drawn "No."

"But you could have him if you wanted him?" Roberta was trying hard to comprehend.

"Yes. Yes, I'm pretty sure."

"He's good looking," she persisted, "certainly better looking than *my* husband, although that doesn't make any difference. He's going to be one of the leading ministers of the Southern Presbyterian Church in a few years, Daddy says. And if you married him, you could probably stay in Kingston all the rest of your life—which is more than I can say. You've got all the females in town from sixteen to sixty drooling with envy . . . And you don't want him! Emily Sydnor will take him fast enough if you turn him down, I can tell you. I just don't understand you, Frances."

"Don't you think I've thought about all that?" Frances demanded in a low, savage voice. She looked down and saw that her fists were clenched; so was her stomach. "Can I help it if I want something more?"

"Where in God's name do you expect to find more than that?" Roberta demanded impatiently. "It's not as though you were the most beautiful woman in three states. Or a famous actress. Or had millions of dollars. Who do you think you are?"

"Not much," said Frances, laughing a short laugh that could have been a sob. She wished she had learned to smoke so she could light a cigarette now and cover the trembling in her hands and in her chin.

"Ah now, I didn't mean that the way it sounded,

Franny," Roberta said, tenderly contrite. "I love you so much, I hate to see you unhappy. Especially when I'm so happy with Claude. I want everybody to be happy too."

I wonder what you'd say if you could have overheard the conversation here before you came in, Frances thought. Would you be so secure then?

The light from the shaded lamps glowed rosily on the polished dressing table and caught the two of them within its warm circle. Beyond the light the room was dark and silent like the street. For a long time they sat without movement while below them, faintly, the party laughed and chattered and was gay. Someone was playing the piano, and the music and the singing drifted up the stairwell to them. They were singing old songs, full of memories: "In the evening by the moonlight, you can hear those darkies singing," memories of hayrides and beach parties and closely woven circles of friends harmonizing on the front lawn under the summer moon. "Bye low, my baby, bye low, my baby, bye low, my baby, good-by, my lover, good-by."

"Let's go downstairs," said Frances suddenly, starting up as from a dream. "They'll think we've fallen in." She laughed and took Roberta's arm. "Sitting up here like a couple of old maids, when you've got a husband waiting for you, and I—well, we shall see what Mis-ter Andrews is up to."

As soon as Frances and Roberta entered the drawing room, Hugh saw them and said, above the singing, "Look who's back!" Immediately he broke away from the group at the piano and quickly came toward Frances. She did not miss the glance which ran around the circle of eyes, the flat, sweet smile resolutely plastered on Mrs. Sydnor's face, Emily's open look of chagrin. She should have pride enough to disguise it, Frances thought.

"I was terribly worried," Hugh said, taking her hands and looking into her eyes. "Do you feel all right now?"

"Oh, mercy," she assured him, not removing her hands from his grasp, "I seem to have been worrying everybody here. I just wanted to talk to some of my friends without a lot of people around."

"I'm glad it was just that," Hugh exclaimed, relieved, and led her back to the piano where the circle opened and let her in.

Millicent, who was playing, leafed through a stack of sheet music. "Let's find something with a good soprano lead," she suggested. "Frances sings in the choir, you know," she reminded Hugh.

"So I've heard," he answered, "but she's never let me hear her sing." Everyone chorused that Frances had a wonderful voice and used to sing solos in college chapel, and Frances wondered how much of their warmth was from pleasure in her mediocre singing and how much from pleasure in Emily's discomfiture.

"Do you know *Ah! Sweet Mystery of Life?*" asked Millicent's young man from Winchester, whatever his name was, pulling the music from a pile and opening it on the piano. Frances smiled up at Hugh and said she remembered most of the words.

While they hummed the parts, she sang it through alone, and she heard her voice lift and soar and take all the high notes without too much difficulty—she certainly didn't sing that well as a rule, not even in the bathtub—and then everyone came in on the second chorus: Mr. Sydnor's deep tuneless bass, Millicent's good alto, from time to time Bruce

Cary's tentative baritone, all the rest happily carrying the melody.

"Why, you have a nice voice," Frances said to Hugh. Good and loud at any rate, she added to herself.

"Yes, you two sing very nicely together," Roberta said to them from across the piano where she was standing hand in hand with Claude.

Smiling apologetically into Frances' eyes, "Yes, indeed," said Emily gamely.

"Have you got *Shine On, Harvest Moon?*" Mary Cary wanted to know, and Mr. Sydnor remarked that he always liked to sing spirituals himself. People began stacking favorite songs in little heaps along the top of the piano, and Millicent flexed her wrists and wondered if she could play all of them. They did love songs and minstrel songs and rounds: "Row, row, row your boat, gently down the stream, merrily, merrily, merrily, merrily, life is but a dream." They did all of Stephen Foster's that they could find, with Mr. Sydnor insisting upon *Beautiful Dreamer* twice over. "I used to sing that to your mother when we were first married," he informed Emily solemnly. "Let's sing that again!"

Across the singing, "Oh, Fran-ces!" called Mrs. Sydnor from the doorway. All the people looked up, and there was Paul.

Everything stopped. It could have been only a moment before Frances broke away from the group and swiftly went across the room to him, for as she walked she could hear, hanging in the air, the echoes of the music. But in that moment when everything stopped, and before she could make a movement, the room, the world, and time itself were suspended in mid-air, like a moving picture suddenly immobilized upon a screen. She could examine all the details of the picture. Here were Millicent's hands, still spread upon the black and white keys, here the sheet of music still waiting to be turned, and the Paisley shawl flung in a careless profusion of color over the vast blackness of the grand piano. Here were all the people turned to stare across the room, immobile, stiff, their eyes straight ahead and not yet cutting around to her to squint and narrow and presume. Behind Paul, as though pushing him into the room, Mrs. Sydnor, sweetly smiling. Paul—dark, dark, dark, and out of place. He looked so dark and Jewish!

s e v e n t e e n

She moved, and the scene broke into a thousand brittle pieces. "Excuse me," she murmured to Hugh, the blood pounding in her ears. "Of course," he said, and stood back to let her pass. Behind her, people began to talk again, and Millicent rippled her fingers along the keyboard. In front of her Paul stood still, and Mrs. Sydnor watched them both with her bright birdlike eyes.

"Hello, Paul," Frances said, hearing the words with her ears after she'd said them, and not with her heart and her mind. Manners, manners, manners. "Mrs. Sydnor, may I present Paul Revkin?"

"He's already introduced himself to me," replied Mrs. Sydnor graciously. "Can we offer you some supper? Franny, take your friend out into the dining room—"

"No, no thanks very much," Paul refused. "I've had supper. I'm sorry to break in on a party like this—"

"Nonsense!" Mrs. Sydnor assured him. "You're not breaking in at all. We're so happy to have you. You must come and meet all these people. We needed another man to balance things anyway." Her fat hands fluttered as gracefully as two birds in flight, and her smile was genuinely happy again.

Paul turned to Frances. She could make nothing of his expression. "I had to come into town unexpectedly to see Dr. Mac about the concert he's arranging for the hospital benefit. He wants me to play—"

"Oh, do you play?" asked Mrs. Sydnor. Frances jerked her head toward her hostess. Already she'd forgotten that Mrs. Sydnor was standing there still.

"Paul's a violinist. He plays beautifully," Frances said with unnecessary emphasis, as if by her very intensity she could atone for the hideous reaction she'd had when he entered the room.

"Frances exaggerates," Paul told Mrs. Sydnor. "One day I hope to be the musician she thinks I am. But—" he looked back at Frances, "after I finished talking with Dr. Mac, I called your home, and your mother told me you were visiting the Sydnors. I thought I might take you home. Mrs. Acheson didn't mention that you were having a party." To Mrs. Sydnor he said, "Please forgive me."

Mother did this on purpose, Frances cried to herself, appalled. How could she? How could she? And I reacted just the way she hoped I would. She was cold, suddenly, clammy on this hot night, and sick with shame. "Paul," she said, putting her hand on his arm, "Paul," and her voice trembled. "Please come and meet all these people."

Before he could answer, standing and looking at her intently as though he could see the thoughts floating like scum on the surface of her mind, Mrs. Sydnor clasped her hands about his other arm and playfully tugged at it. "Come along. Don't just stand there mooning at each other, you two. Come, Paul, and meet the party."

It seemed to Frances that a whole new layer of her consciousness had been skinned, and lay, raw and quivering, exposed to the air. She listened to Mrs. Sydnor's introductions, to "How do you do, Paul, I'm glad to meet you," to "I hear you're playing at Lake Luray," to a dozen polite responses; but she heard a dozen unspeaking voices jangling in her ears, "Is this what Frances has been dating all summer?" and "What does her family say?" and "I heard he was Jewish. I'll bet he is," bzzz, bzzz, bzzz. Trembling, she waited for the time when, by ones and twos, the girls would drift upstairs into the bedroom to gather in the warm circle of the pink lampshades and bzzz, bzzz, bzzz. Like a man trapped by savages, whose eyes ceaselessly rove the underbrush watching for the first arrow, she restlessly looked from face to polite face, finding nothing but politeness, trying to catch a raised eyebrow, a flicking whiplike glance, the look which *must* be racing around the inner circle of eyes, if she could only catch it, catch it, catch it!

But the faces were polite and blank and smiling, a blank wall of eyes and smiles and attention. They listened to him talk, a word here with Claude and Roberta about New York, there some conversation with Bruce about a town in Germany they'd both been through, now answering a question about his music. What did this remind her of? When had she seen him behave so before? This polished surface, charming, remote—it was the afternoon of the concert at the Women's Club, when, ringed in at the bottom of the steps by that twittering aviary of full-breasted dowagers eying him like birds after a worm, he had thrust and parried and dominated the whole group. This was Paul at his professional best, but it was not the Paul she knew. He too was a stranger, among strangers, and she sat alone in misery.

How long the evening dragged on, she did not know; she felt she had sat in her chair, a guarding sentry, alert and unmoving for hours. Suddenly, without warning, it was time to go, time to stand up, to move, to break the rigid pose, to babble the amenities—Thank you for the supper. The supper was delicious. We certainly did have a nice evening. It's been so pleasant meeting you. Perhaps we'll see each other soon. Have a nice trip to Kansas. Come again. You must come to see us—

"Can I give you a lift somewhere?" That was Hugh to Paul. Among the empty noises of thank you and good-by, she heard it clearly. "Can I give you a lift somewhere?"

"No, thank you, Mr. Andrews. It's no distance to the bus station."

"Paul, please," she said to him under the babblings and chatterings. "Please." That was all there seemed to be to say, just "Please" over and over.

"All right. Thanks."

They sat in the car, the three of them, with Frances in the middle. Under the arching lindens the street was dark and silent; there were no lights in the brooding, ghostly houses. Behind them there was the occasional slam of a car door, last hushed good-by's. The whole world was asleep, and this too should be a dream, but it was not a dream. It was all too real.

Cautiously Hugh started his car, explaining all the while in great detail to whoever was listening where he got it and how he got it and how wonderfully it ran. On and on his voice droned in Frances' ear, requiring no answer. She was aware only of Paul beside her, dark and silent as the night.

At the bus station she let him go without a word. She could not say what she wanted to say—for after all, there was Hugh, filling the night with words, words, words—and she would not say what she could have said: a pleasant evening, so glad you came, please come again, good night, good-by. Without a word she let him go, and watched him walk across the faintly lighted platform of the bus station, watched his long black shadow flickering and spreading behind him.

"Where did you meet *him*, Frances?" Hugh asked.

"At my church." —Don't ask me any more.

"Is he a member there?"

"No."

"Just visiting?"

"He played for us once."

"How long have you known him?"

"Two months, two weeks, and four days." —Please stop, Hugh. Please, please stop.

They pulled up in the driveway to her house, and in her haste to escape from him, she opened the door herself and scrambled out onto the porch steps. "Don't bother seeing me to the door," she called. "Thanks for a pleasant evening."

But he would not hear of it. "Just a minute, please, dear," he requested, coming around behind the car and following her up the steps.

Hand on doorknob, she glanced impatiently over her shoulder. "What do you want?" Her voice was barely civil.

Hugh came across the porch to her and stood close, his big body blocking her within the deep casement of the door. "You're angry with me, aren't you?"

"No," she said frankly. "Should I be?"

"I thought—you were behaving so strangely—"

"Yes?"

"Well, maybe because of Emily—" he floundered.

Good Lord, she thought, I'd completely forgotten all that. "What do you mean, 'because of Emily'?" she inquired deliberately. Let him flounder a bit; it wouldn't hurt him.

"Well," with a manly determination to confess and be done, "most of the evening there, I managed to let Emily and her mother make a fool out of me, push me around, and so forth. I couldn't seem to get away." He sighed. "I don't wonder you're angry."

"Oh, Hugh," she said wearily, "I'm not angry with you. I wasn't even paying any attention to you and Emily." In passing, it occurred to her that indifference would hurt his feelings much more than jealousy. "Don't get so upset." She leaned her head back against the door and pressed her hands hard to her temples. "Oh Lord, Lord, Lord."

And Hugh leaned down and kissed her.

"Don't!" she cried in panic. Dammit, she should have gone in right away. "Don't!" She drew away from him as far as she could, pulling her neck into her shoulders and holding her hands up in protest.

"I'm sorry, Franny," Hugh said gravely. "I certainly didn't mean to upset you."

Past his arm, wordless, she slid, out of the door's casement and onto the porch, to stand by the railings and pull leaves off the wisteria vines. A word, an explanation, an apology, she owed him something for the brutal rebuff he'd just received, but she could think of nothing to say.

"Hugh—"

He came to her and stood, again too close; instinctively she dropped back a step. Like pawns in a chess game, she thought, I wonder who's planning these moves?

"Frances," Hugh said, his arms straight down at his sides, "I know you haven't known me very long. Five or six weeks at the most." He cleared his throat and, almost imperceptibly, his vowels began to round and his phrases roll. "But in that time I think you've come to know what I stand for, and what my prospects are for the future. Your family likes me very much, I think. And certainly your home is a second home to me."

"That's very important, isn't it?" said Frances numbly, gazing out into the night.

"We share the same interests, you and I, the same background, the same friends—"

"This is all a little too contrived, don't you think?" Frances said aloud.

"Excuse me?"

"Nothing—I guess I was addressing God."

Stupefied, he stared at her. "Sometimes I don't understand you at all, Frances."

She faced him. "Do you think I understand myself?" she demanded.

Ignoring what he could not understand, Hugh returned to the theme of his discourse. "Of course, I haven't said anything to your father yet. But Frances"—here he took her shoulders in both his hands—"do you think you could learn to care for me?"

Slowly she said, "There was a time when I was like a

book. It's trite but it's true. I could read myself, and so could anybody else. There I was, all black and white and words of one syllable. Just open me anywhere and read me. 'This is a cat. A cat has four legs. This is a dog. This is right. That is wrong. This is white and that is black.' A primer for minds in the first grade—"

"You're tired, dear," Hugh said tenderly. "I shouldn't have chosen such a bad time to talk to you—"

"And now it's like trying to read Sanskrit," she went on, unheeding. "Or hieroglyphics or Greek. The symbols don't have any meaning any more. White is black and black is white. Everything used to be so simple, and now they've turned it all around backwards."

"You don't have to give me an answer now—"

She looked at him. "Is there an answer?"

"An answer to the question I am asking you. Of course there's an answer. But I won't press you. Just promise me you'll think about it."

"I promise. I think about it all the time."

"That's all I could ask." He squeezed her shoulders once, then dropped his hands. "Now you run along to bed and get some sleep. You've had a hard day."

He did not try to kiss her again, but taking her by the elbow, led her to the door and opened it for her. "Good night, dear."

"Good night, Hugh."

She stood in the doorway until his car had vanished around a curve in the road, and for many minutes thereafter. Before her lay the night, serene in dark, impenetrable beauty. She looked for the wall of mountains that, cradling, sheltered the sleeping land. Even without light, she knew the mountains were there, as they had been always, as they always would be.

Softly she shut the door and went upstairs to bed.

Beyond the mountains that enclosed the town, on the lawn of the Lake Luray Hotel, Paul stood in the moonlight and contemplated his shadow. He turned his back on the moon and saw before him his shadow long and black on the grass. He faced the moon and walked a step and over his shoulder watched his shadow following him. He could not escape it.

He could not escape it. This way and that he ran, a few steps here, a few steps there, zigzagging, dodging, twisting, all the while knowing that running was hopeless. His shadow dogged his footsteps all across the lawn.

Finally, belligerent, he turned and faced it, shoulders hunched and fists clenched; he took an angry step toward it and it retreated, just one step. He took another, quicker; it fell back and waited too. And another, and another . . . until again he was running as fast as he could across the lawn in the moonlight, headlong, blindly, wildly—with his shadow wildly running ahead of him, just one step away.

By the squat stone wall which surrounded the lawn of the hotel, gasping, exhausted, he threw himself down on the grass with his head in his arms, lying so without movement until the heaving in his body flowed off into the earth and he was still. He had not cried since he was a very small boy and he could not cry now and he knew he would never cry again.

In a little while he sat up and put his back to the wall and lit a cigarette. Without humor he laughed because his hands did not tremble when he lit the cigarette. How wonderfully strong you are, he sneered to himself, looking at his hands in the moonlight. How bloodless-cold and without emotion! Isn't it fine to be a rational, unemotional human being! To see things in the white, harsh light of reason, to accept them as they are and to act accordingly. He flicked his cigarette into the grass and watched the sparks fly upward. Sparks fly always upward and shadows always pursue and from the roots of cabbages lilies never grow. That was the way it was always, the way it was to be.

So Frances was not for him. Perhaps she knew it, perhaps she didn't; that was unimportant. For in the end it was his decision, and the decision had been made. In that tiny moment, when he had walked into the Sydnors' drawing room and had seen her, from the closed circle at the piano and out of the shadow of Hugh's arm, turn upon him with a look of stark fear and denial, his decision had been made. In that tiny moment, she had faltered; she had lost. Until that moment there had been in him a hope which he had nursed and kept alive, even while he watched her slow withdrawal, even while he listened to her silences, because he made himself remember that she once had strength enough to act with the courage of her convictions. But with that look of fear, which so truly mirrored her inner denial, she had killed his flickering trust in her strength, and he knew he must relinquish her, cleanly and painlessly as possible, to the deep-rooted forces which pulled her away. To compromise with reality and let her inner weakness wreck both their lives; or to make the break now, while there was still time—he had no choice.

Across the lawn the old hotel lay sleeping quietly, its windows blank and unseeing. The moon had gone and the night was very dark. Far off in the mountains a train whistled, and Paul wondered where it was going. He stood up and began rapidly to walk across the lawn to the hotel.

e i g h t e e n

The concert for the benefit of the Kingston General Hospital was a great success. Everyone said so. Although the evening was sultry ("I declare, you'd never know it was September already," the ladies murmured dispiritedly among themselves, fanning their faces with programs), the auditorium of the high school was crowded, and the audience was indiscriminately enthusiastic. The quartet from the Rotary Club was brought back for two encores, and both times sang *The Bull-dog on the Bank and the Bull-frog in the Pool* because the mayor of Kingston sang bass. The Glee Club of the high school burst forth with *The Palms* and *Jerusalem the Golden;* the few persons who recalled that both these numbers had been given at the Easter pageant last spring were graciously silent, and the students were loudly applauded, especially by their parents.

At Dr. McDonough's express invitation, Tiny Lee had come down from the nightclub in New York where he had his own band. Some of the ladies could remember when he mowed lawns for them in the summertime or cleaned off February's snows, and they exclaimed to their husbands that it was wonderful, this big, free country of ours, when a little nigger boy without an education could get to be a famous pianist in a nightclub before he was even thirty. Their husbands wondered how much money the little jigaboo was making. Not only did Tiny play solos, he accompanied Paul Revkin, whom the program called a "brilliant young American musician," while he rendered a few selections on his violin, and at the conclusion of the performance, the two of them cordially shook hands. During intermission, Dr. McDonough, who was the chairman of the benefit, made a few remarks about the future of democracy and the brotherhood of man, to which everyone listened with patience.

Many residents of Kingston who had spent the summer at the beach were back in town, and there was lots of visiting going on in the aisles and in the lobby. Miss Victoria Bardwell, the society editor of the *Bugle,* scurried around examining ladies' new dresses so she could describe them in her next Sunday's column. Mrs. Acheson had to help her spell *crepe de Chine.*

"What that program needed," said Hugh to the Acheson family when the performance was finally completed, "was you, James." Mr. and Mrs. Acheson were standing in the lobby with Hugh and Frances; around them flowed streams of laughing, chattering people leaving the building.

"What did you say, Hugh?" Mr. Acheson leaned close to him and raised his voice above the noise.

"I said they should have asked *you* to play on that program," Hugh repeated. "Don't you think so, Frances?"

She had been trying to watch every face at once. "I'm sorry, Hugh. I wasn't paying any attention to you. What did you say?"

"Must we stand here?" Mrs. Acheson wanted to know. "We're in the way, and I declare I can't hear myself think."

"Well, why don't you all go along then?" Frances inquired of them brightly. "I guess I'll just stay around and see who I know."

Neither her mother nor her father altered expression. They merely looked at her.

"I'll stay with Frances," Hugh offered, "if you two want to go on home. There are probably some old friends she hasn't seen for a long time."

"You don't have to explain me to my own parents, Hugh," Frances said sarcastically. "They know what I'm waiting for better than you."

"Frances," said her mother coldly. "Where are your manners? Hugh is only trying to be helpful."

"We'll all wait," Mr. Acheson declared, glowering, and lit a cigar.

When Frances promised Paul that she would wait for him after the concert, she'd been afraid that Hugh and her parents would insist upon waiting with her. There seemed to be no getting away from them short of breaking and running down the empty aisles of the auditorium, through the stage door, and with Paul out into the darkness. She knew she wouldn't do it, but she toyed with the plan, imagining the shocked looks on everyone's face, half-hearing the startled whispers that would crackle like fire behind her—until she saw Paul coming through the crowded lobby toward them.

Along the way he was stopped several times by greetings and congratulations. He bowed a little to the ladies, shook hands with the men, smiled pleasantly, thanked them all, but with that same strange remoteness Frances remembered so well; and when, lithe, taut, and somehow wary, he approached the Acheson family, she felt that she

2 3 3

knew him no better than the strangers who had murmured pleasantries to him in the aisles.

Finding a breath, "Hello, Paul," she said. "Mother, Daddy, you all remember Paul Revkin, of course?"

"Of course," said Mrs. Acheson graciously smiling, and Mr. Acheson har-rumped something that might have been anything. Neither he nor Paul offered to shake hands, but the ugly moment was lost in Hugh's hearty greeting.

"Glad to see you again, Mr. Revkin," he cried. "That was a fine and ennobling experience, listening to you play. A privilege."

"Thank you," Paul said. All the Achesons murmured that the program had been wonderful, wonderful.

"I'd like to invite you to come and play at First Presbyterian Church some Sunday soon. That's where I'm pastor," Hugh continued. "When would it be convenient, Mr. Revkin? That is, I mean, if you'll be kind enough—"

"Not at all," Paul assured him. "I appreciate your invitation. But I'm going back to New York tomorrow night —the season at the hotel is over, you know—" He did not even glance at Frances. "So I'm afraid I'll have to postpone the pleasure until some other time."

"What will you be doing in New York, Paul?" Mrs. Acheson asked.

"Studying. More studying. I've a long way to go yet. Maybe I'll be able to play a little here and there."

"How long do you think it will be," Mr. Acheson broke silence, "before you're—uh—before you can support yourself, make a decent living—"

"Never, perhaps," Paul answered him calmly. He

looked directly at Mr. Acheson and did not amplify his remark.

There was an uneasy silence. "Oh, but Paul is bound to make lots of money," Frances cried out. "Look at all the applause he got tonight. He was far and away the finest thing in the show." She glanced from one face to another and was conscious that words were tumbling out of her without thought or meaning. "Why, you all heard it yourselves. Everybody's sure he's going to be a great concert violinist—"

"Are *you* sure, Frances?" Paul's voice cut across the torrent of her words. It was tender and full of love. Abruptly she stopped talking and looked at him.

Mr. Acheson cleared his throat. "It was a very good program, Paul," he said at last. "And you certainly deserve all the compliments you've been receiving."

Frances looked from her father to Paul. Paul said nothing.

"But I think Dr. McDonough did you a great disservice," Mr. Acheson went on, "having you appear on the same platform with a Negro—"

"Oh, no, Daddy," said Frances wearily, "not again. Don't you ever change your tune?" She looked pleadingly at Hugh who ignored her.

"—and that business of your shaking hands afterwards, Paul. I'm sure you appreciated his playing the piano for you, but if you expect to make a success of your career, you've got to watch those things." His voice was as calm and pleasant as if he'd been telling a bedtime story. "I'm sure you just didn't realize."

"Shall we all go and have a nice cool drink at our

house?" Mrs. Acheson suggested. "Paul, you'll come, won't you?"

"Excuse me just a minute," said Paul, still looking at Frances' father. "I'd like to get something straightened out right now, Mr. Acheson. There are no barriers in music. I respect Tiny Lee as a musician, and in the short while we've been rehearsing, we've come to be good friends. It's as unimportant to him that I'm Jewish as it is to me that he's Negro. The important thing is that we make music. I should be proud to have him as a guest in my home for dinner."

"Well I'll be goddamned," Mr. Acheson exploded, "if any daughter of mine will ever sit down to dinner with niggers!"

—Or Jews either if you can help it, Frances added to herself, feeling the blood drain out of her face and pound through her body. Their swords, sheathed so long, were bare now and glinted in the light.

"Why don't you let Frances make up her own mind?" Paul asked coldly.

"Good God, I know what's good for my own daughter. Do you think I raised her just so she could ruin her life?"

"Well, how could eating dinner with Negroes a couple of times ruin Frances' life?" Hugh inquired seriously. "I think that's a little far-fetched myself."

Frances burst into shrill laughter. "Oh, Hugh, Hugh," she said when she could get her breath. "It must be wonderful to be a vegetable."

Mrs. Acheson put her hand on her husband's arm. "James, we're the last people here. They're waiting to put out the lights." She turned to the others. "Please come over to our house for iced tea. Hugh? Paul?"

Glowering but quiet, Mr. Acheson stared out of the high-school doors into the darkness.

"Thanks just the same, Mrs. Acheson," Paul refused, "but I have to go back to the hotel and pack a few things. I'm afraid I can't come tonight."

"It's been nice seeing you again, Paul," Mrs. Acheson said courteously. "Have a good trip to New York."

Jovially Hugh said all the right things, shook hands, reminded him to come back and play some Sunday in the First Presbyterian Church. Even Mr. Acheson made an effort and said good-by. Only Frances stood stockstill, silent, watching him walk across the lobby and out of its swinging doors.

"He's a swell person," Hugh declared. "You'd never even know he was Jewish."

Suddenly Frances flung "Excuse me!" over her shoulder, heedless of her mother's outstretched hand, rushed through the lobby doors behind Paul, saw him silhouetted against the streetlights at the end of the walk. "Paul!"

He waited as she flew to him down the long stone path.

"Paul," she said breathlessly, "Paul—I—" She had no idea what she wanted to say. "Thank you for playing *Intermezzo*."

"You knew I would, dearest, didn't you?"

"I hoped you would. It was wonderful."

He seemed content to stand quietly, watching her face as though he were memorizing every line of it.

"Paul, you haven't forgotten our picnic tomorrow?"

"Oh no," he said. "I'll meet you in the Square at one?"

Suddenly, impulsively, she threw her arms around his

neck. "Oh, Paul, I love you so much I think I'm going to die."

"I know, lieble, I know."

She laid her cheek against his and kissed his ear, feeling a surge of desire so strong that she trembled and leaned heavily upon him. "I'll never stop loving you, never, never, never!"

He kissed her once, gently and with infinite tenderness, removed her arms from his neck, kissed the palms of her hands and her finger tips, never removing his eyes from her face. "You'd better go back to your family, darling," he said. "They'll be worried about you."

"Oh, I don't care!" she cried, and then with a sigh, "I guess you're right. One o'clock tomorrow?"

"In the Square?"

"Yes. And Paul, I'll have the car, so we can go up to our special place!"

"Fine." He didn't kiss her again, but he waved once and walked away down the long street without looking back. She waited until she could no longer hear the echo of his footsteps, and then she turned back to join her family.

Sometime after midnight—she was lying on her back in bed, staring wide-eyed into space—Frances heard a tentative rapping on her bedroom door, and her mother's murmur, "Franny, are you awake?"

She scrambled to a sitting position and drew the sheet up over her nakedness. "For heaven's sake, what's the matter?" she demanded in a hoarse whisper.

Mrs. Acheson came in and sat on the side of the bed. "Don't put on the light, dear." With one hand outstretched toward the lamp on the night table, Frances peered through the darkness at the dim shape of her mother. "Is something the matter?" she asked again, leaning forward and pulling her knees up.

"Franny, I'd—I'd hoped I wouldn't feel the need of this. But I cannot—" Mrs. Acheson swallowed, and in the stillness Frances could clearly hear the little gulping noise. "Franny, I *can't* let you go on any longer without talking to you."

"Couldn't—wouldn't you please rather wait until tomorrow or sometime when we aren't so tired?" Frances suggested, although she knew the effort was hopeless.

"Tomorrow may be too late. I want to talk to you about Paul."

"Paul?" What a quavering little sound that was! "What about Paul?"

"Frances, you're a grown woman, twenty-three years old. You are not a child, and shouldn't be treated as a child. That's why I want to talk sensibly to you, and I expect that courtesy in return. I haven't said anything to you about your relationship with Paul, I haven't asked you to stop seeing him, I never even questioned you about where you've been or what you've done—because I thought it was a passing infatuation, a romantic school-girl crush which you'd get over as soon as you saw things in a sensible light. Now I'm not so sure. It may have gone too far. Paul's leaving for New York tomorrow night. Did he ask you to go with him?"

"No," Frances whispered.

"Are you in love with him?"

"Yes."

"And you think he's in love with you?"

"I know he is."

"Did he—have you discussed marriage at all?"

"Well," said Frances, considering her words, "we haven't talked about it much. At first we just sort of knew we would get married, but we never discussed anything specific." She was silent for a long moment. "Recently we haven't mentioned it at all."

"Where does Paul live in New York? I mean—"

"He lives with his family, just like I do, if that's what you mean."

"You never told me anything about your trip to Washington, Fran, the day you met his father—"

"His *uncle*," Frances interrupted. "I never told you because I didn't think you'd be interested."

"Was that the only reason?"

"What else?"

"Would you be proud for Paul to bring his family here, to Kingston, and introduce them to your friends and relatives as in-laws?"

"I wouldn't care," Frances said stubbornly. As soon as the words were out of her mouth, she realized the confession implicit in them, and she grew angry that her mother would deliberately trick her. "I don't see what difference it makes to you and Daddy anyway," she went on. "I've been living in a house with two strangers this whole damn summer. You all pretended Paul didn't even exist. It was cruel, that's what it was—"

"Honey, honey," Mrs. Acheson said, leaning over and taking her daughter's hands. "Please don't be angry. I love you so much. I want you to be happy, that's the only thing in the world that matters. What happened to the fine feeling we used to have, you and I? We sat together by the hour, not having to talk, just being together. And all the walks we took, and the places we visited. Ever since you were knee-high to a duck, you'd come running in and tell me everything that happened to you that day. You'll never know, 'til you have a little girl of your own, what that meant to me. You know in your heart that your happiness means more to me than anything in the world, don't you? You do believe that, don't you?"

"Oh, I believe it all right," Frances mumbled. "But that doesn't necessarily mean you know what's going to make me happy."

"You want to pull away from everything that's made you happy in the past—your family, your friends, your home, your background, your church—and go off into a void with one man. Do you honestly think he'll make up to you everything you'll lose?"

"It wouldn't be a void," said Frances desperately. "Paul would be there."

"How would he take care of you? Tonight he admitted he might never make a decent living—"

"Stop it, Mother! Stop it!" Frances pressed her hands to her forehead. "Stop picking on me! Everybody's been picking on me for so long now." It was almost a wail. "Don't you think I've considered all that?"

"In other words you're going to sacrifice decent living and social position and respectability and a chance to give your children the good things in life—just to follow an infatuation, a dream left over from a fairy-tale book? Frances, Frances, wake up, darling, wake up. He's nice enough and all that, but he isn't good enough for *you*."

"He's *too* good for me," Frances said in a flat, dead voice.

"Why do you say that, Franny?"

"Mother, I honestly don't think you'd understand."

For a long time they were quiet, and in the stillness Frances heard odd little sounds like the creaking of a floorboard downstairs and the stirrings of the canary in his cage at the window. Above everything she could hear her mother's slow, heavy breathing.

"Dearest," Mrs. Acheson's voice came softly out of the darkness. "There's something I want to tell you. I never thought I would, but now I want to. When we went into the war, the First World War I mean, I was living at home. This was before father sold the place down on the peninsula and moved into Williamsburg. I used to go to Newport News on Saturday nights to work in the Red Cross canteen. Let's see, I was—seventeen and then turned eighteen those years."

She straightened her body as though steeling herself to go on. "I used to meet a sailor. His name was Jan, and he was stationed in one of the Navy yards there. I thought he was very handsome—"

"What did he look like?"

"Yes, he *was* handsome," Mrs. Acheson mused, "in a coarse sort of way. He was blond and big-boned and he was a wonderful dancer."

"Mother, I can no more imagine *you* dancing!"

"In those days I could dance for hours without stopping, always with Jan. For a big man he was as light on his feet as—as—well, you've never seen anything like it."

"What was his name? Jan what?"

"Wensi- Wenski- I never could pronounce it. A Polish name."

"Were you in love with him, Mother?"

"Yes I was, Frances," Mrs. Acheson said with dignity. "I've never tried to deny it. I wanted to marry him very much. That would have been the greatest mistake of my life. You know how precious my mother was to me. She saw the whole situation much more clearly than I could, and she persuaded me to stop seeing Jan. After a little while I got over him, and now I can think about him without any feeling at all."

"But how could you marry Daddy if you loved somebody else?"

"I respected your father, Frances, and admired him, and I knew he'd make a good father for my children and give them every advantage I wanted them to have. I learned to love your father after a while, and we've had a very successful marriage."

"I think that's obscene!"

"My dear, you're a highly emotional girl, and Paul has undoubtedly aroused—stirred you physically to some extent." Mrs. Acheson waited expectantly. I wish I had something to confess, Frances thought. "How long do you think the 'passion' lasts, my dear? When the 'love' dies down, what will you have left? Come out of the clouds, Frances, and consider the alternatives."

"Mother, honestly, believe me, it's more than passion or the kind of love you're talking about, the kind that flares up and dies down. Paul has changed my whole life! Surely you've seen that. He's strong and aware, he's alive and he brought me to life. When I'm with him, *I'm* strong and aware too. And when I'm not with him, I'm squeezed back into the mold, but Mother, I don't fit the mold any longer. The different me that belongs to Paul breaks through. I love him. I'll be in love with him all the rest of my life."

Her mother's long silence frightened her. "Mother?"

She put her hand on her mother's arm and felt it shaking under her touch. Panic seized her. She clutched her mother's shoulders and in the dimness tried to look into her face. Only then did she realize that her mother, her calm, poised, beautiful mother, was sobbing—horribly, noiselessly, without tears and without control, dry gulping sobs that shook her whole body. Frances pulled her mother frantically into her arms and rocked her back and forth, crooning softly over and over, "Mother, Mother, honey baby, don't. Don't carry on so. It's all right. Everything's going to be all right." Hot tears spilled out of her own eyes, and her throat constricted so that she could barely speak. "Dearest Mother, I love you so much. Please, please."

"Oh, Franny, Franny, you're all I have," her mother gasped. "If you marry this boy, it will hurt me worse than the death of my own mother."

Frances held her mother close against her breast until the racking torturing sobs died away. In the next room she could hear her father snoring. Numbly she stroked her mother's hair and listened to her father's snoring. There was nothing else to do.

n i n e t e e n

They drove as far as they could along the bumpy dirt road and then they stopped the car and climbed the rest of the way to the top of the hill. There was a little path, rocky and twisted and full of exposed tree roots, barely wide enough for the two of them to walk together. Among the trees it was still and damply cool, and all Paul could hear was the caw-caw-caw of a crow jagging across the green silence.

He knew the way well. Together they'd been to this "special place," as Frances called it, all summer long. As they neared the top, he could see the old wormwood fence that marked the edge of somebody's property and the three-stepped stile going over it; beyond, the massive oak tree and the stretch of sun-washed hillside which commanded a sweeping view of the valley. Even if he closed his eyes, he could see everything clearly: it was *here* he would remember her all the rest of his life.

Slowly Frances climbed the three steps of the stile and stood on the broad wooden top looking down at him. "Want me to take the basket?" Her voice was listless and there was no expression on her face.

"No, darling, I have it all right," Paul said, swinging the picnic basket over the fence and following Frances across the stile.

As soon as they had sat down, she busied herself with lunch, spreading a square white cloth on the grass and pulling sandwiches and fruit and packages of hard-boiled eggs from the hamper as though she were engaged in the most important work in the world. She arranged and re-arranged the food on the cloth, concentrating hard and nibbling on her lower lip. Paul knew she was afraid to face the moment when there would be nothing to do but talk. "I don't see the thermos bottle. I know I put it in," she murmured, scrounging around in the bottom of the basket. "Oh, here it is. Thank goodness."

"You must have got up early to fix all this," Paul said.

She glanced up at him and smiled nervously. "Not very. It wasn't any trouble. Please just help yourself. Here's ham and these are cheese, I think, and over here"—carefully she peered into a sandwich—"peanut butter and jelly. Just take what you want." She sat back and dropped her hands in her lap.

Below him in a checkerboard pattern of greens and yellows and rich browns, the land rolled away to the hills. In the valley someone was burning a pile of dry leaves, and the smoke rose straight up in the hazy air. The valley was as peaceful as a valley he remembered in the Vosges in northern France before his tank company had crashed across it and met the Nazis in the blue hills on the other side.

A movement from her pulled his mind back to now, and he saw that she was wearily running her hands through her hair. "Frances, you aren't eating anything, dearest. You surely don't expect me to finish all this?"

"Must we talk about food on a day like this?" she said with a small smile, but she took a ham sandwich and began intently to pull it into bite-sized pieces.

Odd, that there was no pain, Paul thought to himself. The pain had come and gone and it would come again, but now there was only the old numbness. How long the numbness would last, how long he could force himself to remain pleasant and superficial and unthinking, he did not know. Though lulled now by the day and by being with Frances and by sheer strength of will, the pain was familiar to him and had been for a long time. He would not allow himself to contemplate how long it would be with him through the days and years ahead.

Part of his deadly aching pain was for her. He remembered telling her, on their first evening together, that she was going to get hurt, very hurt. He would have spared her that. For him this was only the newest and deepest pain in years of old, deep pains and would merge at last into the whole and be absorbed. But Frances had achieved self-knowledge, a two-edged sword, and deliberately she was cutting the heart out of her body while her mind looked on and understood.

There was one thing only he could do: he could spare her having to answer out loud and give the lie to her bleeding heart. He could spare her having to say, "No, Paul, I can't go away with you." Perhaps in time to come she could salve the wound by saying, "It was only a summer's flirtation. He never even asked me at all." She would need that salve if she had to live the rest of her life with Kingston, with Hugh, and with herself.

"Do you want a piece of cake?" she asked him, unfolding a large linen napkin and revealing thick yellow slices covered with chocolate icing.

"Did you make it yourself, lieble?"

There was a flicker of the old Frances. "You know as well as I that I can't cook. Don't you pick on me, too!"

He took a piece of cake and broke it in two, offering her half. "Please have part of mine. You haven't touched a thing." She accepted it, not looking at him, and they sat a while in silence, watching the smoke from the leaves burning down in the valley.

"What time does your train leave?" she said at last. It was the first time she'd mentioned his leaving.

"At seven tonight."

"Seven." It was neither a question nor a cry, just a breath escaping.

He wanted to reach out across the unbridgeable chasm between them, to take her hand, to say a word. But there was nothing to say and he dared not touch her, though it took all his strength to sit silent and still.

"Well—how long does it take to get to New York?"

"About eight hours."

"Eight hours. You'll get home in the middle of the night."

"Yes, but it's a good time to travel. The train won't be so crowded and—"

"Oh, Paul!" Suddenly, desperately, without warning, she pulled him to her and kissed him with wild abandon, over and over. Her tears and her desire smashed his control to pulp, and in a fury of passion, he threw her back upon the grass of the hillside, kissing her open mouth and her eyelids, her ears, her throat, her breasts. "Yes, yes, please," she gasped, lifting her body to his, eyes dilated, breathing hard and labored.

Convulsively, with all his strength, he tore himself free and leaped to his feet, cramming his clenched fists into his pockets and walking away from her over to the oak tree. Trembling, shaking, he leaned against it—God, how much need a man stand!—until he could breathe again and control his thinking. She lay as he had left her, limp and sprawling on the earth, her head turned to one side; from beneath closed eyelids tears trickled and slid into the earth. After a few minutes he went back and sat down beside her, lighting a cigarette and looking out across the land to the wall of mountains that sheltered the valley.

"Please don't cry, dearest," he said, and his voice was even again and gentle. She neither moved nor spoke. "I love you so much I'd rather die than hurt you." He looked at her then, but she lay with closed eyes as though she were dead. What else was there to say? The banalities were not in him, and the truth could no longer reach her. He smoked his cigarette down to the end, crumbling a handful of moist earth between his fingers and feeling within it the decay of old dead things which nurtured the roots of the new.

Finally he flipped his glowing butt into the grass where it smoldered to ember. "Frances," he said, "I'm going now." Still she did not open her eyes. "Do you mind very much if I leave you here alone and walk back? I'd like to remember you in this special place."

She took a deep breath and held it, tightening her lips so that the air could not escape, then sighing a long, quivering sigh. At last she opened her eyes and they were full of tears. "No, I don't mind," she said faintly.

Gently and with great tenderness he leaned down and kissed her. "I'll love you all my life," he said and went away without looking back. Down the grassy hillside in the afternoon sunlight he walked faster and faster. But no matter how fast he walked, his shadow ran before him and no matter how fast he ran, he could never catch it.